Praise for *Dear Dickhead*

"Zoé [offers] blistering polemics that are ferocious, provocative, and often intensely funny . . . [Her] righteous fury is electric, and Despentes compellingly presents her as a casualty of male privilege . . . In *Dear Dickhead*, the letter becomes a venue for this kind of ruthless taking stock of one's self through frictive, uncomfortable dialogue with another person . . . Rebecca has a way of whittling complex insights about sex and gender into sentences that have the compressed fury of a two-minute punk song." —Anahid Nersessian, *The New Yorker*

"Frank Wynne swings Despentes's French into confidently contemporary English . . . Despentes pulls it off with a brio that's wholly characteristic . . . The energy of Despentes's voice kept me on her side, and rooting for Oscar, Rebecca and Zoé as they navigated their lives with varying degrees of failure, distress and, occasionally, hope." —Erica Wagner, *The Telegraph*

"[Full of] lots of highly entertaining Bernhardian rants on the subject of men v. women, generation v. generation, and more." —John Self, *The Guardian*

"A bitingly humorous conversation about addiction, lockdown, cancellation, and, ultimately, friendship." —Jasmine Vojdani, *Vulture*

"A rare beast—a literary work that successfully uses an old-fashioned form . . . to speak refreshingly to the current moment . . . A novel of uncommon depth and poignancy . . . Subversive, disruptive, and infused with a punk sensibility . . . [A] triumph." —David Vogel, *Words Without Borders*

"Epic . . . Brash and provocative . . . [A] riveting exploration of feminism and sexism . . . Readers will be awed."
—*Publishers Weekly* (starred review)

"Rebecca, Oscar, and Zoé come across as real people and their interactions with each other manifestly change them . . . Grounded in real human emotion and experience." —*Kirkus Reviews*

"Despentes's unsparing directness and fluid style are well served by Wynne's translation; nothing is lost . . . Funny, raw, compelling."
—*Library Journal*

VIRGINIE DESPENTES

DEAR DICKHEAD

Translated by Frank Wynne

Virginie Despentes is a writer and filmmaker. She worked in an independent record store in the early 1990s, was a sex worker, and published her first novel, *Baise-Moi*, when she was twenty-three. She adapted the novel for the screen in 2000, codirecting with the porn star Coralie Trinh Thi. Upon release, it became the first film to be banned in France in twenty-eight years. Despentes is the author of more than fifteen other works, including *King Kong Theory* and the acclaimed Vernon Subutex trilogy.

Frank Wynne is a literary translator from the French and Spanish. The authors he has worked with include Michel Houellebecq, Patrick Modiano, Javier Cercas, and the late Ivorian novelist Ahmadou Kourouma. He has won numerous prizes, including twice winning the International Dublin Literary Award, with Houellebecq for *The Elementary Particles* in 2002, and with Alice Zeniter for *The Art of Losing* in 2022.

ALSO BY VIRGINIE DESPENTES

Baise-Moi

Pretty Things

Bye Bye Blondie

King Kong Theory

Apocalypse Baby

Vernon Subutex 1

Vernon Subutex 2

Vernon Subutex 3

DEAR DICKHEAD

DEAR DICKHEAD
VIRGINIE DESPENTES

**TRANSLATED FROM THE FRENCH
BY FRANK WYNNE**

**PICADOR / FARRAR, STRAUS AND GIROUX
NEW YORK**

Picador
120 Broadway, New York 10271

EU Representative: Macmillan Publishers Ireland Ltd, 1st Floor,
The Liffey Trust Centre, 117–126 Sheriff Street Upper, Dublin 1, D01 YC43

Copyright © 2022 by Virginie Despentes and Éditions Grasset & Fasquelle
Translation copyright © 2024 by Frank Wynne
All rights reserved
Printed in the United States of America
Originally published in French in 2022 by Éditions Grasset & Fasquelle, France, as *Cher Connard*
English translation published in the United States in 2024 by
Farrar, Straus and Giroux
First paperback edition, 2025

Grateful acknowledgment is made for permission to reprint an excerpt from *Darkness Visible: A Memoir of Madness* by William Styron, copyright © 1990 by William Styron. Used by permission of Random House, an imprint and division of Penguin Random House LLC. All rights reserved.

The Library of Congress has cataloged the Farrar, Straus and
Giroux hardcover edition as follows:
Names: Despentes, Virginie, 1969– author. | Wynne, Frank, translator.
Title: Dear dickhead : a novel / Virginie Despentes ; translated from the French by Frank Wynne.
Other titles: Cher connard. French
Description: First American edition. | New York : Farrar, Straus and Giroux, 2024. | "Originally published in French in 2022 by Éditions Grasset & Fasquelle, France, as Cher Connard."
Identifiers: LCCN 2024008326 | ISBN 9780374611613 (hardcover)
Subjects: LCSH: Man-woman relationships—Fiction. | LCGFT: Epistolary fiction. | Novels.
Classification: LCC PQ2664.E7895 C4413 2024 | DDC 843/.914—dc23/eng/20240315
LC record available at https://lccn.loc.gov/2024008326

Paperback ISBN: 978-1-250-39766-9

The publisher of this book does not authorize the use or reproduction of any part of this book in any manner for the purpose of training artificial intelligence technologies or systems. The publisher of this book expressly reserves this book from the Text and Data Mining exception in accordance with Article 4(3) of the European Union Digital Single Market Directive 2019/790.

Our books may be purchased in bulk for specialty retail/wholesale, literacy, corporate/premium, educational, and subscription box use. Please contact MacmillanSpecialMarkets@macmillan.com.

Picador® is a US registered trademark and is used by Macmillan Publishing Group, LLC, under license from Pan Books Limited.

picadorusa.com • Follow us on social media at @picador or @picadorusa

10 9 8 7 6 5 4 3 2 1

For Jean-Claude Fasquelle

DEAR DICKHEAD

OSCAR

Chronicles of chaos

Bumped into Rebecca Latté in Paris. Memories came flooding back of all the extraordinary characters she played—the dangerous, venomous, vulnerable, poignant, heroic women—how many times I fell in love with her, the countless photos pinned up in countless apartments over countless beds where I lay dreaming. A tragic metaphor for an era swiftly going straight to hell—this sublime woman who initiated so many teenage boys into the fascinations of feminine seduction at its peak, now a wrinkled toad. Not just old. But fat, scruffy, with repulsive skin with that foul-mouthed, female persona. A complete turn-off. Someone told me she's become an inspiration for young feminists. The fleabag sorority strikes again. Am I surprised? Fuck no! I curl up on the sofa in the recovery position and listen to Biggie's "Hypnotize" on repeat.

REBECCA

Dear Dickhead,

    I read your post on Insta. You're like a pigeon shitting

on my shoulder as you flap past. It's shitty and unpleasant. Waah, waah, waah, I'm a pissy little pantywaist, no one loves me so I whimper like a Chihuahua in the hope someone will notice me. Congratulations: you've got your fifteen minutes of fame! You want proof? I'm writing to you. I'm sure you've got kids. Guys like you always reproduce, they worry about carrying on the line. One thing I've noticed, the dumber and more incompetent men are, the more they feel a duty to carry on the line. So I hope your kids die under the wheels of a truck, you have to watch them die without being able to do anything, their eyes pop out of their sockets, and the howls of pain haunt you every night. There: that's what I wish for you. And leave Biggie in peace, for fuck's sake.

OSCAR

Wow—seriously harsh. Okay, I asked for it. My only excuse is I never thought you'd read it. Or maybe, deep down, I hoped you would, but never really believed it. I'm sorry. I've deleted the post and the comments.

Still—that was pretty harsh. At first I was shocked. Later, I have to admit, it made me laugh out loud.

Let me explain. I was sitting a couple of tables from you on a café terrace on the rue de Bretagne—I didn't have the nerve to talk to you, but I stared. I think maybe I was embarrassed that my face didn't even ring a bell with you, and also by my own shyness. Otherwise, I'd never have written those things about you.

What I wanted to say to you that day—I don't know

whether this will mean anything to you—is that I'm Corinne's little brother, the two of you were friends back in the eighties. Jayack is a pseudonym. My actual surname is Jocard. We lived in an apartment overlooking the place Maurice Barrès. You, I remember, lived in a housing project called Cali, your apartment block was called the Danube. Back then, you used to come over all the time. I was the kid brother, so I spied on you from a distance, you rarely talked to me. But I remember you standing in front of my toy race track, and all you cared about was showing me how to cause a pileup.

You had a green bike, a racer, a boy's bike. You used to rob sackloads of LPs from the Hall du Livre, and one day you gave me David Bowie's *Station to Station* because you had two copies. Thanks to you, I was listening to Bowie when I was nine. I still have that record.

Since then, I've become a novelist. Though I haven't achieved anything like your level of fame, things have gone pretty well for me, and I've had your email address for ages. I got hold of it because I wanted to write a theatrical monologue for you. I never had the courage to get in touch.

Best wishes.

REBECCA

Dude, screw your apologies, screw your monologue, screw everything: there's nothing about you that interests me. If it makes you feel any better, I'm even angrier at the dumb fuck who sent me the link to your post, like I need to be up to speed with all the insults being hurled at me. I don't give a fuck about your mediocre life. I don't give a fuck about your collected literary works. I don't give a fuck about anything related to you, except your sister.

Of course I remember Corinne. I hadn't thought about her for years, but the minute I saw her name it all came back to me, as if I'd opened a drawer. We used to play cards on a sled she used as a coffee table in her bedroom. We'd open the shutters and smoke cigarettes I stole from my mother. Your family had a microwave long before anyone else, and we used it to melt cheese and spread it on crackers. I remember going to visit her in the Vosges mountains—she was working as an instructor at some chalet where they had horses. The first time I ever went into a bar was with her, we played pinball and tried to look cool, like we'd been doing it all our lives. Corinne had a motorbike—though, given how old we were back then, it must have been a souped-up moped. She smoked Dunhill reds and drank beer with a slice of lemon. Sometimes she'd talk about East Germany and Thatcher's politics—things no one around me gave a shit about back then.

I hated Nancy, I rarely think about the city, and I don't feel remotely nostalgic about my childhood—I was surprised to find I had any pleasant memories of those times.

Tell your sister I googled her name but couldn't find anything, I'm guessing she's married and she's changed her name. Give her my love. As for you: drop dead.

OSCAR

Corinne has never had any social media accounts. Not that she's a technophobe, she's a sociopath. I remember when you used to come over. Then, later, you became a movie star and I couldn't get my head around the idea that the girl who used to sit in our kitchen had her fifteen minutes of fame at the Oscars. Back then, fame wasn't something within the grasp of most people, it was for the select few. It seemed insane to me that it could touch someone who came from our neighborhood. I don't know if I'd even have dared look for a publisher for my first novel if I hadn't known you. You were living proof that everyone in my family was wrong: I had the right to dream. I feel like a complete dick that I wrote something vile about you. You're completely right: it was a particularly pathetic way of trying to get your attention.

You didn't go to the same school as my sister, so I don't know how you two got to be friends. When you were in elementary school, your favorite thing was to build housing projects for dolls out of huge cardboard boxes. It was a massive undertaking, and even my mother, who never had much imagination, let you get on with it and never complained about the mess you were making in Corinne's bedroom. One Wednesday, you brought a fridge packing crate over, and you filled it with shoeboxes to make apartments. The ceilings were too low for Barbies, so you raided the collection of folk dolls my mother had on the shelves of the living room. I thought she'd go ballistic when she saw her precious dolls from Brittany, Seville, Alsace, and wherever living in your development. The moment is burned into my memory, because my mother couldn't even pretend to blow her top. A sense of joy overrode her sense of propriety. She kept saying, "You're pushing it," but before she gave the order to put the dolls back in their clear plastic display cases and tidy the bedroom, she crouched down in front of the installation, shaking her head and saying, "I can't believe it." She was only grumbling for form's sake, and it was obvious. We rarely managed to make Maman laugh, us kids. You managed to cut through her bad moods. Years later, whenever she saw you on the little television set in the corner, she'd say the same thing: "Remember the time she and our Coco took all my dolls down off the shelf and put them in her big cardboard housing project . . . She always had a way about her, that girl. And she was so pretty, even back then."

I wasn't even old enough to play Go Fish at the time, but I knew you were beautiful, but I only truly realized how stunning you were one year at the end of summer, a few days before school started, when you walked into our place and said, "Shall we have a coffee?" From that day on, there was no more playing with dolls. Suddenly, you were a grown-up. And I hardly recognized you.

REBECCA

Listen, honey, I'm guessing you know you're not the first guy to tell me I'm beautiful, or to point out that I'm famous . . .

But I have to admit, you're the first slimy bastard who's had the nerve to insult me and, practically in the same breath, follow up with "We come from the same neighborhood, we've got shared memories."

At this point, your sheer dumbfuckery commands a certain respect. But it doesn't change the basics: I don't give a shit about you. All my love to your sister, she was a wonderful friend.

OSCAR

I don't know whether you ever figured out that my sister was into girls. She didn't talk about it back then. I could see that she was rough, and cruder than most of her friends, and I was embarrassed that she didn't make the effort to look better, but I never drew any particular conclusions. Years later, our parents had gone to Spain one August and I was staying in their place looking after the cat. There was a heat wave, and Corinne, who was already living in Paris at that point, came over because she wanted to make the most of their little garden. She would put down a towel and lie in the shade of the peach tree, reading or listening to CDs on her Discman. Sometimes, we'd take the car and go to the swimming pool. We were never particularly close during vacations. We gave each other a wide berth, each spending the day doing our own thing. Then one day she stumbled on a VHS box set of the *Mad Max* trilogy in a box in the garage, so we curled up on the sofa, closed the shutters, and drank cold beers while we watched Mel Gibson. We were both a bit drunk, and between movies I talked to her about this girl I was seeing who I didn't have the guts to dump even though I was fed up with her. Corinne listened without laying into me like she usually did. I have to force myself to phone her, I was saying, because otherwise she'll make a scene, but actually I'm happy she's working all the time, because she stifles me, I'm bored to tears, it's all a bit shitty. I just couldn't understand why I was scared to tell her it was over. It's not like we were living together. Deep down, I was afraid that if I left her, I'd end up single for the rest of my life, and I thought having a girlfriend who drove you up the wall was better than being alone all your life. But I didn't dare say this aloud, so I asked my sister how things worked for her, dating boys. She never had a boyfriend. Not that that surprised me. She wasn't very pretty, and she wasn't exactly easygoing. I was scared of her, and I assumed she terrified other guys too.

She didn't beat around the bush, she just said: I date girls. That's how she came out of the closet. She'd been living in Paris for three years by that point. I thought, my sister is lesbian, and it didn't square with reality. "Dyke" wasn't even one of the insults in my vocabulary. I had a whole bunch of pejorative terms for my sister—but "dyke" had never occurred to me. I'd never wondered whether women like that really existed, I certainly didn't know any. Corinne warned me that if I told anyone, she'd smash my face in. I told her I never ratted her out, and she said, that's true, at least you can keep your big mouth shut, that's one thing I managed to beat into you. This made her laugh. Not me: when I was little, she'd whack me if I so much as went near her. I didn't appreciate her smugness. I wanted her to tell me she was genuinely sorry.

We put on *Mad Max Beyond Thunderdome*, and I was feeling awkward. It seemed crazy that something so shameful should happen to our family. Being a fat, ugly woman with no redeeming features was one thing, but being a dyke, well, that was something else entirely. I felt bad for her—imagining her life in Paris, people throwing stones at her in the street, girls laughing in her face and calling her a pervert, employers firing her because she made them sick. A few days later, she took the train back to Paris; we didn't talk about it again.

I thought it would be a shameful secret we'd have to live with our whole lives. But a year and a half later, when the whole family was together for Christmas up in the Vosges and we'd all had too much to eat and drink, she and I went for a walk in the woods. I can see her now, the orange mittens she'd borrowed from our aunt, her nose red with the cold, smiling, surrounded by fir trees, reveling in her bullshit, talking about "boorish heteros" with infinite contempt. These days the word is banal, but this was the first time I'd heard anyone use it. The dignified, discreet coming-out phase was over. She was a butch dyke now, a "political issue." I'd snuck some champagne out under my puffer jacket, and I watched her chug it straight from the bottle, I was shocked by her sense of joy. She should have fallen to her knees among the fir trees and begged the gods to let her be normal, have a bunch of kids with a decent guy, take out a loan, buy a car, have the kind of marriage the family could respect. I had some champagne myself, and that gave me the courage to ask her: "This thing with dating girls, you don't think maybe it could be just a phase?" She stuffed her hands into her pockets. "I hope not. As a straight woman, I'm a dog, but on the lesbian market, I'm pretty much Sharon Stone." Her answer shocked me. Ever since we were little, we'd both been losers when it came to love. That day, it felt like she was letting go of my hand and leaving me alone in the dark while she headed off to frolic on sunny beaches. She'd found *her thing*; I hadn't.

We got lost on the way back, she couldn't stop talking about the joys of being a lesbian. I could partly identify with what she was saying: I'd never wanted to be like the other members of our family either. Back then, I dreamed of being a journalist, but I'd never have admitted that at the dinner table. I knew exactly how everyone would react—the belly laughs and the rolling eyes, the "He always did think he was a genius," "Come on, you really think they'd take someone like you?"—the whole litany of the middle class inured to the daily grind, to doing a job for the money rather than for love. The most important thing of all was knowing your place. As we walked, I got the sense that, for my sister, refusing to follow the path trodden by the women among our family and friends offered the same sense of liberation.

Later, I pieced together her evolution. In school, she'd had a couple of girlfriends who hooked up with her on the down-low but dated guys whenever they got the chance. She'd had a shitty time of it, secretly living through the heartbreak of lousy affairs, and I know what girls are like, they're ruthless when it comes to losers. And back then, being a lesbian was worse than being a loser—lesbians had no right to exist. In the cage fight of traditional femininity, she couldn't even get her gloves on.

As soon as she finished high school, Corinne left for Paris, enrolled in a university, and initially lived off odd jobs, though pretty quickly she found full-time work as a receptionist in a gym and dropped her classes. She fell in love with a girl at work, it was her first serious relationship, they shared loads of experiences, exhibitions, movies, gigs, weekends in Normandy. And then one day the girl told her she was getting married. Corinne was one of the witnesses at the wedding. She kissed her one last time in her white bridal dress. Assuming my sister actually has a heart, I think that was the day it shattered. After that, things were different—the gym closed down, she was on welfare for a few months while she hung around in bars. This was where she met the woman who changed everything, the one who would tell her, my folks know I'm a dyke whether they approve of it or not, fuck them and fuck anyone who has a problem with me. They moved in together. They hung out in lesbian bars and Corinne started to get into politics. She changed the way she dressed, got rid of every external sign of femininity—no long hair, no jewelry, no high heels, no makeup. All the things she had clumsily borrowed from the regulation-issue female repertoire but had never become a part of her. Like skin grafts that her body rejected.

It was the birth of my daughter that really changed things between us. My sister might like to scream and yell that she'd never re-create the concentration camp of grotesque neuroses that is the nuclear family, and that the lesbian's superiority over the straight woman lies in that fact that she doesn't feel obliged to be a mother in order to exist—but she took to the role of auntie with a seriousness bordering on fanaticism.

We can rely on her for anything. My daughter's name is Clémentine, and even I wouldn't claim that she's easy to live with. In fact, if being a pain in the ass was a sport, she'd be an Olympic champion. But she never complains when we tell her she'll be spending a couple of weeks with my sister. The mother of my daughter, Léonore, who is suspicious of everything and everyone, is happy for my sister to take her.

My sister lives near Toulouse in a vast, ramshackle house where Clémentine has a bedroom up in the attic, and I remember the first time we dropped her off there, I was convinced as we drove away we'd have to turn around and collect her before we got to the end of the street. But Léonore didn't insist that we cancel our weekend plans. She trusts Corinne completely. And she's right. I'll tell her you send your love, she'll like that.

REBECCA

Don't you have any friends you can talk to? Before I even had time to ask how your sister is, you've gone and sent me a full-length biography. Luckily, I'm interested; I spent the afternoon reading your email.

No, I never guessed that Corinne liked girls, but now that you've told me, I can't help but wonder why I didn't catch on. When I picture her at the local youth center in a pair of shorts using her ping-pong paddle to bash people's heads in, it's obvious that she was almost a caricature of a dyke. But no one thought about it back then. There were a couple of queer guys in our group. But back in the eighties, as far as I knew, girls were straight and that was that.

I could easily have fallen for her. Thinking about it all now. There was something special about her—I wouldn't have laughed in her face. But at the time, the whole thing didn't seem ambiguous. Looking back now, I realize it was. She treated me like a princess back then, I called her a really good friend. It's quite possible that there were times when I was tactless. If so, please apologize to her for me. I spent a lot of time talking to her about guys I liked.

Our mothers had worked together at the Geiger factory. Mine couldn't put up with factory life for very long, but that's how Corinne and I first met. It's weird that I completely forgot that you existed—I mean, Oscar's not a particularly common name. I forgot you, but I can remember every detail of your apartment, the little kitchen on the left as you went in, the living room straight ahead, Corinne's bedroom on the right at the far end of the corridor. It overlooked the place Maurice Barrès. Back in the day, people had a sick sense of humor when it came to naming places and buildings. We lived in a seedy housing project called California. If that wasn't a "fuck you!" I don't know what is. Though I don't feel nostalgic about my childhood, it wasn't a bad neighborhood to grow up in. The fact that our apartment was tiny and cramped was annoying. I had two older brothers who made a deafening racket and exuded an animal energy that made the place feel like a cage. I liked going over to your place. Corinne had her own bedroom. Your parents were never there. It was quiet. I really liked the neighborhood. It never occurred to me that where we lived was ugly.

But these days, when I go back to visit my family, I see where we grew up through other people's eyes. It's not the terrible poverty. It's something different. It's neglect. It's having grown up in a place that no one gives a damn about.

When I went to high school in Nancy, some of my new friends lived in spacious apartments in the city center, or in charming little houses in new developments. I found that as boring as I did my own home. And their parents were no better. It was obvious that their mothers were hitting the bottle and their fathers were pretentious assholes. It never occurred to me to feel ashamed. During that brief period I turned fifteen. I didn't give a shit that at home we didn't buy Nutella but a cheap store-brand spread. I had only one thought, to get the hell out of that hick town and go to gigs in Paris or London. And I wasn't about to change my mind because of a Hermès scarf worn by some dumpy airhead on the terrace of the Café du Commerce. I wanted to leave that whole life behind.

OSCAR

Or maybe you didn't give a damn about how rich kids lived because you were beautiful. At fifteen, beauty trumps wealth. It's even more true for boys than it is for girls. A teenage girl might feel overwhelmed by the effect she has on others, she might be dismissed as an airhead because she's pretty. But a handsome young man has the whole world at his feet.

As a teenager—maybe it was masochism on my part—my best friends were always jocks. The sense of superiority it gave them about everything was grotesque.

Me, I was academically gifted. Being good at school was for kids who were ugly and for kids who were poor. Something for the deserving. My parents didn't tolerate poor grades. Not from my sister, and not from me. The least we could do was get good grades since we'd been given the opportunity to gain an education that might get us into a good profession. I'm from the last generation who were taught to believe that if you worked hard, you could move up in the world. The crash of 2008 did a lot to temper our expectations.

My mother would always tell us that we wanted for nothing, and constantly compared us to people who had really had it tough—I learned to check my privilege before I learned to read and write. It would never have crossed my mind to say that I wanted a Sony Walkman or a pair of Levi's—my parents would have thought I'd gone insane. In high school, I discovered rap. The son of an old teacher of mine was a tough guy who wore a black leather jacket. He'd been held back a year, and he had an older brother who'd done time in prison. I was in awe of him. He was a tall, blond, violent guy, but he liked me. He bought a compilation called *Rapattitude* and made me listen to Public Enemy, and Eric B. & Rakim. I became completely obsessed with rap, and within six months I was the one introducing him to new music. That was when I knew I really wanted money.

When my first novel was published and took off, I immediately tracked down your address because I dreamed of writing something for you. I'd run into Philippe Djian at a book fair, he was very kind, he was the one who told me that, for an author, writing plays could be lucrative. And I thought about you—almost every guy from my generation had a thing for you, but for me it was something special, because I'd known you when you were young. People called me a liar, and I had no photos to prove I was telling the truth. I dreamed of watching you perform a play that I'd written, most of all because I love your voice, the cadences when you speak. But I pretty quickly realized that, among my newfound literary friends, there weren't many who'd spent their summers working in a factory or stocking shelves in a supermarket so they could earn enough money to pay for their driving test. Once, I wrote a screenplay with a director my age who'd spent a summer working at the reception desk of a luxury hotel—he talked about it like he'd fought a war, like it was this exceptional achievement that meant he was more enlightened than other people, more able to understand the real me. That was another reason I wanted to write for you. I needed to feel closer to people who were like me.

I contacted your agent to discuss the project. He said we could talk about it again after I'd written the piece. That was more than a decade ago. I was just starting out, I thought I was hot shit just because I'd been on TV. Since then, I've seen guys much younger than me break out on YouTube, and they have the same arrogance I had. It's easy to get drunk on your fifteen minutes of fame. I don't mean that you get a big head or think you're better than you actually are, but you feel like people recognize you, that they're talking about you, that they're jealous of you. Critical success—narrow as it may be—takes up all your mental space. It's like a baby elephant you have to constantly feed and care for and exercise and entertain. A benevolent monster. You wake up one morning, you walk out of your house and, as Biggie puts it, "Sky's the limit." Everyone wants a piece of you, people fight to get your number, to hang with you, pay for your pizza, take your photo, get you to come to their gig. It makes you moronic. I haven't met many people that fame has made happy, but I've met lots that it's turned dumb as rocks. When I called your agent about my project, I expected him to do handstands because a young author of my caliber was interested in one of his actors. I thought he'd set up a dinner with you then and there and give me the keys to his country house so I could use it as a refuge to do my writing.

He put me in my place. I wrote a few lines. A young woman who's just gotten out of prison after a long stretch. I read a bunch of articles by women who had been inside. One of them said, what really struck me is that in women's prisons the visiting room is always empty. And I realized I'd never met a guy who said, my wife is locked up, I go visit her every week.

But I never wrote the script. I am among the authors—and we are legion—who practice the art of procrastination. The internet doesn't help matters. I open up a Word document thinking I'll do some work, and five minutes later I'm watching porn online.

Lately, I've been spending my days playing dumb games on my phone. When I say "day" I mean the whole day. At about nine in the morning, I roll my first spliff. I put on a CD, turn on the radio, or look for a podcast—and I start playing. Until it's time to eat. By then, I've usually had a couple of spliffs, so often I'll fall asleep and wake up at about five, when it's time for my first beer. Either this gives me the urge to go out and meet people so I can indulge in more booze—or something stronger, if the opportunity arises—or I go back to skinning up spliffs and end up binge-watching some TV series. I keep playing on my phone while the TV is on. I can spend six or seven hours a day playing—my phone is a narc, every week it tells me how much time I've spent playing. And when I say dumb games, I mean dumb games. Free downloads. I'm not talking fantastical worlds filled with heroic quests and magnificent graphics. Oh no. Games for morons. If anyone ever stole my phone, I'd be ashamed to go and pick it up, that's how bad it is. We're talking completing every level of Candy Crush. And I pay for the bonus levels, of course. I'm one of those people who get completely sucked in. People say gaming has the same effect on the brain as taking cocaine. I believe them. Nothing is more calming than spending three hours glued to my screen.

Apparently, some of the most sophisticated minds in the world are tirelessly working to figure out how to keep you playing for as long as possible. It's the science of addiction. People who could be researching ways to improve our lives or make the internet less damaging, people who could be analyzing how the web could make work easier and people happier, use their talents to make sure you spend as long as possible playing Zombie Apocalypse.

I procrastinate. It's very different from having writer's block. My head is filled with reams of dialogue, detailed scenes, I know what I want to write. Instead, I do something else. I don't do something interesting, or something fun. It's hard to explain. Being a writer is a pain because all your friends imagine you spend a couple of hours a day effortlessly churning out some bullshit, and you're done. It's impossible to make them understand that the very simplicity of the process makes it difficult to write, and all your time is taken up trying to get started.

So I never did write the monologue about a woman being released from prison after fifteen years and rediscovering Paris. I am procrastinating. Right now, it's serious: I'm completely blocked. I've just published a novel, and everyone's talking about me, but not because of my book. I've been MeToo'd. Something I wouldn't wish on my worst enemy. I feel like the whole world knows. That's why I'm telling you. Maybe now that you know, you'll never write to me again. I can't say I would understand. But you wouldn't be the first.

ZOÉ KATANA

Chronicle of my fist in your face

I've been writing a feminist blog for years now. I'm used to the vicious pile-ons, the rape threats, the death threats, the comments on the size of my ass or the pitiful state of my intelligence. I'm used to your male rage.

But until now I've never named names. Hence the thunderous outcry since I named Oscar Jayack. I dared to tell my story. My point of view is a terrorist attack. I'm confused about my feelings. Someone should rip out my tongue and let him speak. I say: being sexually harassed for months means waking up one day and not recognizing yourself. It means taking years to admit that you'll never come back, that the woman you were is gone forever. It's the fear you feel on a day-to-day basis, it's becoming a different person. It's the shame that someone looked for your weak spot, found it, and destroyed you. The shame that it was so easy. And the fact that no one gives a damn. I said: I didn't have the means to defend myself. And I've told others, if it ever happens to you, get out. Get out as fast as you can. I say: it's time the shame was on the other side. You're the ones blowing this out of all proportion. Not me. And your rage validates my decision.

When I say, "It's unbearable," I'm told, "Everything was fine until you opened your big mouth." Everything was fine for as long as it was possible to coerce my body into this equation of desire; my body, but not my words. On set, I'm needed, I'm the young ingénue that the hero has the hots for. But no one wants to hear about what I feel. And it's not just men who tell me to shut up. Women do it too. They tell me that what's happened to me has always happened, and that they managed to put up with it. Centuries of women before us managed to deal with it in a dignified fashion. And I say that they've choked back their shame and pasted big smiles over their sleepless nights. I say that every time a man forces his pleasure on a woman he is instinctively submitting to the laws of the patriarchy, and that the first of those laws is to make sure that we are excluded from the domain of pleasure. And to force us, from an early age, to be part of that structure. Keeping us shackled is the duty of the foot soldiers of the patriarchy. They fear what might happen to the world order they have created if they allowed us to flick the bean in peace. That murky, primal fear—that is the dark continent. Female sexuality was referred to as the dark continent because it was vital not to disclose the practices that shape it. Incest, rape, coercion, harassment. The ways in which female desire is thwarted had to be concealed at all costs. The things we are exposing today are not chance accidents. Our bodies are forcibly drawn onto the battlefield, because they must be mutilated. Our saying no is merely part of the spectacle. We can identify with the bull in the bullring: like the bull, we have been reared and nurtured for the sole purpose of being put to death in an arena where we stand no chance. The patriarchy is and always has been a display of strength and power staged in such a way that it protects the killer and allows the crowds to cheer him on, for the sheer beauty of the ritual. What is being celebrated when a man rapes a woman—rapes her good and proper—is the very essence of the patriarchy: a mindless, macabre ritual intended to bring power to its knees, to confirm that, even stripped of power, violence can triumph over what you most fear.

But today I belong to the army of abused woman stepping out of that silence. You can track me down, threaten me, insult me. It won't change anything. We have broken the wall of silence. It's time the shame was on the other side. When a teenage boy posts a picture of a girl giving him a BJ, he needs to know that one day his name will be published and he will be humiliated. We need to teach our daughters to be proud of their fellatio. It's absurd that young women might contemplate suicide just because someone has photos of them having sex with guys they fancy. It's the guys using their male privilege to demean them who should be thinking about offing themselves. Teenage boys should venerate girls who give good blowjobs. Instead, we're pilloried for wanting to fuck them. And when we refuse, it's worse.

So the problem is my voice joining the hundreds of thousands of other voices, where there should be silence and erasure. My voice is a single snowflake in the avalanche that will bury you. I choose to speak out, to say that I went to work every day with a knot in my stomach. My disgust making me feel disgusting, but going anyway. Ashamed of my rage and my inability to articulate it. Not all the men who worked for the company were bastards. But all the men were complicit, because it was an unwritten rule: the public space is a hunting ground. Not everybody hunts. But they all stand aside to let the hunter pass. And I am convinced that I am a fool.

I was hired to work for the publisher because I had several degrees, had done a number of internships, because I was hardworking, meticulous, punctual, because I was a fast learner. And I was also hired because I was young and slim, because I had long lustrous hair, big blue eyes, pale white skin, because I dressed well, because I painted my nails. It wasn't just me they were hiring, it was my youth.

And in one-on-one situations with him, I never really knew how to handle things. I babbled and took a step back, looked away, left the room, I sat pressed against the door of the taxi, I squeezed my knees shut, I blushed, I forced myself to laugh, I left early, I moved his hand away, I hugged the walls, I wore flats, I ran around a desk when he was drunk and he found that hilarious, I gritted my teeth when he groped me, then, one night, I just ran out of the place. I scurried away like a pathetic little rabbit. People saw me leave, sobbing, defeated. All they could see was the colorful little scene. The big macho author and the little PR girl.

Oscar would phone me in the middle of the night—and I'd be too terrified to go back to sleep. In hotels, he'd knock on the door of my room, and I'd be too terrified to go back to sleep. I'd throw up before I went to work, but I'd smile and say *bonjour monsieur* like nothing had happened, because if I shouted I was a hysteric who couldn't control herself and if I sulked, I was unprofessional and unwilling to make an effort: it was like those nightmares where you try to scream and nothing comes out. I screamed in silence while around us the little drama entertained the gallery—people were waiting for me to give in. He was flirting with me. I was playing hard to get. We each had our roles.

Today, when he says that he couldn't possibly have known how devastating it was for me, what he's really saying is that I was the only person who didn't think he was great. The author as drunken, red-blooded, hardscrabble son of an unemployed steelworker from the east, the wunderkind who played up to the image people expected of a fucking prole like him. He was the great author, he sold lots of books. When the situation deteriorated and he started to complain, someone suggested assigning him a different publicist, there could be no question of losing the great writer. And, as far as I know, Oscar Jayack never bothered to wonder what became of me. I've come back to tell him. I never got another job.

There are hundreds of thousands of us, all telling the same story, and there are hundreds of thousands of bosses pretending it's a big joke. Telling us, "We can't hear you." They never change the record. They summon up the memories of feminists long dead and gone, and claim that things used to be better. Because, obviously, even feminism belongs to them. Good old Simone de Beauvoir wouldn't have complained about a hand on her ass, oh no, Simone was part of the golden age—when rape victims kept their mouths shut, ugly women were happy to be wallflowers, and lesbians hid in the shadows while the little secretaries that men knocked up were sent off to die somewhere else. The good old days when domination was crystal clear to the dominated.

Men's liberation never happened. Your fantasies are submissive. They say "domination," and you can only get it up for domination. They tell you to enlist and fight in the war, and you say that weapons are more important than the air we breathe or the water we drink, that weapons are the bedrock of humanity. When we attack bosses, you panic. You fall over yourselves to defend the bosses. That's what you're doing: falling over each other to reassert the right of the boss to do what he likes. We can hear what you're saying: whatever you do, don't throw off your chains, you might break ours in the process.

REBECCA

Are you maybe a bit clueless when it comes to choosing who to piss off? If talented sociopaths can instinctively sniff out a perfect victim, as narcissistic perverts go, you're the runt of the litter. Of all the women currently working in publishing, you had to pick the only one going gangbusters on the internet.

Quit bitching, it's not like she went to the cops. These days, you get the impression that girls treat the local police station as a second home, give them the slightest pretext and they're there. Zoé Katana is just expressing herself, it's not clear what exactly you did to her, but she took it badly. Which is fair enough—I mean, I've seen interviews where you claim to be left-wing, so you must be thrilled that women who have never had a voice are starting to say what they think about the world.

Besides, there's no such thing as bad publicity. It's a bit of a cliché to say that, and I know from personal experience what it's like to take one on the chin. But, actually, it's true. Public figures like you and me, we're streetlights. People hang stuff off you, they piss on you, they lean against you to think or to throw up. They do what they like. All that matters is that your streetlight is on a busy street. And once you get enough passing traffic, it's automatic, people assume you're a decent guy. The problem with the internet is that the people who support you are less inclined to shout it from the rooftops than those who want to string you up.

Even so, to be crystal clear, if you're writing these long emails in the hope that I'll publicly defend you, I'd rather die. There's no way I'm about to piss off my card-carrying feminist audience to defend a moron like you. You're a writer, so write! I've heard you bitch in interviews all over the place, but I haven't seen you publish your side of the story anywhere.

I have to say, I find Zoé pretty funny, I can understand why she's so successful. She's of a generation that is easily worked up. And she has no shame in exploiting it.

Why not? My generation of women are famous for our ability to put up with shit. We were told, "No feminism, it turns men off," and we said, "Don't worry, Daddy, I won't bother anyone with my little problems." But all around me, I saw women being broken. That it all happened in a dignified silence didn't help anyone.

Personally, I thought the game worked in my favor, so I played it. I never had to force myself to love men, and they repaid the compliment. But now I'm nearly fifty. And my problem isn't that they love me less than they used to. It's that I find them less attractive. Men don't age well. You constantly need someone to take care of you, reassure you, understand you, help you, nurse you. It's too much work. Younger women are right, your masculinity is fragile.

Anyway, that aside, I found your stories about your theatrical monologue and your writer's block infuriating. When I was ten years younger, anyone and everyone would get in touch and suggest this or that project. And guys like you didn't suffer from blocks of any kind. Stop reeling off all the problems you face in an attempt to justify why hardly anyone offers me work these days. If I wanted peace and quiet, I've got it—I have all the time in the world to relax. I could probably learn a dead language with all the time I've got. I'm an actress. Other people's attention is my livelihood. I'd like to be philosophical, to tell myself these are the rules of the game. But don't come crying on my shoulder that the only reason you haven't written something for me is because you have problems with your attention span. Fifty might be a little old to play ingénues, but it's a little young to disappear completely. I don't like feeling sorry for myself, and you'll note that it's something I never do publicly. I get it, this is the game. It lasted as long as it was going to last, I have nothing to complain about, at least I made the most of the times I lived through. But don't take me for an idiot. You didn't write a piece for me because you know that any theater director—private or public, it doesn't matter—would advise you to cast an actress who can fit into a size 2 and wouldn't recognize a VCR if she saw one. No one gives a damn whether my name would still be enough to fill a theater. No one gives a damn whether audiences want to see me. It's not the audiences who decide that no one writes parts for women my age. That comes under another law entirely.

You make me laugh with your pitiful grievances: "You can't say anything anymore, you wind up being canceled for the slightest thing, it's an affront to culture and to civilization." You want to know what it's like to be canceled? Talk to any actress my age. And believe me, I'm lucky, my decline has been a gentle slope. For most women in acting, it starts when you hit thirty. And I don't know a single male actor who supports us. Oh, they don't revel in the fact that things are difficult for us. When you meet them in a restaurant, they don't gloat that you've been sidelined while they've never worked so much in their career. But it would never occur to them to say, in this movie I'm screwing a girl of twenty, I'm fifty years old, why not cast an actress closer to my age, at least that way they wouldn't all be unemployed. They know the producers would look at them like losers. I asked my agent, why does no one ever give me a role written for a guy? Just look at me, I'd be a lot more convincing in a male role than two-thirds of the men working in French cinema . . . He laughed at that. But I wasn't joking. I've always loved bruisers, I've hung around with them all my life, I know what I'm talking about. At my age, I don't care if you ask me to mess up my hair, make myself old and ugly—but prissy little male actors . . . Not that it matters, no one asks me to do anything these days. Not me, or any other actress my age. When I was the center of attention, I knew it was because of my beauty. I knew that when I turned fifty, no one would hire me to do nude scenes, the scenes where a naked woman on a bed takes a phone call, where she takes a bath, or chats to another woman in a steam bath. I was eager to read screenplays where I didn't have to ask the director, "Why does she take her clothes off before watering the plants?" I didn't realize that no one would give a shit that I'd spent my life on stages and film sets, that I knew what I was doing, that I'd built a rapport with the audience. In a way, I assumed that things would evolve as I grew older. That never happened. It's one of the reasons why, when I read Zoé Katana, part of me is thinking, "Why is she so bent out of shape?" and another part knows that she is right. Things don't evolve if you don't force them to.

Given that guys of your generation have a tendency to parade private messages on social media and that I'm not entirely convinced of your intelligence, let me spell it out for you: if you publish a single word I've written to you, online or anywhere else, I'll gouge your eyes out. Call the tabloids, you'll find that I'm on good terms with most of my exes and that I have a thing for toxic masculinity. So when I say, "I'll gouge your eyes out," it's not a trope, it's a threat. Within my inner circle, I can easily find an ex-boxer, a Hells Angel or a mercenary to track you down when you least expect it and gouge your eyes out with a spoon.

OSCAR

I'm not writing to you in the hope that you'll support me publicly. A selfie of the two of us eating cotton candy at a carnival wouldn't fix my reputation. It would definitely tarnish yours, but without clearing my name. I am the focus of hatred for half the population of the country. It's unfair, and I wouldn't want anyone to have to go through it. I took a fancy to a PR agent years ago. If you google my name now, you'd think I rape kids in elementary school playgrounds.

I'm writing to you because I feel like I'm dying alone, because I've lost everything and I don't know what to hang on to. I'm writing to you because I haven't drunk a drop of booze, because I haven't snorted a line of coke, dropped an E, smoked a spliff, or popped a pill to help me sleep for more than two weeks, and I feel as fragile as a child. I'm writing to you because I'd rather talk about the past than wade through the daily shit that is the present.

The day I saw you from a distance on the terrace of that café on the rue de Bretagne, I'd just come out of a Narcotics Anonymous meeting. I'm embarrassed even to mention it, but I force myself to go. I've always scoffed at people who don't get loaded. Real men drink whiskey, smoke blunts, swig codeine syrup, and snort rails as fat as girders. They eat greasy food, pump iron, and don't give a fuck about woke bullshit. And real men don't feel utterly destroyed because some slut starts whining ten years after she had her ass groped. When it comes to being a real man, I've failed on every level. I'm puny, I eat like a bird, I'm borderline hypochondriac, and I'm losing sleep because I'm being crucified on Twitter. The only macho thing I was ever any good at was getting wasted. That was the only difference between me and some dorky highbrow asshole. I was more devoted to my identity as a poly-addict than I thought. In a way, it was the only thing I had going for me.

But instinctively, I know I have to stay the course. I don't even understand myself. When I go back over the shit that's happened, play it over and over in my head, it always ends with the same closing scene. The moment when I go home and I know that my only hope of getting through this is to stop getting high.

This whole MeToo thing was previewed to me weeks before it happened. I'd run into Katelle, an editor who was taking one of her novelists in for a radio interview. We bumped into each other going into the studio, when we were emptying our pockets before going through security. Seeing them together, I wondered if she was fucking him. The guy's got a pretty ripped body, for a writer. He's from Brittany, has piercing blue eyes and something of the sailor about him. I was thinking, if they're not getting it on, why would she come with him to an interview for France Culture?

We were waiting for the elevator when she suggested I wait for her at the Bar des Ondes, across the road. I was only there to read a couple of passages of Calaferte for some program. People always think of me when they're doing something about a working-class writer. Which means rarely. I had nothing in particular going on that evening so I said, sure, I'll wait for you, suspecting there was some kind of problem. Katelle and I know each other a bit, we regularly see each other at book fairs out in the sticks, and we're both leading members of the association of piss artists. It's one of the great things about alcohol—with the exception of uppity intellectual pricks, people are generally much nicer when they're shit-faced. So everyone gets along, but not to the point where you'd phone and suggest meeting up for coffee one-on-one. Katelle's invitation was intriguing. I didn't think she was likely to make a pass at me—she's way out of my league. All the affairs she's had have been with serious big shots, government ministers, major TV journalists . . . I'd need to have won a Goncourt at the very least to have a shot at screwing her. That said, I would have been thrilled at the idea of things between us taking a turn. One year at the Crime Writers' Festival in Lyon, I realized that beneath her floaty, exquisitely chosen clothes she's hiding a magnificent pair of breasts. It's all the more surprising that she should hide them since it's pretty rare for a super-hot babe to do everything to hide the fact. But while I waited, I didn't have my hopes up, I thought maybe she wanted me to write an introduction for some guy who'd written a novel about working in a factory.

I know the Bar des Ondes well. It's where you wait when you're running early. Or where you end up if the program has been a disaster and you need a little stiffener before you crawl into a taxi. Katelle showed up, she said nothing, just sat watching the cars and the bicycles flash past the window, and then eventually she said, like someone dropping a heavy bag they're giving back to its owner:

"I wasn't sure whether I should say anything, but I like you, and there's this rumor going around . . . but maybe you've already heard?"

From my expression, she could tell I had no idea what she was talking about. She continued, "You remember Zoé, your first publicist?" and, not seeing how this could be a delicate subject, I said without a second thought: "Of course. I loved her. She did an amazing job on the book." I could tell that Katelle was distressed. "She doesn't work in publishing anymore. But she writes a hugely popular blog. On social media, she's considered a very influential feminist." Great, I thought, I didn't give a damn. I should have savored that moment, because it was the last time I'd hear the word "feminist" without shuddering.

"She hasn't published anything yet, but she's working on something at the moment. You know, the whole Me-Too thing . . . and it's true that in the publishing industry we're way behind the curve." I was listening to her calmly, still convinced that what she was about to tell me concerned someone else. Someone who'd really fucked up. There's no shortage of pretty embarrassing stuff in the business. I could see that Katelle was waiting for me to say something. I probably babbled something inane like "It's important that word gets out," and she realized that I had no idea where this was headed. "Oscar, she's planning to write about what happened between the two of you." I burst out laughing. Excuse me, but if one of us had the right to complain about what happened, that person was me. I had no desire to humiliate myself going back over the whole sorry story, but I'd been madly in love with her. And utterly miserable, because she turned me down. It's the story of my life, really—all around me I see soulmates and they look at me like some disgusting bug that's landed in their cup of tea. Katelle had to spell it out. What Zoé was intending to call assault was just me being a bit too flirtatious with her. In the run-up to the publication of the novel, three months, max. I never tried to force her into anything. I'm as vanilla as it gets, and besides, I'm used to being rejected. I don't jack off under tables, I don't strut around naked under a bathrobe in provincial hotel rooms, and I have no desire to push a girl up against a wall unless she specifically asks me to. At the height of my passion, I might have lunged for her lips when we said goodbye. I thought she was stunning, I loved spending time with her. Had I fallen in love with a girl who didn't want me? Absolutely. Did I harass her, humiliate her, break her? Absolutely not. But that night, I found out that for months Zoé had been bitching that I completely fucked up "her career."

Katelle glanced at the waiter and traced a circle above our empty glasses. She was annoyed. I was not reacting the way she had expected. I was denying the facts. She said, "The problem with that, Oscar, is that there are lots of people who remember what happened. She was constantly in tears—she talked about it to journalists, to other publicists, to people in publishing . . . and since things obviously couldn't go on like that, she was the one who was forced out. Your editor was hardly likely to ditch you given your book was a huge success. She was a brilliant PR rep, but she never found another publisher willing to take her on. And she said as much to lots of people. When she publishes her piece about you, her version of events can be easily corroborated." I said, "I don't really remember much about her leaving. But I never saw her in tears." Katelle's tone was flinty now. "You were drinking like a fish to celebrate your success. And it wasn't just the booze. It's not surprising you don't remember anything. But she talked about it. One evening, you cornered her in her office and threatened to kill yourself if things didn't go your way. She ran out. She ran for her life, Oscar, while you were screaming after her like a lunatic. The whole office heard you." I never did that. Or at least I don't remember doing it. The problem is that the whole story carries with it so much shame that a lot of details don't come back to me. I'm not ashamed because I wanted to force her to do anything. I'm ashamed because I told her I was madly in love with her and she didn't want to know. And because it's a familiar scenario: I'm not what you'd call a player. By now I couldn't stop Katelle, who ordered a third round of drinks. "You've had a string of scandals—take me, for example, now I don't really care, but how many times have you humiliated me in public, talking about my amazing tits? That kind of thing doesn't cut it anymore." I was tired of listening to this bitch. Deep down, she was getting off on what was happening to me. This whole MeToo thing is just revenge of the sluts. The point where we can no longer avoid listening to what they have to say—and, let's face it, it's complete bullshit. I gestured to the waiter for the bill. I could tell she was offended that I'd cut short her tirade. I thanked her and got into a taxi. The driver was an elderly gentleman, and his car smelled of sweat. He was listening to samba. I sat, staring out the window at the Seine, waiting for the Eiffel Tower, because I've always loved seeing it up close, especially at night. I was trying to convince myself that this whole thing was bullshit. Who cared about little Zoé's career? Her parents had paid for her to go to private school in Lyon, and they were probably the only ones who were disappointed. She wasn't cut out for publishing, end of story. I'm guessing that her parents are the reason she's cooked up this story about me, so they'll forgive her. The real truth, as everyone will realize, is that she wanted to take advantage of MeToo to get a little publicity for her blog. I didn't say anything to Joëlle, my girlfriend, when I got home. I rolled a fat two-skin, which, after three straight whiskeys, left me feeling sick. I was just starting to relax and think about something else when I had the brilliant idea of typing in Zoé's name on Instagram just to see. Over a hundred thousand followers. A terrible feeling began to spread through my chest. One I knew all too well. Sheer terror.

The following day, I'd almost managed to shake off this feeling of foreboding when I ran into Françoise dithering over a prepackaged salad in my local Franprix. Seeing me, she explained, "I always buy salad, but then I never eat it. I like having something green in the fridge. But when you think of the price." I suggested she split the difference and buy a cheaper, less gourmet salad, but she wouldn't hear of it. "The rest are all disgusting. This one has pine nuts and parmesan—I even eat it sometimes . . ."

Françoise has the voice of a heavy smoker and the seething rage of an old-school trade unionist. A lifelong feminist, she's made of tougher stuff than the snowflakes you get these days—not the type to be offended by a dirty joke. Just the opposite, when you're with her, anything is red meat to make people laugh. She's a regular at the bar just opposite my apartment, it's open late and I sometimes stop by for a late-night snifter. Her father was a schoolteacher, she knows whole pages of Victor Hugo by heart and is only too happy to recite them once she's got a couple of grams in her bloodstream. She's the same age as my mother, and she calls me "the author" and "handsome." She flirts with me with grim determination but no illusions—even when she's drunk, she's realistic about her prospects. To me, she is the embodiment of dignified feminism, that kind that came before the farce.

It was chilly at the salad counter, and I was happy to see her.

"Have you got time for a quick one? Something weird has just happened to me, and I'd like to know what you think."

"Affirmative. Why don't we go upstairs to mine? I need help replacing a mattress. With my sciatica, I can't do it on my own."

I agreed, and we headed to the checkout together. Already, I felt reinvigorated. I could picture her with a beer in one hand, slapping me on the back and dismissing any girl capable of mistaking me for a predator as a mononeuronal muppet.

As we walked back to her building and squeezed into the cramped elevator, I recounted in minute detail what I'd been told the previous night—which also allowed me to get my thoughts in order. In her place, the tiny living room was full of oversized dark furniture, and the ancient curtains were stained yellow with nicotine. Next to the television, a Chinese lucky cat sat cheek by jowl with a bronze bust of Karl Marx. A poster for a Basquiat exhibition on her bedroom wall clashed with the antiquated furniture; piles of books lined the walls. I had no idea she read so much. She left me to get on with replacing the mattress, it was a tricky job, and I'm not exactly built for heavy lifting. She watched me work, disappointed to see me struggling with such a simple task. Then she took out her iPad and her reading glasses, and asked me to take the old mattress down to the street while she did a little research on Zoé. I was sweating in the elevator, and as I dragged the mattress out and stood it next to the door, I thought it was a little inconsiderate of her to leave it there as though the sidewalk were a dump.

When I went back upstairs, she was deftly scrolling on her iPad, serious and focused. She gestured for me to sit. I asked if she had any beer in the fridge, she said no, she had coffee. I didn't feel like going back down to the store. I waited. I was starting to regret coming. I realized that we rarely saw each other during daylight hours. Finally, she delivered her diagnosis, stroking her chin with her thumb and forefinger, imbued with an air of wisdom and competence I'd never seen in her.

"I'll give it to you straight: you're in love, you're a sweetheart, your conduct is beyond reproach, you're a great guy, and some crazy bitch is making up stories to destroy you. Problem one: that's the same bullshit excuse spouted by every stalker rapist predator in your world. The way you guys see it, you're all innocent. Which means that you have thousands of victims on the one hand, and on the other, a bunch of great guys who don't understand why this is happening to them. Problem two, and this is more important: the only thing messed up about Zoé Katana is that she's got a blog, which even I know is so last century. Apart from that, there's nothing remotely deranged about this young woman. She's young, and young people are stupid. That much is true. But compared to the average, she's Einstein. Don't look at me like that, Oscar, you're hardly going to get up and storm out just because I'm not saying what you want to hear . . . I've seen you hanging around the bar for years. You are the personification of the friendly, thoughtless guy. Personally, I find it funny. But back in my day, women considered self-mockery to be a sacred duty. That's all over now. The best thing you can do is get out in front of it, write and humbly apologize, and ask if there's anything you can do to clear your name."

"Apologize? For what?"

"That's for you to think about . . . Maybe for abusing your impunity as a big-name author to harass a female employee? I mean, if you think about it, people should be able to get up in the morning and go to work without worrying about Oscar Jayack drooling over their tits."

"I never told you that . . ."

"No, but you told me that you were shit-faced most of the time and your memory of the period is vague."

"Françoise, I thought you were a warrior, a truly political animal, not like the sanctimonious snowflakes they churn out these days."

"Sorry, handsome, I spent my whole life earning minimum wage, one of the countless women who were told that they were lucky to even have a job. I know exactly what it's like to be the anonymous scapegoat who gets terminated as soon as there's a problem. When you're telling your story, she's the one I identify with. You're just a middle manager in the book business. And I've worked with enough middle managers to know how you tick."

"I'm gobsmacked that you see it like that."

"Smack your gob all you like, but your story is all too familiar, I've heard it a thousand times, it's the same story every drunk guy tells: how one day his wife went crazy and started accusing him of beating her. Except that when you meet the wife, her face is black and blue and you have to wonder why she'd do that to herself. I've listened to you, and I'll tell you straight: what you're saying doesn't hold water."

"The truth is you've got no choice, Françoise, you're siding with the baying mob because they terrify you. I've always thought of you as brave and reckless, but when you're sober you're just like all the rest. A scared little snowflake."

I got up, disgusted, she thanked me for dealing with the mattress, and when she walked me to the door, I saw pity in her eyes and I wanted to punch her. I was angry at myself for being so stupid, for walking into the lion's den. I should have known, I'm not a kid—the friends you make in bars should only be seen at the appropriate time in the appropriate state. As she opened the door, she stared hard into my eyes and said:

"Cut out the booze. Cut out everything."

"Yeah, yeah, you old lush, just because you're two days sober doesn't give you the right to bust everyone else's balls."

"You've got a lot of shit coming your way. If you can drag yourself out of your shitstorm of addiction, you'll have a fighting chance of getting through this thing and limiting the damage. But if you carry on the way you're going, as sure as death and taxes, you'll find yourself washed up, chief mourner at your own pity party and looking increasingly pathetic."

I stepped into the elevator without saying goodbye. Mentally, I was calling her a crazy old bitch. The fucking nerve of her, lecturing me, left me feeling murderous.

I went home, opened the bottle of champagne I always keep chilled, and cranked up Big L's *The Big Picture* on the speakers; two hours later I was in the bar with a bunch of friends, and I didn't sleep for the next forty-eight hours. That took my mind off things.

A few days later, I got the first text message from a B-list writer assuring me of his support. I knew instantly that it had started. I didn't read Katana's statement. I never read it, but I heard so much about it that I feel as though I know it by heart. More text messages. Every offer of support was like a stab wound. Nothing is more crushing than the pity of people who looked up to you. At the time, I thought, fine, I don't care. I thought I could take the hammering. I didn't fire up my laptop, I read a book. I didn't doomscroll on my phone, I took a walk. I felt confident. I told myself, something will come along and dethrone me from *trending topics*.

There was an article in *Marianne* mocking the girl for being a delicate snowflake. And it went viral—the insanity of the online world that entails reposting anything and everything about you and calling it "sharing." I throw a stone along with the rest of the crowd at the ritual stoning and I call that "sharing." I felt the reality they call "virtual" flooding into me, like water coming in under the door until you have to wade through it.

I felt alone.

I know lots of people. I have no friends. My only friend, since forever, has been booze or weed or Klonopin. Drugs gave me the illusion that I might be alive, as they say in NA. There are some I prefer over others according to the season—but any form of gear made me feel alive.

Being a writer means having zero power. That's why you see them all struggling to network, to get a little side gig as columnist on TV, on the radio, anything but write. You have to be dumb as a bag of hammers like me to devote yourself exclusively to writing.

Wiping me off the map is as easy as crushing a cockroach on a kitchen wall. These days, I'm the epitome of the white male. The daughters of academics, lawyers, and film producers are tossing aside their nail files to ream me out online. Zoé's given them the perfect excuse to forget to mention their own privilege. It makes me feel bitter. And ashamed to realize how proud I was to have gotten to where I am. You and I come from the same place—you know as well as I do that people like us weren't destined for literary stardom.

Françoise gave me a call. She cheered me up, I found her gravelly voice comforting. "At first you're convinced you'll never get through this, but all things pass. For better or for worse. This too shall pass. Focus on your next book," and I hung up feeling better than I did before her call. Then I remembered her advice to me as she showed me out: "Cut out the booze." I was coming down off a coke binge and crawling the walls with fear. I had the curious hunch that she genuinely wanted to help me, so I called her back. Three hours later, she took me to my first Narcotics Anonymous meeting. And it's become the only place in the world where nobody gives a shit what's going on in my life. The moment I say, "I want to be clean," they accept me as one of their own. I've been feeling like an outcast for weeks, so these meetings are precious to me.

I cut out the booze. Then the weed. Then the coke. I avoid going to any place where people do coke. I don't go out much. Maybe it's magical thinking, but I believe that if I stick with it, maybe this too will pass. And Françoise is right. I really can't afford to come out with some stupid shit when I'm rat-assed drunk. Not now.

REBECCA

When I read your email this morning I thought, this Françoise of yours should mind her own business and keep her advice to herself. But now that I think about it, maybe it's not such a bad idea. The correlation between men's alcohol consumption and their being assholes is underestimated. You can always claim you're making an effort and subtly imply that the booze and the drugs were the only reason you sexually harassed girls. As a strategy, it's a little weak, but you might pull it off. Good call, Françoise.

Besides, I've always thought people who can't handle their drugs should pack it in. I see lots of them, it's not their thing, they should quit. In my case, it's different. I manage the whole addiction thing so well, it'd be a shame not to carry on.

The first guy to ever give me a fix was a kid, just like me. We were seventeen. I never saw him again. I knew exactly what I was doing; we'd been warned that taking smack could mean life in prison. From the first minute, I knew that it would change my life, that it was what I needed. I was on heroin for twenty years. You must know—I was famous for it. I can't count the friends, husbands, lovers, agents, and directors who tried to get me to quit. Back in the eighties, men who regularly fried their neurons with cocaine and vodka went all judgmental if they found out you were on smack. When it came to getting shit-faced, there was a hierarchy. Booze and blow were fine; heroin, you had to quit cold turkey. It was ridiculous. At least these days people are puritans, they can't even stand cigarettes and red meat. This way, it's clear they're jerks.

So I was dragged to one of those Narcotics Anonymous meetings. I don't have particularly bad memories of it, but it wasn't for me. The clue is in the name: I may be many things, but I'm far from anonymous. This was about twenty years ago. Everyone at the meeting was hooked on smack. We were absolute scum. When the meeting was over, eight of the ten junkies came up to me to offer to score me some junk. I found the whole thing hilarious, but I never went back. Besides, I don't see why I should give up drugs when they give me such pleasure.

I've heard that the atmosphere is very different these days, that NA meetings are more serious. I even know a bunch of people who managed to come off crack through NA. That's impressive. Heroin is to crack what great literature is to Twitter—a whole different story. I say that because it sounds good. Deep down, real junkies take drugs because they know they're worthless. Whether you're shooting dope or smoking crack, what you're really doing is reminding yourself that you're shit. When you become a junkie, you're saying to the world, you really think you're better than me? You're deluded. Shooting up and fucking up is our way of telling other people how much we despise them. Their pathetic efforts to stand on their own two feet. I'd rather die than do yoga.

Then I quit. One day, I just got bored. I fell in love with a guy who didn't approve, and rather than lying to him, rather than doing like I always do and putting junk before everything else, I got clean. It wasn't the first time, only this time I never went back to it. I saw myself in photos. For years I'd had a slender, willowy figure, a regal, airy, indifferent look. But gradually my face became haggard, my eyes vacant, my complexion pasty. It didn't suit me anymore. And besides, I was tired of all the hassle, having to arrange for a dealer to meet me at the hotel every time I went to a different country. I took a bunch of other things and wound up somewhere else. I gave up a drug I adored and replaced it with others that I don't really enjoy. It's like an obsession. I can't tell you why I do it. But I'm not planning to stop. I always knew that me and drugs were made for each other.

I read online that the boozing, the blow, and the spliffs were all part of your persona . . . like a Bukowski or a Hemingway. A good choice, since it's pretty much the only macho thing about you . . . It's hard to square being a writer with any kind of vigorous masculinity. What you do is like embroidery. You'll disappoint a lot of fans if next time you publish a book you announce you're clean and sober. Fans like their heroes to self-destruct, it's fascinating to watch. There's this myth that artists lose their spark when they go clean. I don't believe it. I've got too many friends who never quit drugs yet went on to become total losers. The real problem is that as you get older, you're more of a pain in the ass. If recreational drugs stopped that from happening, we'd know all about it. Most artists have only three things to say, and once they've said them, they should find a different occupation.

Watching your friends grow old is the most unsettling thing I've ever experienced. You're blithely minding your own business and then one day you see it—a reflection, a gesture, a figure recognized from a distance, a particular way of walking. Your friends are old codgers. When this happens to you, you can train yourself to avoid mirrors. But the decrepitude of your inner circle is irrefutable evidence that you've lost the very thing that made your world. These friends still dazzle you with their charm, their wit, their humor, their curiosity. I've never been much interested in clothes, I like money because I like to squander it, I don't like to invite people into my home, I don't buy elegant furniture, and I don't keep my books. I am the people who surround me. The remarkable thing about my life is that I've always been surrounded by people I truly admire. That was my great success. More so than my films, when all's said and done. The thing that truly validated me, my equivalent of a private jet or a luxury mansion, the proof of my extraordinary life, was the friends who surrounded me. Oh, sure, we left a trail of empty bottles everywhere we went, used needles, coke straws, and punctured plastic bottles. We weren't model citizens. Until it all fell apart. There's nothing fair about getting old. Some people are wrecks by the time they're fifty. Idiosyncrasies you once adored have turned to caricature, impudence has turned to bitterness, jokes smell of piss and incontinence, all charm has been obliterated. Ultimately, it's a lot like adolescence, only more disgusting. Few people manage to preserve the same voice, the same quick-wittedness. You care for them like precious gems, the old friends who still make you happy. A new beau monde begins to emerge of people who have become wiser, more interesting, or more gentle. You cling to them as though they were the survivors of a shipwreck.

I don't know any debonair old smackheads, there are no Keith Richardses in my circle of friends. All the people I still love have gone clean. Except me.

So maybe at your age it's not a bad idea to quit the booze and the drugs. Writers are famous for early-onset old age. I don't know what it is about literature, but all the writers I know are unfuckable. You're bald before you're thirty, you've got hairy hands, you deliberately choose to dress like shit, it's like you've declared all-out war on the female libido.

Drugs are an extreme sport. You have to have the urge to blow all your identities to kingdom come: gender, class, race, religion. You, on the other hand, seem desperate to cling to the little scrap of respectability you've managed to acquire.

You seem bloated with the importance of your vocation as a writer. If you weren't, you wouldn't find it so difficult to actually write. If your books really are that important to you, quit bitching. I don't remember Camus, Genet, Zola, or Pasolini getting an easy ride. What was good enough for Victor Hugo should be good enough for you. When he published *The Hunchback of Notre-Dame*, it's not like all the fashionable people in the literary salons got together to congratulate him. He got a vicious drubbing, and he didn't spend the next year kvetching. If he'd wanted to be left in peace, he'd have written letters from his carriage to the nearest available marquise about how *stupendous* her ball was. You're happy to pose as the disruptive author but don't want the flak. Suck it up—it comes with the territory—and if you can't grow a pair, go buy some.

OSCAR

This morning, on Yahoo News on my iPhone, I saw my face next to the headline "Breaking the Silence: #MeToo Hits Literary Publishing." I didn't really want to read the article, but I skimmed through it and read some of the comments. Obviously, it was a complete shitshow. Every time I think the nightmare's almost over, it starts up again. I've been sleeping a little better recently. After this thing blew up, whenever I dozed off, I'd be awakened by a jolt of fear. When you've got the whole country baying for your blood, it's not easy to stomach. But I hear you when you say I can't take a drubbing. The thing is, when people tell me I'm a piece of shit, I automatically agree. You're the only one I've talked to about this. With the people in my circle, I pretend I don't care. And I don't bring it up during NA meetings either. I'm ashamed of seeming weak. More precisely, I'm ashamed to realize how proud I was of how far I'd come. In my family, being proud of your success was the cardinal sin. I mean, who the hell do I think I am? Who died and made you king?

It's like I'd had a Maserati for ten years and forgotten what a thrill it was to drive such a beast, and then totaled the car. And now I'm driving around in a beat-up wreck with flat tires and steam coming out of the radiator and I look like a slob. I can tell that the people who love me are embarrassed for me. The subject is pretty much taboo. I feel terrible that I've disappointed them. It's as if they're finally seeing my true self. As if what was unjustified was the praise and admiration they lavished on me.

I had to laugh at your list of authors who've had a shitty time. I never thought of you as a serious reader. I don't mind talking about Genet and Camus, but as for the rest of them . . . I have nothing in common with the writers you mentioned. Talk to me about Calaferte, about Bukowski, or even Violette Leduc and Marguerite Duras, but don't go bringing up bougie writers who from the day they were born were told: you're destined for greatness. You and I come from the same place, so don't tell me you don't know how vulnerable that makes me feel.

REBECCA

Fear of losing respectability, now that's bougie. In the worst possible sense of the word. Claiming to be an artist and wanting to be loved is absurd. I'm an actress. If nobody loves me, I don't exist. But I've never privileged the adulation of the masses over my own sincerity. I'm not a new brand of fizzy drink being marketed to kids. I'm not running in a presidential election I can only win by appealing to the majority. Daring to be truthful and sincere, that's what I'm selling. Being utterly myself, whether people like it or not. That's why I've been cast over other actors in major roles, it's not because of my looks or my voice. It's because I have the guts not to look like everyone else. To risk people not liking me—that's part of being an actor. You can't make a real impact if you're afraid to be who you are. It's not the mess you're in that's made you powerless. It's the fact that your next-door neighbors have stopped greeting you like a rock star. You talk about your lowly birth, the jobs your parents did, to play the victim and justify your weakness. But we both know that's just an excuse. Rich kids are no different from you. Everyone's in the reputation management business these days. That involves producing aesthetically consistent messages that directly target the client. They don't give a fuck about the truth, all they want is to win people over and not piss them off. You want your work to be taken seriously, but you're afraid of offending or putting yourself at risk. It's not that there's not enough blood in the inkwells, it's that what you want is to wear the crown of thorns without scratching your forehead or carrying the cross. No one wants to be provocative anymore. People just want to be well thought of. They want to be *nice*. The class clown who sits at the back, comes out with stupid shit, and creates merry hell isn't popular anymore. The dunce in Prévert's poem might as well pack his bags and leave—the only language people recognize these days is corporate speak. Serious, official, on the side of the angels and of the highest possible profit. Nowadays, people will put up with provocation only from those with power. But it's not fun when it comes from the top down. Wreaking havoc is only fun when you're a filthy little rat.

I'm a child of the eighties—our personalities are forged by the decade when we turned twenty—and let me tell you, back then, it was all good. The minute you came up with some bullshit theory, you'd get up on a chair and proclaim it to the world, and there was always someone in the audience who found it interesting. It was the antithesis of what happens on social media: the smaller your minority, the more important it seemed. We weren't fishing for likes. It was the opposite: we were determined to be hated by dickheads. As a strategy, it had a certain charm. Make the most of what's happening to you. It's more interesting than winning a prize from the local supermarket.

OSCAR

You were vicious even back in those days. You used to punch me in the back if I disturbed you and Corinne. I felt terrible, because I worshipped you. What you and I experienced was very different from childhood these days. We assumed disappointment was a fact of life. Our parents were never really around. They'd had children when they were young and still had their own lives to lead. My sister was often burdened with looking after me, but on Wednesday afternoons when she had a handball game— I don't know if you remember how shit-hot she was—I'd be home alone, even back when I was in first grade, and everyone thought that was normal.

I have a twelve-year-old daughter. If I left her on her own all Wednesday afternoon, my ex-wife would call the cops and take out a restraining order for child neglect. My daughter takes a bus that drops her off right outside my door, but from what she tells her friends, you'd think I forced her to cross Afghanistan on a donkey. When I was her age, I'd cycle five miles to go and play with my friends in Tomblaine and I didn't have a cell phone to reassure my parents, who wouldn't have worried anyway. And this wasn't because I was a boy—when she was my daughter's age, my sister regularly got caught sneaking out at night. She'd go to an abandoned train station where kids would sit around huffing glue from plastic bags. My parents didn't know about the glue. But they didn't call a shrink because their daughter was sneaking out.

Since I'm seven years younger than Corinne, when I talk about what she got up to at twelve, I tend to embroider a little, what I'm recounting is more the legend of Corinne. She was ahead of me in everything, so I was always hearing about the things she'd done before me. She left home when I was eleven. After that, whenever I saw her, she'd say she was worried I was retarded. She worried that I was being bullied at school, but she said it in a tone that implied "I think it would be pretty logical given how dumb you are." When I was little, she'd make me watch *The Exorcist* and *Scarface* and I don't think it did me any harm. I was scared, that's all. Afterward, she'd crawl under my bed and grab my ankles when I came in to go to sleep, my screams would echo through the empty house and she'd giggle. I don't have any good memories of her. I haven't gotten around to telling her that I'm in touch with you.

When I look at my daughter and her friends, I'm not sure their childhoods are any happier than ours were. At least in our day, grown-ups knew what to say to us.

Maybe they didn't hover over us 24/7, but they were full of convictions: work hard at school and you'll get a good job, for example. They were unshakable, and we believed them. What can you say to a twelve-year-old kid today? What can I say to my daughter? Perfect your Insta feed and you'll rack up lots of followers? Never answer emails after ten p.m.? Learn to pack a suitcase fast—you never know how much time you'll have when the order comes to evacuate the city and leave your home forever? What do I know about the life she will lead? Ironically, the greater the real risks to which we expose our children, the more we fuss about the details of protecting them. There's something grotesque about the contradiction.

I don't know what to tell my daughter about the world she will live in. We walk past refugees sleeping under bridges, and I tell her that back in their own country, they had a life but probably not much money, otherwise they would have stayed there. Maybe one day we'll have to pack up and leave for a foreign country too, I tell her. I don't know what possible use she could have for such information. And I'm not very good at educational support. She needs help with her homework. That's another new thing. She won't open a notebook unless there's an adult watching over her. I'm easily annoyed. I don't know how to explain things to her, and she's not particularly academic. I wish I were different, but the anger boils over faster than I can stop it. I end up screaming, she's crying, I feel like I'm watching the scene from the outside and it's heartbreaking.

I quit drinking the year she was born. I've been thinking about that a lot recently. I was madly in love with her mother, who was also a pretty heavy drinker back then. Since she had to give up everything when she found out she was pregnant, I said, nobly: I'll quit with you. I stuck it out for ten months. Long enough to realize that being sober was not remotely what I'd imagined. I assumed it would be like going on a diet, taking up a sport, or giving up smoking. A virtuous, challenging decision. One that wouldn't change my identity. A routine I needed to adopt. But I quickly realized that when you stop drinking, you lose everything. You lose your best self. I wasn't a maudlin or aggressive drunk. When I drank, I was chill, funny, at ease with my own bullshit and that of other people. I had often stayed home without having a drink for two days straight. But I'd never tried going to a friend's for dinner without touching a glass. I had no idea how gloomy, fretful, and quick-tempered I was. A miserable bastard. I'm a miserable guy. When you quit drinking, you don't just lose the person you were, the person you loved being, you also lose all your drinking buddies, the haunts where you hung out, the endless possibilities of the night, and the feeling that anything could happen. When you're sober, by eight o'clock you know exactly what's going to happen: three hours later you'll be in bed, and there's not much chance of anything happening to change that.

I felt like a solitary child on a makeshift raft drifting through dark, icy waters, and on the distant shore I could see a tight knot of people laughing, hooking up, happy to be alive. When Clémentine was born, I was close to having a nervous breakdown. I managed to hold out for another month because her birth was like a tornado— a never-ending round of sleepless nights, shopping trips, and bottle-feeds. At first it felt like one endless night. No one tells you the truth about babies. No one ever tells you what they're really like. Later, I realized it's because they've forgotten.

The first time I went out fully intending to fall off the wagon, I was convinced it would be an amazing night, but I was bitterly disappointed. The booze made me sleepy and the coke made me grind my teeth, the feeling of euphoria was meaningless and although I was shit-faced, I was still bored. But I didn't give up. I made it a point of honor to go out whenever I could, and gradually the pleasure of being shit-faced returned. Or at least I got back into the routine.

Now here I am, twelve years later, sober again. The difference is that in the meantime my love affair with drugs has palled. I've heard some people say "The party animal machine is broken." That's what happened to me. I take drugs and they make me feel great, but deep down they make me miserable and spit me out at dawn in a pathetic state. For me, the party's over. Or that party, anyway.

REBECCA

When I read about your sister sneaking out at night, it brought back the smell of solvent. I remembered the plastic bags we used to huff Pastali glue. We would bike to the hypermarket where they sold it. Between the housing projects, there were patches of vacant lots everywhere.

We'd hang out in derelict railcars and deserted farmhouses. We'd sit drinking on the banks of the Meurthe. There was no one watching out for us. We'd get eaten by the leeches. We'd make loud noises as we walked because we were terrified of snakes. We alternated between concrete wastelands and overgrown lots.

It's strange, but since we've been writing to each other, I've realized that not all my memories of that place are bad. I've never had much time for poring over the past. I had too much going on in my life. First off, because film shoots can be grueling. Each one eats up several months of your life. It wears some actors down, they get tired of constantly having to leave home, of putting their lives on hold to submit to the laws of the film set. Personally, I always loved it. In a way, I don't care whether the film is a success or not. When you're an actor, what matters is the journey. Every shoot is a world unto itself.

But it wasn't just films that took up all my time. I was constantly falling in love. Now, it feels astonishing to spend so much time not being in love. The most difficult part is not flirting less. It's desiring less, not getting swept off your feet.

Some love affairs are like hard drugs. You don't walk away, even after it's turned into a train wreck. You're convinced that if you're faithful, gutsy, and determined, things will go back to how they were at the start. When everything was amazing. Your mind knows that it's over, but your gut takes over, tells you not to walk away. In my case, it always happened with guys who felt like me. Who were trying to fill a void as deep as an abyss and blindly believed they could make it work.

If, after three weeks, a guy can tell me, "Sorry, can't see you tonight, got too much work," there's no chance our relationship will ever become toxic. Toxic is the meeting of two hopeless cases. I speak from experience. There are as many reasons for staying with a guy who's hurting you as there are love affairs. In my case, the problem is my need for things to be intense. The guys who were the best fucks were always the ones who hurt me most. It's danger that attracts me. If I don't feel threatened, I get bored and go off with someone else. And in situations like this, there's always a point when the machine for polishing rough diamonds breaks down. All you're left with is the ugliness. And still you can't leave because you don't want to admit that you fucked up. Again. If you walk out on the relationship, you'll see things for what they were. A succession of pathetic scenes with an asshole who threatens to throw you out the window if you so much as talk to another guy.

It's a question of education. When I was young, people told me over and over that the most beautiful thing in the world was to die for love! For a woman, there could be no more tragic fate. Except being a long-suffering mother. It's always the suffering in motherhood that's venerated. Never the fulfillment. And for lovers, it's the tragic death. If you enjoy having sex with men, you have to be ready to die.

We're completely at ease with the idea of men killing women just because they're women. Unless of course they're little girls or old ladies. Which means we're comfortable with the idea of a woman being the victim of a man as long as she's of an age to be sexually active. It doesn't matter whether she's married, a mother, or even a nun—from the moment she reaches puberty until the age of seventy-five, she's a suitable victim. And I think it's precisely because she could be sexually active. Society understands the murderer. Oh, obviously it condemns him. But above all, it *understands* him. He can't help it. Whether it's his wife or a stranger.

Imagine if instead of men killing women, bosses were killing their employees. Public opinion would be galvanized. Every other day there would be a news story of some boss killing an employee. People would say, things have gone too far. A person should be able to go to work without running the risk of being strangled, beaten to death, or gunned down in a hail of bullets. Now, if an employee murdered their boss every other day, it would be a national scandal. Imagine the news story: three times the boss filed for an injunction and got a restraining order, but the employee waited outside his home and shot him down at point-blank range. It's only when you swap killer and victim that you realize how broadly femicide is accepted. Men can kill you. This fact hovers over us like a cloud. We know it. It's like someone suggesting you play Russian roulette. I've never had a death wish, but I've always loved hard drugs, brutal men, and speed. I've had a lot more people lecture me about hard drugs than about men.

All my life, I've been warned about myself. I'm glad I did whatever the fuck I wanted. I was drawn to violent men, dangerous men. It's a phase that goes by so quickly. When I meet women in their twenties, I want to say: make the most of it, in twenty years' time, nothing will ever taste as pure as this. I was beautiful before beauty became an Olympic sport. We didn't give it a second thought—we were sexy, we drove men out of their minds, and women too, we were happy. These days I see girls come on the scene and they have a career plan that borders on madness—they see themselves in parts, as though they were made of Legos—ass nose feet hips inner thigh lustrous hair dazzling teeth plump lips breasts collarbones eyebrows. I feel like telling them, you're not a cartoon character and flirting isn't rocket science, stop worrying, stop wasting your time. Enjoy yourself. Stockpile glorious memories. Oh, and money. I didn't give enough thought to money. That's my one regret. As for the rest, I put myself in harm's way, I was destroyed. That's my story. I never learned how to be in love without being in danger.

And now I'm faced with a problem that's very new for me: passion is no longer a shop window where I can pick and choose according to my whim. Nothing appeals, nothing dazzles, nothing moves me. I'd rather suffer a thousand times and die from unrequited love, I'd rather be dumped, cheated on, humiliated, abused, I'd prefer any amount of wounded pride to this tedium.

OSCAR

A few years ago, I fell head over heels for a Spanish singer after seeing her on stage. I'd never have dared speak to her if she hadn't been ten years older than me. She sent me packing. She wasn't so helpless as to find me attractive.

I mention her because I've been thinking about what

you wrote a while ago about actresses not getting movie roles. It's something I'd never thought about. I don't expect much from movies. I find women who are over forty attractive. I think maybe I find them attractive because they don't remind me of anything. My mother didn't idolize me. Not as a boy, as a teenager, or as a young man. When I've compared my experience with that of my friends, I've noticed that some mothers are in love with their sons. People talk as though the objectification of a teenager or a young man is charming. Some people claim it's the little boy who wants to sleep with his mother. I think it's always the adults who desire the children. But the sons aren't allowed to complain. And I think that when you're fifteen, and you realize that every man in your mother's life has treated her like shit, and now she only has you, you freak out. And you can't complain. You can hardly take away your mother's sole remaining pleasure. The pleasure of smothering you with her boundless love—which must be chaste because it's maternal, must be benevolent because it's maternal. Sons are locked up in homes with mothers who desire them. They didn't get what they wanted out of life, they'll never get it now. Actual sex is the only thing off the table. Otherwise, they can give in to their passion. And I think that twenty years later, mama's boys are terrified when they encounter women who are the age their mother was when they were growing into men. They're frightened by the memory of the mother they couldn't escape. We don't allow fathers to talk the way mothers do. You can't imagine how many times I've heard mothers talking openly at the dinner table about the size of their son's prick. I have a daughter. I used to change her diapers. Her infant body was a thing of wonder. But it would never occur to me to talk about her lovely little pussy at a dinner party. People would give me strange looks. Even an ignorant slob like me, who'd never heard of feminism before it was compulsory, always knew my daughter's body didn't belong to me. That I had no right to talk about it in public. We set no bounds on the excruciating voracity of what we call a mother's love. And we do nothing to help these boys, we just leave them to deal with it. They have to say they enjoy their mother's obsessive love, because it would be too cruel to tell the truth: I find her wrinkled skin repulsive, I'm embarrassed by the way she looks at me, I find her loneliness upsetting, I can't stand the sight of her. So, when the time comes, they say these things to other women of her age.

My mother never took much interest in me. People take maternal love for granted. But when I see myself in photos as a child, I understand her. I wasn't particularly lovable. As a kid, I had an ugly little face: jug ears, lank, greasy hair, and these beady little eyes. I had no charm. I didn't come out with the childlike expressions grownups find so enchanting, and I whined a lot. In my teen years, my mother would complain that the stench from my bedroom infected the whole apartment, and would throw open the windows as soon as she got home from work. Looking back now, I can't say she was a horrible old woman—she was absolutely right: I hated showering and I stank. By the time I was fifteen, I was jacking off four or five times a day—I'd leave wads of toilet paper strewn around my room. It was disgusting. I know I should complain that my mother never loved me. It's something all mothers are expected to have in their blood, regardless of what the offspring looks like. Even when my mother was physically present with me, her mind was elsewhere. There was no animosity—she just found me boring. If I took to the streets shouting that it was an affront to my human rights, people would listen. Mothers are supposed to love their children, I don't know where that idea came from. It's difficult enough just taking care of them, I don't see why you should have to love them too.

There was no love in our house. We didn't miss it. I wasn't beaten. I wasn't neglected. My parents signed my report cards, they sent me to summer camp, they'd call the doctor if I was running a temperature, and they'd make cannelloni for my birthday because it was my favorite. It was the same for my sister. We felt no sense of injustice. All we wanted was to leave home as soon as we were old enough, we knew that our lives could only really begin somewhere else. At home, we represented a series of constraints. Like work in a way. A series of obligations. It's a view I find less ridiculous than the palaver of families today—at least our parents didn't rely on us so they could feel good, or to fill some kind of vacuum. These days, children have become essential to their parents' self-image.

REBECCA

I'm of two minds. Are you a complete moron or a genius? It can be a fine line. As for your theory—I'm not going to get into it because I feel it's riddled with holes, but I like the fact that it's provocative. Now that we've gotten into the habit of sending each other reams of emails, I can tell you—I found it hilarious that in the middle of a major Me-Too pile-on, you had nothing better to do than insult my looks. For such a delicate flower, you can be pretty reckless, which has a certain charm.

As for mothers, I've noticed that people always find some reason to criticize the way they care for their children. They're either too present or they're absent, smothering or selfish, overprotective or neglectful. Bullshit. Mothers do the best they can. Like fathers, by the way.

My mother worshipped my two brothers. In her eyes, they were more important than I was. She never pretended otherwise. She thought that was normal. But let me assure you—there was nothing sexual or lustful about it, and I never heard her talk about my brothers' pricks. True, she believed having sons offered greater validation. And she saw no reason to challenge the status quo. My mother was never much interested in feminist issues, to say the least. She was a stunningly sexy woman. And she was surrounded by men who were always being shat on from a great height. Being shat on when they had a job, when they were in prison, when they were unemployed—whatever their logic, they felt they were being shat on and she knew it. And she felt it her duty to ease their pain. She considered it natural to teach me to follow her example—with a slap in the face if necessary. She wanted to get me used to the idea that my role was to cater to the needs of men, a sort of lifelong stewardess. And my brothers took it all for granted. They wanted to be like the local thugs who kept an eye on their sisters and sowed fear and terror. As for me, I only wanted one thing: to date boys. I quickly realized that the best way to get my brothers off my back was to date guys they were scared of. At the age of fifteen I realized that, whether they were thugs, boxers, or Hells Angels, a "good guy" was one who scared my brothers shitless.

You really got to me with your little story about the singer. I don't want to sound cruel—though you're old enough and ugly enough to realize that you are ill-favored in the looks department—but it's a horrible moment when you realize that ugly guys feel they're entitled to try their luck. It's one of the most humiliating things about getting old. If some hunky bruiser gives you the brush-off when you've made your interest clear, it's a surprise, it hurts, but there is a certain dignity about it. Like cloaking yourself in your wounded pride—you can still make a dramatic exit. In the moment, it's awful, and I think it always comes as a shock to any woman who was once beautiful. But in a funny way, you know it's all part of the game. But when some average slob starts groping you and going for it, you discover to your horror that it's not because he's misread the signals; it's because you haven't yet realized how low you've sunk. Now that is truly grim. I'm not calling you a slob—I'm not trying to be aggressive here. It's just . . . well, I feel sorry for the singer you were flirting with. Whoever she is—even if she's a first-class bitch—I feel sorry for her. When you're young and some meathead who doesn't stand a chance tries his luck, you only have to look around to see the amused looks of "Who the hell does this guy think he is?" And it's genuinely funny, you almost have to admire the cojones of guys who have no self-doubt. But one day, one of those leeches sticks to you and when you look around, all you can see in the eyes of your fellow guests is "They'd make a lovely couple" so you clench your fists under the table and adopt a faintly ironic smile to hide what you're really feeling. An icy hopelessness.

ZOÉ KATANA

The angel of vengeance

I don't get only insults and threats sliding into my DMs. I mention this because I've noticed readers are starting to worry about me. I really treasure your messages of support. Some people tell me they've become feminists through reading my posts, and that makes me feel really fucking weird. But it makes me happy. It means it's all been worthwhile. Some ask me for advice. As though I have privileged access to some kind of feminist Mount Olympus where I gather pearls of wisdom from the founding mothers. One woman asked—and I could tell she was genuinely distraught—how she could reconcile her love of French rap with feminism.

What the fuck do I know? It's not a trivial question. There can be no simple answer. But what I can say is: Why don't we take a tip from that blazing star Lydia Lunch? She says, "Talking about 'feminism' is like saying 'potato.' What kind of potato are you talking about, and what are you going to do with it? You need to be specific: You're a feminist . . . with whom?"

Being a feminist with Audre Lorde is not the same as being a feminist with Catharine MacKinnon. You have to make clear "with whom." Me, I'm a feminist with Valerie

Solanas. It was the *SCUM Manifesto* that rocked my world. I shrugged off my shame like a coat I no longer had any use for. A certain kind of femininity—meek, compliant, permanently guilty—was miraculously stripped from me. Thank you, Valerie. I always recommend Solanas. With her, you can listen to all of Orelsan or La Fouine and still feel completely comfortable with your feminism. Solanas is so problematic that you'll never end up with the Mormons. She's demanding, but she's not restrictive. You feel comfortable with her, she's like the athletic wear of feminism. You're an all-terrain feminist, no one gives you any shit.

I also get messages from a radical lesbian. She's twenty years older than me. She tries to win me over. We end up finding common ground. She says: get off social media. Protect yourself. Publish your books, a bookshop is a lot less terrifying than the online world. She tells me: I set up a Twitter account just to find out what you write there, and an hour later I was so full of murderous rage that I deleted my account. She says: protect yourself, get off social media.

But I'm an online activist. It's dangerous. I don't give a fuck. This is where I spread the word, where I respond, where I represent, where I meet people. I give precisely zero fucks about being a "real" writer like that asshole Oscar Jayack, who thinks that what he writes is important because it's part of the old, lamestream media. All he stands for is his pathetic little name on bookshelves.

My radical lesbian friend says she's a feminist with Monique Wittig. According to her, my being heterosexual is a tragedy. You don't suck cocks, you cut them off. I beg to differ: sex is the only area where guys make themselves useful. Everywhere else—at home, at work, out in the streets—you never really know what they're doing besides being a fucking pain in the ass. But you can't deny that, in the sack, some of them really make an effort. I even know a few guys who are gifted at it.

She tells me that's just because I've never experienced sex with a woman. She writes to me about William Burroughs. Who murdered his wife when she was twenty-eight, put a bullet through her forehead. He claimed he was drunk, that it was an accident. She says Burroughs hated women the way Solanas hates men, but not in a funny way, because he's on the side of murderers whose crimes we hush up. He didn't quote Solanas because he knew that men erase women's names when they write history, but he picked up her idea, only in reverse: Burroughs dreamed of a society where women were no longer needed to reproduce. She laughs and adds: but that's science fiction, there's no way of propagating the species without women's bodies just yet.

She sends me a quote from an interview with Burroughs where he says: "I think that what we call love is a fraud perpetrated by the female sex, and that the point of sexual relations between men is nothing that we could call love, but rather what we might call *recognition*." She tells me it's all in there. The idea of a feminist conspiracy. Subordinates constantly plotting behind the bosses' backs. The idea that women are responsible for what is done to us. The victim is always the guilty party. And the notion that there can be no solidarity, no "recognition." To men, we are the alien sex, the enemy sex. The opposite is not true. But that's the problem—how can you peacefully coexist with someone who refuses to "recognize" you?

OSCAR

I want her to quit talking about me. Every time Zoé Katana mentions my name some fuckhead among my friends always lets me know. It's like some gruesome thing clinging to the back of my neck. It reminds me of the thing in *Alien*. A slimy creature grafted onto my body and slowly sucking out the marrow. I wish she could just forget about me. I don't understand why she is so desperate to cling on to me. I can't believe I'm the perviest guy she's ever met. It's transference. Some other bastard gave her a rough ride and she's taking it out on me.

And, if I'm being totally honest—which for some unknown reason I want to be with you—the worst thing about it is that I want her to like me. It's horrible. It reminds me of the kid on the playground who'd give anything to be friends with the school bully who's tormenting him.

When I fell in love with her, it wasn't some bullshit ploy by a big-name author who struts around with his cock out wondering why women aren't fighting each other to sit on it. I wasn't lusting after all the girls who worked for my publisher, or the journalists I met, or anyone at all. At the time, I had a girlfriend, things were going well between us, I didn't want any grief. I'm not a stalker— I'm well aware that just because I'm obsessed with some girl doesn't mean she'll fancy me. Okay, I'll admit that I always seem to have a potential love interest, a romantic obsession, it's like I need the reassurance of a possible relationship. Usually, I keep my fantasies to myself. But

I felt like she and I were made for each other, and that she knew it. It's related to the head rush that comes with having a successful debut novel. It was no accident that the girl I fell in love with was the person who ushered my book into the world. Zoé was the one who told me all the good news. She kept phoning to ask if I was available. She'd sit in a taxi outside my place and spend hours talking to me about myself because that was her job, and I got the wrong idea. I fell in love with her, and I didn't realize that her attentiveness and the impression she gave that she was fascinated by every aspect of my life were part of the job. I got worked up. I didn't think of her as pretty or sexy: she was the love of my life. I trusted her implicitly. I never for a moment imagined that she would be my downfall.

I was cautious. About everything. I'm keenly aware that it is a privilege to be where I am, to do what I do. Not having to grovel or beg for a job. It's something I often think about when I wake up. I think, I'm going to get through the day without having to deal with a single person I don't want to see. It's a luxury. Nobody can fire me. Even now that everything is going to shit, they can't take my name off the books and replace it with the name of some guy who doesn't have a MeToo target on his back. And I spend my life doing something that is meaningful to me. Very few of us are so fortunate.

I always knew it was precarious. Those of us not born into privilege know that it's just a benevolent twist of fate. It can all go away. And it comes with certain responsibilities. No one owes me anything. When I was fifteen,

I watched bailiffs storm into our home because my father had racked up debts. And even then, it wasn't the glamour of the badass gangster or the tragedy of the social misfit, just a middle-class mediocrity who couldn't do his accounts. Money a bit tight, a few too many months of unemployment benefits. Where we come from, you make the slightest mistake and you have to start over from scratch. And the older my father got, the harder it was for him to reinvent himself. When you're a wage slave, there's no networking. You accept a shittier job, and that's it. And what my mother was earning wasn't enough to make ends meet. I watched my parents' whole world fall apart. In slow motion. I know that my position is precarious, that anything can happen. I have no right to make mistakes.

So I was cautious about everything. Like a decent working-class guy amazed by his good fortune—by that first fat check, which amounted to four times the annual minimum wage, because when I started out, I calculated everything in terms of the minimum wage. I wrote crime novels. Back then, I used to knock them out in a couple of months. So I was making a fortune. And as soon as I raked in a little money, I was cautious. Tax returns. Never leave anything out, never make mistakes. Don't try to be clever. Pay taxes where you actually live. Pay your rent on time. Never have dinner with politicians. Turn down honors and medals when they're offered. Steer clear of white-collar criminals, the least respectable of all. Steer clear of friendships with drug dealers, thugs, and pimps. Don't post shit online—although, if I'm honest, in the early days I was tempted to set up accounts under fake names just to let off steam. At worst, I sent spiteful, slightly insulting emails for a couple of years—before I realized that anything from my account could potentially become part of a lawsuit, where asinine jokes can be ticking time bombs when taken out of context.

I was careful about what I said when sitting on café terraces or leaving restaurants at closing—the minute the first camera phone was launched, I knew that the only place I could say whatever the fuck I liked was in my own home, with the doors locked. I was careful about the people I hung out with: anti-Semites, homophobes, rapists, racists who didn't even have the middle-class vocabulary to be subtly racist. I gave these guys a wide berth, even if I really liked them.

My middle-class conscience told me: Your novels and articles pay all your bills, you get to travel all over the world because your books are translated and the taxpayer is footing the bill for those little jaunts, so when you're on a plane, behave yourself. You have to keep your nose clean. And I did. Actually, I was pretty paranoid. I was smoking shitloads of weed. That only heightens your paranoia.

I didn't think about women. It never occurred to me to police my love life. That was one part of my life where I never thought I needed to be cautious. I couldn't see the harm. I'd thought about everything—except girls. Nobody thought about girls. When it came to the taxman, the alt-right, the Blacks, the Jews, Twitter, we bit our tongues and kept our heads down. But girls? We couldn't see what the problem might be.

We assumed that women were happy. I grew up in a

world where it seemed that turning a guy on was the best thing that could happen to a woman. And, let's be honest, they played it for all it was worth. On TV, they primped and preened, they giggled at all the guys' jokes, they were constantly telling us that we had class, how much they loved macho guys. They fluttered around powerful men, they were kind to wimps and losers, they never made bitchy comments. Girls were one of the best things about life. We honestly had no idea they were angry.

How could I possibly know that falling in love would cost me so dearly? When MeToo happened, I watched from a distance. I had no idea it would ever affect me. Not because I'm so much better than other guys, but because I know most girls don't fancy me and I've made my peace with it. I collect rejections—I never thought it would be fun to force someone to have sex with me. I don't deserve any credit for that; it's just not one of my fantasies. My fantasy is being with a girl I fancy, she adores me, I'm really into her, I fuck her like a god, and she needs me like a drug. I'm not saying it's more ethical than any other fantasy, but it's legal. And out of my league—I've never managed to get the girls I fancied or to get what I wanted from the ones who fancied me.

I didn't rape Zoé Katana, I didn't raise my hand to her, I didn't try to blackmail her into having sex with me. I didn't try to get her sacked. These days, she tells anyone who will listen that the publisher was forced to make the decision because the situation was unmanageable and I was threatening to kill myself if she didn't give in to me. But that's not true. And all the vile comments online calling me a rapist, a dirty old man, and a disgusting pig—

they'll be there forever. My books might pay my bills, but I don't have enough money to hire the lawyers to clean up this shit. It's permanently associated with my name.

Other guys know—they know I've done nothing wrong, that I'm just a sucker who walked into a trap. They pray it won't happen to them, but they know it can happen to anyone. And they know what this whole thing says about me: that I'm a pathetic schmuck that women don't want to sleep with despite my success. And it's not like I set my sights on some young starlet on the red carpet. I went for someone in my league. A young PR person. After she left my publisher, I didn't write to her, partly because I'd been asked not to, and partly because I knew I had no hope—I figured she'd quit her job so she didn't have to bump into me. I gave up.

My girlfriend dumped me during all this mess. Things hadn't been great between us even before the scandal broke, and she didn't feel like going through all this shit with me. I suspect she got ahold of the password for my laptop and was reading the WhatsApp messages from my phone as they happened. It took me a while to figure it out. I was careful to delete any dubious messages before going home. But on my laptop, she could read what I was writing to other people. She was insanely jealous. She'd been cheated on by some bastard when she was young, and she never really trusted me. My version of events. Actually, I rarely lied to her because I rarely had the opportunity to cheat on her. Not because it was a conscious choice. Some girls are turned on by the media coverage, some are genuine readers, some are out for what they can get and think it'll help them get published, some girls think you'll make them the heroine of your next novel—some girls were attracted by my fame. But the attraction has rarely been mutual. Been there, done that. I cheated on the mother of my daughter shortly after my career took off and quickly got bored with it. Girls don't realize how pushy they can be. How they start from the assumption that if they're up for it, then I have to go along. I've had girls burst into my room and take their clothes off before the door has even closed. Girls I never asked for anything. I've also learned: never allow a woman you don't want to fuck into your hotel room, even if she insists, even if she sneaks into the elevator next to you. Long story short, the women I find attractive are the ones who don't want anything to do with me. But my last girlfriend must have been reading the WhatsApp messages I was sending during that awful period, and I think that's why she decided to leave. It was cruel—but, strangely enough, it didn't break me. I wanted to be alone.

And now I am. Completely alone.

REBECCA

Stop playing the victim all the time. Honest to God, it's exhausting, and I haven't got the energy to feel sorry for you.

You've probably fucked up more than you're prepared to admit to yourself. Your friend Françoise spotted that: you don't make a convincing innocent abroad. Something particular must have happened between you and Zoé

Katana for her to bring it up a decade later. She doesn't come across as dumb. If she wanted to make something up to get at you, she'd say you raped her. That it was harrowing, that she still can't sleep at night. If she'd set out to ruin your life, believe me, she'd have gone about it differently. If she accused you of rape, you'd be off the hook, there would be no evidence, but you'd have a rough year. And your reputation would be in tatters.

I don't believe that every victim's word is sacrosanct. Obviously, women sometimes lie. Either because they have no principles or because they think it's fair game. But the number of pathological liars among victims is infinitesimal, whereas the percentage of rapists among the male population speaks volumes about the sorry state of male heterosexuality. Yet I suspect you're far more shocked by the possibility of an unfounded accusation than you are by the fact that some of your friends are rapists. On this basis—how can I put this delicately?—even with a supersize dose of compassion, it's hard to feel sorry for you.

The whole feminism thing hit me quite late. For a long time, talking to me about sexism was a bit like debating capitalism with the CEO of Louis Vuitton: I understood why some people were critical, but personally, I only saw the upside. When Catherine Deneuve and Brigitte Lahaie signed an open letter defending the right of men to aggressively hit on women, I said to my new feminist buddies: calm down, girls, it's hardly surprising that Catherine and Brigitte think everything's fine and nothing needs to change. I mean, just think about how stunning they used to be. Taking down the patriarchy speaks to me now because I'm old. Twenty years ago, if you'd talked to me about Monique Wittig, I'd have said send in the legionnaires, let's have a blast.

But when the Créteil International Women's Film Festival organized a retrospective of my films, I discovered that the passionate, generous, female audience knew much more about my career than most film critics, and could expound dazzling and completely new theories about my work. It happened to coincide with my first major setback as an actress. Oh yes, I had to wait till the grand old age of forty before I saw someone else being cast in a role I desperately wanted to play. Just because it comes late in your career doesn't mean it hurts less. On the contrary.

Looking around at the sea of women who had turned up to give me a ten-minute standing ovation, I realized how trapped I was by the mentality of women my age. No men? It's not noteworthy, there's no money in it, it's not that important, it's nothing special. Yada, yada, yada. But times have changed. That's what I gradually discovered as I accepted invitations to women's film festivals around the world, a lot of them in the sticks. Women under thirty insist on women-only spaces. And it doesn't mean ditching the glitz and the glamour. You've got everything on tap. So I've moved with the times.

Up to that point, I'd never thought of feminism as fundamentally important to me. On films sets and in theater, it wasn't a major concern. Not to mention the fact that when feminists condemned me in the eighties and nineties, they were boring as hell. Some of them were obsessed with the idea of woman-as-sex-object, and since I was usually half-naked on the posters for my movies, half a dozen might turn up to a premiere and hand out leaflets protesting against my objectification as though I weren't there. Other times, they'd pen spiteful articles because I'd shot a torrid sex scene they didn't like, so I'd take it on the chin. But I can't say they really annoyed me, because for thirty years in France you barely heard a word about feminists.

I didn't think it applied to me. So, when the whole MeToo thing kicked off in the film industry, my initial reaction was to say to anyone who'd listen: "Mr. Weinstein always behaved like a perfect gentleman with me." I'm not a moron, so when I was asked to appear on television to discuss the subject, I politely declined. But privately, I left it at that: I'd seen so many actresses at Cannes behave badly, trying to get his hotel room number the minute they realized who he was, that at first I didn't particularly sympathize. Zoé Katana is right, the weirdest thing was his entourage. For decades, Weinstein was king of the world. I didn't just see women fighting to get close to him, I saw film distributors send girls into the front lines. They knew precisely what they were doing. And nobody said anything. I've seen parents whose careers didn't pan out like they hoped dispatch their teenage daughter as an offering. But now that he's been dethroned, you don't hear from any of those people anymore. This applies as much to Weinstein as to all the guys who've been MeToo'd. Not a single person in their entourage thought to say "Excuse me, but what you're doing is a crime."

Then I talked to one of my female friends. She gave

me her Weinstein story. He'd always behaved like a perfect gentleman with her. Then one day, he grabbed her by the throat, lifted her up with one hand, and pinned her against the wall. She was saved by a TV executive who was trying to find a quiet place to do a line of coke and stumbled on them in a corner. When she got back to her table at dinner, she told the men at her table what had happened, and they burst out laughing and pointed to the dress she was wearing. She laughed too. I told her I was sorry, and she asked me if anything similar had ever happened to me, and I said, "No, thirty years in the business, and I've never had any problems." She said, "I'm not surprised. The guys you date are seriously terrifying."

I hadn't thought about it like that. I genuinely believed that the guys around me behaved like gentlemen because I was also impeccably behaved. But she's right. My boyfriends were always thugs and gangsters, and no one wants their kneecaps broken. And besides, it wasn't hard to sustain my famously irreproachable behavior since I was born bankable. I never felt inferior in a film producer's office. They were the ones who had to pull out the stops to keep me happy, because they desperately wanted me to sign the contract.

After that conversation, it was like the scales fell from my eyes. I have a lot of female friends in the film business, and not just actresses, but makeup artists, stage managers, casting directors, and assistant directors, and every single one has a story to tell, a story we'd never talked about despite spending weeks on set together. So I changed tack. I stopped believing that a positive attitude could change things. And, simultaneously, I realized that even stupid little gold diggers I'd seen doing things I disapproved of had every right to complain. But they didn't. Nobody feels sorry for an actress who puts out to get a role and doesn't get it. It's unfair. Women who sleep their way to the top have unique qualities. They should be admired. I was wrong to judge them when they were simply playing the game. It's not like they made up the rules of the game—I'm sure they'd much rather things had worked out for them as they did for me. No hassle, first major role just after eighteen, and international stardom. But they're too nice, they smile too much, they had no choice. I've seen brilliant women directors simper like teenage girls to potential financiers. That doesn't make them airheads or gold diggers. They just happen to work in the movie business.

As your friend Zoé so succinctly puts it, there's something for everyone in the MeToo movement: activists, ballbusters, airheads, and brilliant women. I seek out people who I understand and who like me. That way everyone's happy. I've always been the most individualistic woman on earth, and the most elitist. But I realized that, as an individual, there was nothing I could do to change attitudes about my age in my profession. I couldn't force movie producers and TV channels and film distributors to give me work. It's humbling to disappear simply because I've grown old. But I'm not ashamed, because I can see that it's not my fault.

Zoé Katana speaks a language that I've learned to listen to. The language of angry young women. Five years ago, I wouldn't have gotten through the first paragraph of one of her posts. I'd have thought, she has to be a snowflake, only snowflakes allow themselves to be victims. But menopause has changed me, and I now know that when you find yourself in a shitty situation that, as an individual, you can do nothing to change, you need to say so. So that others can say "Me too" and "I hear you."

And I hear you too, buddy. I've always liked men. Some of you have made me happy. I have no hard feelings. A lot of you still behave impeccably toward me. And not just guys my age. And while it bothers me that I don't get offered roles anymore, it doesn't bother me that older men have stopped coming on to me. I'm not remotely interested.

I like young men, fighter jets: buff, self-assured guys with a thuggish attitude and a fierce spirit in their eyes. Ugly, brainy guys are constantly telling women like me, in an apologetic tone, "Beauty is fleeting." As though intelligence and talent weren't. I don't just find guys my age unattractive, I find them boring. But I've already told you all about that. You'll think I'm fixated.

So, yes, I hear you. I understand. What's happened has come as a nasty shock. You'll get used to it . . .

OSCAR

I'm not complaining. But the only time I can forget what's going on is when I go to NA meetings. Usually, I have to force myself. Beforehand, I'm convinced that this time it won't work, that it's not worth it. And every time I'm wrong. The veterans told me that for the first three months I should go to a meeting every day. When I heard that, I thought, never in a million years. One of the great things about NA is that we're all hopeless cases. It's designed for people whose response to advice is thinking "Never in a million years." And I end up going to a meeting every day. To me, it feels like a little bar in the middle of nowhere. No one is expecting you, you go if you want to, you never know who'll be there, there are famous faces, fuckheads who drivel and ramble on, and people you like—and gradually it changes, the people you liked turn out to be bores and the ones you thought were morons will say something you find moving and you see things differently. Sometimes there'll be a girl I find attractive, and I'll glance at her from time to time, being careful not to come on too heavy because the last thing I need is to be on the NA list of sexual predators. That's something I don't think I could bear. So I never try to chat them up after the meeting. I keep romantic crushes to myself.

Whenever I go to an NA meeting I haven't been to before, I feel shy. As shy as I was before I hit my teens. There's something childlike and fragile about the feeling that's unfamiliar to me. I never thought of myself as shy. Ever since I was fifteen, whenever I felt anxious, I'd order a whiskey. Usually before I felt anxious, to be honest, I'd be looking for something to get me shit-faced, to make the day more interesting. Getting blitzed is my antidote to boredom, to embarrassment, to shame, to the blues; it's my way of celebrating, of relaxing, of finding inspiration, of chasing away nostalgia. It's the Tabasco sauce of the everyday, the thing that counteracts the blandness.

It's been my one-stop solution for everything. And if one particular poison becomes problematic, I change things up, or change the people I'm taking it with. I've never thought of myself as a timid guy, and now I'm realizing that I am one. I never thought of myself as a coward. After all, I'd taken any fix that was offered to me, I thought of myself as a daredevil, a kamikaze, a head case. Now I have to fess up to the fact that, without drugs, I'm a forty-something guy whose heart starts hammering when he walks into a room full of strangers.

The weather was fine that morning, so I headed off on foot at about eight o'clock; I love Paris at that time of day. When I reached the church on the rue Saint-Maur, there was already a little crowd gathered outside—the guy with the keys was late. A couple of them nodded or waved, I just stared at my phone and wondered if they recognized me. We make up a curious congregation. A riddle that's hard to fathom when you see us from the outside: What do these people have in common? A young Black girl, earbuds screwed in, straight hair pulled back, inscrutable, beige turtleneck, huge gold earrings. A woman in her sixties, pale eyes, a shock of white hair, wearing a brand-new tracksuit. I thought she looked like a madwoman, but later when she spoke during the meeting, she was very articulate, gentle, not at all what I'd imagined. A good-looking guy, about my age, close-cropped hair, manicured hands, protruding chin. He looked like a veteran, maybe gay, but when he spoke, I decided he was just a supercilious dick of no interest whatsoever. A fifty-something Arab, a big, hulking guy with a face like a gangster, one look and you knew he'd been in prison for years, but when it was his turn to share, he wasn't the goon I'd imagined: quick-witted, killer quips, pithy phrases. He knew the NA program forward and backward and gave a flawless presentation on working the steps. He had the whole room laughing. He had the face of a killer, but no one was afraid of him. Next, a twenty-something guy straight out of a photo shoot, with that beauty that transcends gender and has a devastating effect on everyone, and when I saw him, I thought, with a face like that, you must feel a little cut off from the world. He spoke in a low voice, wringing his hands, he was having a really rough time, all he could think about was using, but he'd lost everything, he talked about his shame, and I felt like interrupting the meeting and saying, are you insane? How can you hate yourself so much when you look like an angel? A sallow curly-haired girl with wonky teeth, a weird woolen jumper, and a hideous mid-length haircut suddenly became luminous when she spoke during the meeting. She talked about how grateful she was for the program, about how far she'd come, and her gentleness was contagious; I could almost see her lighting up the room. An elderly gentleman, gargantuan, hideously ugly, seeing him I thought, I'm just kidding myself, I can't believe I've got anything in common with these people, because this guy really looked like a human wreck, but I was surprised once again when he took the floor and talked about his recent trip to Algeria to see his father, who chugs beer from sunup to sundown, and about his impossible desire to save him. And what he's saying is devastating because I realize that I also wish I could have saved my father—not from booze, but from his fatalistic sadness—and for me too, that's impossible.

I was getting up every five minutes to pour another coffee. I couldn't sit still. At the start of the meeting, during the reading from the basic text, always the same reading, I was thinking, that's it, this time it won't work, this is the point when I realize that even here, I don't fit in. The first person to raise a hand looked like a bank manager, he had a rasping voice and spoke so softly you had to strain to hear what he was saying. "I'm happy to be here with you all, I need this fellowship to get me through what I'm dealing with right now. My eldest daughter is in a really bad way, she's been hospitalized, she's suicidal and I've spent my whole life avoiding her, I've ducked out at every possible opportunity, and, yeah, I could say it's because I wanted to get wasted but actually I think it's the opposite, I got shit-faced as much as possible so I didn't have to see my children or think about my wife, who I hate, and now the sense of guilt is the one thing that is bearable, what's really devastating is the realization that all I can do is mourn our relationship, that it's all my fault, that it's too late. I fucked up at being a father. And I need this group so I can talk about my regrets and my doubts." He was getting all choked up, so he quickly ended, "To be able to say these things, to have people listen to me and not judge, is miraculous. I don't feel that I deserve it. I've come here to try and find the strength to do my best from now on, instead of brooding over my mistakes and making no attempt to put things right." I became aware that I was crying. I was stunned, because my mind was telling me one thing—that I didn't care, that I didn't fit in—and my gut was telling me a different story. One that said I'd come home. I can't remember ever crying in front of other people. I don't remember being told not to cry at home or at school, so I don't know where I learned not to. The girl sitting next to me gave me a smile, she wasn't trying to say "Take it easy" or "Let it all out" or "I've written a book, could you introduce me to your publisher?" She was smiling because she felt moved too. And it didn't bother me. I tend to be suspicious of people, especially right now, I'm always wondering about ulterior motives for their kindness. But that morning, I just accepted the rules of the game. There's an atmosphere of benevolence that's part of it. It's free. I raised my hand, but there were too many of us, so I didn't get to speak. It didn't matter. Every word from these strangers—unemployment, Tinder, housing, work, the dentist, the neighbors, porn, sugar, rage—touched me as though I were saying it too. At the end, I told them how long I'd been clean: it's been three weeks already. I've never gone that long without taking anything. I'd never even thought about it. I wasn't thinking of quitting when Françoise took me to that first meeting. I was thinking, maybe quit booze for a while, just until things settle down. Someone said, "It took me years to realize that the only way not to take drugs is never to take drugs," and I laughed. But it stuck in my mind. And that's where I am now. Right now, I'm genuinely happy that there is one place where people applaud me, where they congratulate me, and for something that's not a sham. Some of them know what's happening to me with Zoé Katana. They don't really give a damn. It's none of their business.

REBECCA

I admire your approach. This clean shtick of yours is a long day's journey to the end. It takes courage to put yourself out there. I'd be surprised if Zoé and her cohort appreciated the effort. After all, they mostly exist online, they're not interested in engaging in a dialogue, in reconciliation, or in reaching out to anyone. The online world is all about rage. Oh, occasionally you see someone using it the old-fashioned way, to express complex ideas and respond to counterarguments. But as a rule, online activism is sheer fanaticism: once people convince themselves they're morally right, they think it's perfectly acceptable to slit their opponent's throat. I was a bit dubious about your approach. But you seem so genuinely happy with your new friends that I don't want to put a stick in your spokes. For once, you haven't been bitching . . . And in the meantime, I've heard a lot about you. Corinne messaged me. More of a marathon than a message, actually. You gave her my number, she WhatsApp'd, and I replied immediately—which is pretty extraordinary in itself because I get so many messages it's not humanly possible to reply to them all—and besides, I have an agent, and given the percentage he takes, the least he can do is deal with my messages. One of the things I like about you is that you never ask me when we're going to meet up. I don't like leaving home unless it's for work. I don't understand the point of being with people if we're not working on something. I can't bear all the small talk and the social niceties. So I text Corinne right back—oh, great. I instantly recognize the tone, the one I get from people who are really impressed because I'm famous and hate themselves for it. That aggressive familiarity that forcibly reminds you that they're not just ordinary fans, they're not starstruck, they're not talking to you from some lowly position. I let it pass. I know from experience that if things start out like that, they rarely get better. If she's got a problem with fame, I can't somehow remix her feelings and explain that I'm not going to give up who I am just to placate her. It's impossible to separate me from my public persona. I am both of them; you either deal with that or leave me in peace. And then, like clockwork, it came: "I'd really like to see you but I've got my self-respect and I don't trust actresses." I told her to go fuck herself. I don't know what Z-list actress broke her heart, but I'm a legend. If she can't deal with that, she should leave me alone.

And after five minutes chatting with her, I realized that you've been bullshitting me. As far as the people around you are concerned, you're not some guy who drinks a little too much playing the rock 'n' roll novelist. You're a fucking slob. A complete embarrassment. You're the kind of guy who can't hold his drugs but keeps on using. We're not in the same league. I was born for this shit. I'm surprised researchers aren't calling to study my case because I've been using for decades and I'm thriving. In my case, drugs aren't an escape from shyness or from shame—take away the recreational drugs and I'm still perfectly comfortable in any situation. What I'm trying to escape is boredom. Things move so slowly. You've seen the Amy Winehouse documentary, where she's clean and she comes off stage after a gig, distraught, and says, "It's so boring without drugs." I know exactly what she means.

I never use when I'm on set, because you can see it on film and you get takes that can't be edited together. And even though you spend endless hours waiting around on a film shoot, everything is so intense that I don't get bored. The rest of the time, it's so boring without drugs. That boredom isn't for people like me, we're warrior junkies, semi-pro addicts.

I googled the etymology of "addict." "In the Middle Ages, a man who could not keep his promises or his word was declared *addictus* and auctioned off to a master." Sold off to a master, relegated to the status of a woman, or a slave, a citizen dependent on the goodwill of others, and placed at the service of someone else, with no regard for his own interests. So being an addict is a way of relinquishing your power. Of trashing your privilege. Becoming incapable of keeping your promises and paying your debts. Personally, I think that we inherit our debts when we're born, that one day we'll understand the messages encoded in our DNA and realize that it doesn't matter whether Papa sang you lullabies or wrecked the house and beat the shit out of Maman. What matters is the story you inherit. What promises did I break to warrant being an addict? The real question is more like this: What broken promises did I inherit? It goes beyond my heritage in the bourgeois sense of the word. The mania rich people have for their family history. There's always a historical and political context to doing drugs. It's a way of acknowledging that you have a slate and simultaneously wiping that slate clean. Maybe it's the language I speak that stops me from breathing, and I regurgitate it by taking shitloads of drugs. Maybe it's the mortification of the adults all around me I'm trying to ward off by getting wasted. I remove myself from the situation, I extricate myself.

I'm making sure I'm incapable of being a good little worker, a good little wife, good little grown-up, punctual, polite, loyal. A reliable cog in a system. I'm faulty. I'm difficult to manage. I'm an insubordinate soldier. Good little soldiers take the drugs they're prescribed. Drugs are like violence. Lawful when used by the state. Criminal when used by the individual. If I take the drugs prescribed by the doctor, I'm a legal addict. I've noticed that junkies are the most resistant to taking antidepressants. If you're addicted to the legal psychotropic drugs, if you pop the pills the doctor recommends, you're a good worker. A model economic citizen. That's the real reason for getting wasted. Rejecting your country. Rejecting the language you speak. Rejecting the bit part of an honest woman. Rejecting the factory where your mother worked. Rejecting the trench where your great-grandfather died as an unknown soldier.

An addict is someone who makes promises they won't keep. It's saying, I'll be there tomorrow, and not showing up; it's saying, I'll pick the child up from school, and not turning up; it's saying, I'll do my job, and not answering the phone. This brutal, hard-won truth isn't necessarily the one you heard from your parents as a child—the bullshit bourgeois obsession with parenting is really a psychoanalytic obsession, a desperate attempt to prove that the wealth of the aristocracy and the bourgeoisie is the power to keep the world at bay. A middle-class child's bedroom has walls so thick they are impervious to the upheaval in the world. To the stench. To the sound of bombs.

A middle-class child's bedroom has walls so thick that the mother has only to sing the little lullaby and her babe is protected from the world around him. *Bullshit.* When you end up in a police station as a junkie, you're rarely thinking about your parents. Even if they didn't love you, thought you were an annoying brat, an accident, a disappointment, a retard, an ugly little monster. The truth you've come to find in the cell is a political truth.

And as often happens during a revolution, you quickly get swept up. There are always predators lurking on the sidelines of a riot. The problem is not that you're a slave to drugs, or a slave to a single solution. You are a slave to masters who hide in the shadows: the cops, the money launderers, the narcotraffickers, the borders, the mafia, the prisons—a catastrophic chain of futile violence and corruption. In taking what seems like a magic potion, I'm looking for freedom, comfort, joy, experience—and I end up on the dark web lining the pockets of thugs. And maybe that's what every junkie is looking for at the end of the road: harsh punishments, vicious beatings, being locked up in a cell. The genuine abrogation of his citizenship. Of everything that makes him who he is. When you take drugs, you do it because you're sick and tired of hearing anything about yourself or anyone else. It's having the courage to tell the truth: I don't love myself, and I don't love you either. It's your whole ancestry, your language, your people, your country that's in the cell with you, being handcuffed and interrogated. It's your whole ancestry, your language, your people, your country that's stubbornly lying and being manipulated, being mocked, being insulted, being suspected, and being sentenced.

And governments that criminalize junkies know this. Governments know that laws about drugs are primarily laws of economic dignity. Those from whom it's taken and those to whom it's given. The two-bit drug dealer is a criminal. He's providing a community service, he's useful and he does no harm to anyone. And he serves to launder the money of the hotshot stock trader, who serves no purpose and devastates communities. One gets the accolades; the other gets a jail cell.

I'd love to go back in time to the decade when drugs and I were friends and getting wasted served a purpose. I was like an overindulgent parent worried about her kid—protecting her from everything, terrified she'd get hurt or be unable to look out for herself. I picture my evil genie as having the face of a thug. The face of an ex-boxer. Terrifying but charming—and he protects me. He talks to me about boredom shame sadness shyness fear weakness—and I make it all go away. And just like in a fairytale, in the twinkle of an eye, reality becomes malleable. My evil genie is sexy. Why else would I have devoted my whole life to him? But these days, it's more like I'm possessed. The drugs don't work anymore. I know they don't. I'm bored even when I'm using. But I still do it. The part of me that wants to use is like a region fighting a war to take over the whole country. It's not fighting for independence; it's fighting for annexation. It's a dictatorship. But it's my country too. And, besides, it's my war.

Drugs are an undemanding form of rebellion, a revolution that can be smoked, snorted, mainlined, or swallowed. Bargain basement nonconformity. Any half-wit can get wasted. And it doesn't take courage to keep using.

Because the drugs are stronger than you are, it becomes an easy form of disobedience. Because ultimately, disobedience is always choosing to obey something other than the powers that be. To obey your instincts, or to obey justice, or to obey your desires. In the end, disobedience is just a way of sticking it to the Father: you're not the boss of me. Your word is not gospel.

But of course, choosing to submit to drugs means choosing to submit to the word of the Godfather, the word of the money-laundering banker. You become a paid-up member of a parallel economy only to discover that what you're submitting to is the same toxic masculinity. From one brutal act of violence to the next, it's always the same bullshit that ends up crushing us.

I feel like walking away. I feel like taking a different path, I feel like being unpredictable. I'm bored with being on my own. I feel like I'm a well-tended lawn in a middle-class house out in the boondocks. I feel like fucking things up. I'm exhausted by so much positivity. Read my lips: I'd rather die than do Pilates.

OSCAR

It's a war we're all fighting. This staying clean shit isn't easy. I barely recognize myself. I'm totally losing it. Yesterday someone said, "A gust of wind and I don't know where the fuck I am." He's got this lost air about him and this thing that's typical of junkies, a skittishness, an edginess, a willingness to embark on some disastrous or glorious adventure—anything to kill the boredom.

That's how I feel—a gust of wind and I don't know where the fuck I am. For someone like me, having to deal with all the texts, the emails, the overstimulation is a nightmare—I'm coming apart at the seams, I can't focus, the slightest thing wipes me out.

Last night, when I left a dinner I'd been invited to, it was lashing down so hard I huddled in the portico and called an Uber. A silent man quickly showed up in his big black car. He didn't have music on, he didn't ask me if I had a favorite radio station. From his face I could tell that he was completely shattered and I was grateful to him for not trying to make conversation. I felt stunned. I was glad I hadn't had a drink. I was relieved that no one had skinned up a spliff or mentioned calling their dealer. Which is par for the course in the publishing world, where alcohol is the drug of choice. I tried to feel proud of the fact that the minute I arrived I told them I wasn't drinking and no one asked me to explain—but I didn't feel proud of myself, all I felt was exhaustion and a nagging sense of strangeness. At being sober when I got home.

Nobody talked about the MeToo thing over dinner. I've always felt like an outsider in the business. It has nothing to do with the "class traitor syndrome" people talk about. I don't get this whole thing about fish knives, about not knowing which glass to drink from or which cutlery to use. I know I haven't been invited so people can check whether I went to catering college—and if I feel like saying *bon appétit*, I do, because everyone knows I'm not the son of a diplomat. I don't know the social conventions of my new world—what the fuck do I care? That's one of the advantages of being a drunk—at dinner parties, I'd hang out with the people who were drinking heavily, or making regular trips to the bathroom: the social activities most amenable to the mixing of classes. I was a cheerful, effusive drunk, which made me a popular guest. But no one in my entourage ever forgot to mention I was a factory worker's son. I've been publishing books for ten years, and that little factoid is in every article about my novels. The important point isn't "He got to where he is today by sheer talent" but rather "He's not one of us, isn't he exotic?" I embody the exception that's tolerable only insofar as it proves the rule: true privilege isn't about what you've achieved but about where you were born. And people will often say with a sarcastic smile, "But you're a little more middle-class these days, aren't you?" I don't know why journalists always say this in that half-exultant, half-curious tone of a trick question. As though somehow I should feel bad that an appreciation for hotel breakfast buffets, cashmere sweaters, and designer armchairs came to me late in life. As though I personally have to answer for the inequalities of capitalism, and the immobility of social mobility. Or they're rubbing my nose in the shit and snickering, "See—you like all this luxury, you fucking pleb." And I do like being rich, but I get the impression that they constantly need to make sure that they're the envy of the rest of the world. That's the real reason they create so much poverty. To make sure people envy them, because without the poor man's envy, the rich man's happiness is incomplete: he feels crushed. It's something I try not to talk about with them, but by far my favorite thing about being rich is not having to set an alarm clock in the morning. And going back to bed to spend the morning reading if I feel like it. What interests me in life is the royalty check that comes at the start of each year. Since I've been doing NA meetings, I've realized that I'm reluctant to put a figure on what doing drugs has cost me, financially. I never bought an apartment. I never bought a car. I never opened a college fund for my daughter. I pay for whatever I need to pay for. I never look at the price of things in the stores, whether I'm buying them or not. That's my luxury. And it's enough for me. But I know that one day I'm going to take stock: annual expenditure, how much on coke how much in bars how much on hookers—how much getting wasted cost me. In monetary terms—I'm not talking about this notion that's being bandied about that maybe I fucked up relationships, friendships, or working relationships that mattered because I was permanently wasted. That maybe I could have had a better relationship with my daughter. That maybe—and I've got a feeling this is really going to cost me—that maybe Françoise was right and I did fuck up with little Zoé. Maybe I wouldn't have behaved the same way if I'd been clean. First and foremost because I'm shy. It's a strange thing to discover about yourself when you're past forty. I'm as timid as a pimply virgin.

Ever since the shit hit the fan, I can feel people closing ranks. Recently, it's occurred to me that I haven't made myself submissive enough to fit in. If I'd been one of them, they would have muzzled Zoé Katana with the fearsome efficiency they wield so effectively. But not a single person picked up their phone to defend me.

REBECCA

I've had a friend staying for the past few days. I don't like having people in my home. She invited herself and I let her, it's less exhausting than keeping her at arm's length. I don't sleep well, I've got a pain in the upper back, I seem to spend all day twisting and turning my head, I hate it, and I'm in no mood to have to put up with Sandrine.

We've known each other since we were seventeen, we both came to Paris that year. We met at a Jesus and Mary Chain gig at Les Bains Douches . . . Neither of us had ever been there before, and we ditched the concert before the encores because we were horrible snobs and we thought the venue was tacky and square. Too many geriatrics, too many yuppies, too many jerks, too many trophy girlfriends—we were determined not to like the place. Our friendship was based on this mutual contempt. We cadged a couple of tabs of DMT and spent the whole night wandering around Paris telling each other every detail of our seventeen-year-old lives. There was something about her beauty that took your breath away. High cheekbones, eyes that were almost metallic green, and long white hands with supple fingers—she had something otherworldly about her. She wore a white jacket with epaulets and a sailor's cap—she was obsessed with Grace Jones. I've walked down those same streets many times since, felt the exultation in my legs, the sense of an untouched past that brings tears to my eyes. I wish I could go back to that night.

We were beautiful creatures, lost soldiers, and together we were ten times stronger. Our friendship was remarkably long and happy. It had all the advantages of a great romantic affair, minus the possessiveness.

I can't really describe our relationship now . . . I've cut ties with her more than once, but the bond between us is like ivy: you can rip it out and still it grows back. Sandrine knows exactly what she wants from other people, and she's a bulldozer.

She tends to talk with no consideration for who she's talking to. She's another person who talks to me about drugs, she says that if we had reasons to learn to retreat from reality when we were kids, as adults we carry on using strategies to retreat whenever reality hits too hard. Like we're a drawer that can be closed.

I picture the apartment where I grew up. The savagery of the bodies around me, like living among wild animals condemned to share a cramped cage. It wasn't just that the apartment was much too small to accommodate five bodies, it was the horizon too, blotted out by other buildings so that you had to look up to get a glimpse of sky . . . But I don't think it was my own feelings that I learned to run away from as a child. It was my parents' unhappiness. Unhappiness is very different from a lack of security. And children quickly realize that, if they let it, this all-pervading sadness will consume them, will suffocate them. Sandrine says she has cut out alcohol and sugar. She still smokes cigarettes. She plans to quit later. Excessively critical of herself. Of the small business each of us has become. She still drinks coffee. But she hates herself for it. The other day she ate a doughnut, and to hear her talk about it, you'd think she was a crack whore ready to give anyone a blowjob just to get her fix... Inside her head it's like Guantanamo Bay. Nobody could stand to live there. A penitentiary full of psychopathic guards swinging billy clubs and aiming for her ankles. She says, "I wanted to be more present in my life, more honest about my limitations and desires."

Her life is a shitshow, and nobody gives a damn about her desires... If you ask me, what she's doing is handing her inner child over to an abuser. And an abuser rarely says, "I'm going to smash your fucking face," unless he's a shameless self-confessed sadist; abusers prefer to use the logic of the therapist, the moralist, the teacher, the benevolent judge. The abuser creates the victim in order to inflict a series of punishments on them. Just because you're logical doesn't mean you're benevolent.

I'm used to being around Sandrine, but her presence has become insidious. Maybe when I use drugs, I'm granting the unspoken wish of the grown-ups around me when I was a kid, whose lives would have been so much simpler if I didn't exist... They pretended they were happy that they'd finally had a daughter, but they weren't very convincing; daughter or no daughter, my father was a thug. Whatever money he earned—and I think he earned a lot—he blew it all on himself. I was the third child, the one that meant a lot of extra bother for my mother... Going back over the timeline, it's clear that I was one child too many, the last straw that convinced my father to stop cheating on his wife with every woman in sight and get himself a new wife. As for me in all this confusion, I represented more sleepless nights, more days of sick leave, the bed that had to go somewhere, more school books to buy, more meals to make. I was a problem. My stepfather appeared in our lives before I learned to walk, and he always acted like a father. But deep down, I knew the two of them would have been happier together if they hadn't had to deal with the burden of my mother's three kids. So maybe when I get wasted, I'm fulfilling my parents' wish—I don't make a sound, I switch off, I act like I don't exist. I know you understand the concept—you've already told me your life story.

Sandrine never shuts up. "If I don't have the option of assuaging my everyday stress with a glass of wine, I am forced to confront the root causes of my anxieties." This is the phase she's been in for a while now. Fucking infuriating. I'm sitting there thinking: honey, your son's behind bars, you're old, you're alone, and your social worker's a first-class bitch . . . Your one success in life is that you've got a rent-controlled apartment in a half-decent suburb in the south of Paris where you can see trees from your window . . . I listen to her, but from a distance, "I am forced to confront . . ." Forced. Trained. The bullshit psychobabble of women who are merciless toward themselves. Be good to yourself, find your comfort zone, listen to your emotions, go tinker with the root causes of your anxieties. One more thing to take care of. As though it belonged to you—a houseplant you have to keep alive. And if that wasn't enough, you're expected to be happy. "My son just got a seven-year stretch, so I'll seize the moment and deny myself any pleasure." Dragging yourself before the court of your own conscience. In a virtuous gesture that's probably trying to blot out the true reality. A desperate attempt to be in control of something.

Whereas getting off your face is also a way of connecting to other thoughts. Opening doors inside yourself. Allowing the dust to blow in from outside. Withdrawing your attention from the market. And taking pleasure wherever you can find it. Sandrine says: "Addiction is trying to find comfort in something that's destroying you." And I say: unless it's making what comforts you destructive. And I can tell that she'd love to slap me, because she knows that's not what I really think—I'm just saying it to wind her up. And the more I listen to her talk shit about being clean, the more ideas I have to irritate her . . .

I don't know what to do about this old friendship, which has ended up like the matted knots on the head of a girl whose hair hasn't been properly combed. A tangle of guilt, affection, happy memories, hideous memories. The mirror is so tarnished I don't know what I'm looking for in it anymore.

We were sisters. That famous family you choose. We got into drugs at the same time, hung out with the same crowd. We saw each other every day. Then there was this guy who told me about this casting call, and all I saw were dollar signs, I already knew that an amazing life lay ahead of me, but I wasn't banking on the movies—I don't really know what I was banking on. It was a complete fluke. My whole world was turned upside down. It was never a problem between us. We had the drugs in common, and we loved getting wasted together so much that we stayed close. Wherever I was, she was still my best friend. And given her incredible beauty, no one made her feel bad when I dragged her along to a party or a film shoot.

I haven't kept many friends from my former life. Sometimes I hear people come out with some horseshit about how you abandon your friends because they're an embarrassing reminder of who you were before you were famous. It's not like that at all. Fame is a nuclear bomb. It creates a vacuum all around you. You take up so much space that it becomes uncomfortable—so you're drawn to people who are like you. But everyone always remembered Sandrine, they found her interesting even when I was around.

Then one day, she fell in love with some dumb fuck who claimed to be an artist, and she moved to Canada with him. They bought a house. All she could talk about was cooking and decorating. I forgot about her. She had a son. She'd still call me up, but all she could talk about was being a mother. I stopped picking up if I saw her number on the screen. Her boyfriend was a con artist. Things ended badly. She came back to France with her son under one arm and no sign of the father. I hadn't missed her. But when she knocked on my door, I said, sure, no sweat—I was heading to Italy for a couple of months, so I gave her the keys to the apartment. She stayed for a year. I was constantly working, so I'd request a hotel room even if we were shooting in Paris. At the time, it wasn't a problem . . . When I came over, all she wanted was to pack her son off to bed and for me to phone the dealer. We still had a laugh, but it always felt demeaning, she was constantly trashing my friends, my films, my entourage. She was jealous of me. We never talked about it.

Luckily, she found a guy she could aggravate and moved in with him. Suddenly, she was old . . . She stopped listening to music, stopped watching documentaries, stopped hanging out with friends. She sank into the adult life that scared us so much when we were younger. The boyfriend died of cancer, and I had to keep her at arm's length because she just couldn't get over it. She'd show up at my door all weepy and snotty with her son who was now her best friend. The two of them were like a family pack of misery. The son's grown up now, he's just been given seven years for a bank job where no one got hurt—it's a bit harsh, but money is sacred. He's weirdly sexy, not the sharpest knife but well built, and there's something animalistic about him that I find attractive. He needs some serious tattoos to look like somebody. But a friend's kids are off limits. I've been there before. The parents tend to take it badly. And besides, the kid didn't exactly turn out well. Some jackass said, "Come on, we're going to rob a bank, I've got a plan," and this jackass followed. He's locked up in Villepinte prison. So Sandrine is constantly over at my place. She spends the whole afternoon bitching and telling me how she doesn't do drugs anymore . . . When it gets dark, a flicker of joy lights up her face and she says: "Why don't you make a call?" She always insists that it's a one-off, "I just need to take my mind off things . . ."

Usually, I give in and phone the dealer as soon as she mentions it. But last night, I thought about you getting clean and I said, "I've quit." She knows I'm lying, but she can hardly ask me for a urine sample. She was so disappointed that I almost changed my mind, but I didn't. I wanted to get wasted, but not with her. I'd never thought about it like that before. Thanks to you I think I might have found a solution to an old problem—I'm guessing that next time, she'll ask someone else to put her up.

OSCAR

I can really relate to the story about your friend Sandrine. Lately, I've been losing friends the way people lose their hair, by the handful. I hadn't realized the extent to which the people closest to me are the ones I drink with or take drugs with. Cut out the booze and the drugs, and it's awkward between us. Corinne called. She wanted to talk about you. It was clear she'd launched a second—more successful—onslaught. I'm not surprised, she's as irresistible as she is insufferable. I didn't tell her about our emails. That's the basis of our relationship: mutual mistrust.

I'm writing this in the living room of a house in the south of France that I booked online six months ago. The fire in the grate hasn't really caught—there are billows of thick white smoke from all the newspaper I crumpled up to try to get it going. I'm looking at Instagram photos of my daughter by the pool on vacation in Ibiza. To me, she doesn't look remotely attractive. I feel terrible that I'm this ungrateful father. Opposite me is a cluttered bookcase: a beautiful edition of a Bob Dylan book, a row of CDs, a few Taschen art books, and some old decorating magazines. On the wall there's a color photograph of Tibetan monks walking past a waterfall hanging above a white upright piano. I can't play a note. I wish I had an ear for music. I don't even have a sense of rhythm. It seems that no one has been here for ages. The house feels lifeless, used but not lived in.

I find this part of France too windy. But Joëlle loves the Camargue. As I set down my suitcases in the hall, a vivid image arose in my mind of the night my ex-girlfriend sat cross-legged on the bed, scrolling through houses on her iPad. She was wearing a bright pink sweatshirt far too big for her, with sequined snowflakes on the front. She didn't have to do much to persuade me, because the house looked amazing and I worked out that it would come at the end of my book tour, so I thought, that way I'm giving myself a cutoff date. Because otherwise you can end up spending nine months doing signings in small-town bookshops, attending book fairs, doing podcasts, visiting schools, and a whole range of more or less decent activities that authors get offered when they're not mired in some stupid scandal. Joëlle works for the French Table Tennis Federation. This was the only time she could schedule her vacation. I'd imagined I'd spend my time reading, the weather would be glorious, and we'd go back to fucking day and night because, for once, we'd be relaxed.

When I think about the joy we felt as we flicked through photos of the house we planned to rent, it's like we were different people. None of the things that were to come had happened yet. I hadn't been publicly trashed. Joëlle hadn't shown her true colors: the self-centered bitch who's happy to be on the arm of the hot young writer but not prepared to stand by him when the shit hits the fan. I hadn't punched a hole in the bedroom door, she hadn't packed her bags in the dead of night screaming she was going to the cops and then I'd see what happened, she was going to burnish my reputation as a Grade A asshole, and I hadn't called her a fucking bitch. We were screaming so loud that I never took the elevator in the apartment building again, for fear of bumping into the neighbors. She didn't go to the cops. She came back two weeks later to pick up her stuff. It's a scene that plays out in every relationship: the division of the objects that made up a shared life. It's one I can't bear.

That was six months ago. I was knocking back whiskey, my best friend was dealing coke, my girlfriend was talking about going off the pill, and my editor was convinced my novel would be a bestseller, and if you'd asked me how I felt, I'd have said, I'm genuinely proud of how far I've come, "I can't believe we made it," that kind of shit.

But tonight, I'm alone in a freezing cold room, listening to Nas's "The Message" with nothing to smoke or drink. I haven't rented a car, so even if I change my mind, I can't imagine wandering out into the dark on foot, and I'd be surprised if there were many bars open late in this town. I've no idea what I'm doing anymore. And now whenever I feel like I'm going under, I email you.

The sound here is sublime. I listen to a lot of gangsta rap, mostly by guys from back in the day. I was a kid when I got hooked on rap. And I never moved on. I'm a French guy who listens to American music. A white guy who listens to Black artists. A guy who's never broken a law who listens to music by hardened criminals. I spend whole days doubting myself as a writer so I listen to diss tracks by rappers with big egos. Gangsta rap is like drag. Joëlle used to love drag shows on TV. It was while watching RuPaul with her that the idea first came to me. Gangsta rap is the performance of power by the very people it has crushed. It's a playful way of taking over a set of signifiers we've been told are sacred and beyond the reach of the poor, the damned. And I think the reason I've listened to rap ever since I was a kid is because it was telling me everything is performance. When a descendant of slaves appropriates the slave owner's things—the big cars, the mansions, the cool clothes, the hard drugs, the homophobia, the misogyny, the champagne, the provocative bling—he's not saying, glory to the victors. He's saying, "That's all it is," and "I can do it just as well as you." He's not exposing power, he's making it obsolete by appropriating its talismans. Whether we're talking about African Americans in the States or the lumpen proletariat in Europe—when kids get into rap, it's the story being played out. Five generations down the line, it's not the slave master wondering what to do with his shame. It's the man in chains who carries the burden of shame. Like a tattoo, a mark on the forehead. An indelible stain we don't know what to do with. We're constantly trying to forgive ourselves for the wrongs that were done to us.

I can remember every detail of the night we booked this house. I feel like writing to Joëlle to tell her it was a good choice, that the house is just as charming as it is in the photos. I wonder whether she regrets it, whether she feels sad. Over the past few weeks, I thought I was handling our breakup pretty well. But that's because I thought it wasn't for keeps. That we'd see each other again, that we'd start over. Now that I'm here, alone in this house, I realize how much I loved her, our time together, our shared projects. It's always the same: I only ever notice the beauty of things in the rearview mirror, when they're refashioned by nostalgia. I never imagined things would unravel so easily. It's as though my whole life was woven from flimsy fabric and it only took a tug on one thread for everything to come undone without a sound.

At night, I can't sleep. I desperately want a drink. I press my forehead against the windowpane and wait for my eyes to adjust to the shape of the trees. I'm not used to the darkness; I've lived my whole life in the city. It's been a long time since I was on my own. When Joëlle and I lived together, I was angry that she never left me alone. I couldn't bring myself to say: I need my space. I wanted to, but I kept silent, and resented her for my silence. I resented her when she invited friends for dinner and it ruined my concentration. Or when her parents came to visit and it ruined my concentration. Or when she spent every night binge-watching some TV series and I'd sit and watch with her, and it ruined my concentration. But I couldn't bring myself to say: I'm going away for a few days. Because every time I've ever said that to a girlfriend, it was because I was cheating on her. It was like having retrospective guilt—the guilt of past relationships attached itself to this one. An excruciating mess in a confused chronology. Well, Joëlle's not around to ruin my concentration anymore.

REBECCA

Nobody has ever left me. I've been cheated on, lied to, abused, all of that. But never dumped. I'm a love ninja—I glory in the start of a relationship. Guys don't have time to get bored before I've left them for someone else. A few months ago, I looked into the eyes of an ex-lover and saw something like indifference. That had never happened to me before. I'm not a woman you forget. And I don't know what it feels like to be dumped.

Earlier today, I went to see a director. Her apartment on the avenue de Clichy is like a palace: it takes up the whole of the top floor, and it's built around a terrace that's almost a garden. She tells me she's lived here for twenty years. I've never taken any interest in carpets and furniture, and I wouldn't even dream of having a houseplant. But I love the way other people try to create a space in their own image.

I'm staring at this woman and she looks old, much older than me. Actually, she's ten years younger. I can't get my head around the fact that I'm older. When she asks what I want to drink, I say, "Whatever you're having," and she says hopefully, "Maybe it's a bit early to crack open a bottle of wine." I think of you. I've never enjoyed drinking, so this is nothing new to me, but it's true: by not drinking you're disappointing people you meet up with. Refusing their warm embrace. Turning your head away from a kiss. It's a form of rejection. That's where we differ—you seek the approval of others and despise them when they don't give it because you feel you need it to survive. But me, and I say this with zero pride, I don't give a fuck. That's the difference between booze and smack, our respective drugs of choice. From when I was young and started shooting up, I've had nothing but contempt for people who use legal drugs, booze, or sleeping pills, as well as for those who prefer soft drugs. In the same way cats probably feel contempt for dogs when they see them try to get humans to stroke them.

The director wanted me to say, "Come on, it's almost noon, crack open a bottle." That would have been a simple way of saying: let's be friends, let's have a good time together. But I'm not her friend. If we worked together—which after this particular meeting seems unlikely—I might respect her as a director. She has a reputation for knowing exactly what she wants. I'm happy to submit to her imagination for a few weeks. But I'm not here to drink with her to distract her from her pain. I don't care about her problems, her delusions, or her mood.

Most women my age who aren't into hard drugs are alcoholics. For a long time, this was how I could spot girls with other vices. They'd politely decline the offer of a glass of wine at six o'clock without seeming on edge. Nine times out of ten a woman who turned down an aperitif was taking something else. When we were younger, it could mean they were on a diet. But past the age of thirty-five, it was a sign of addiction to something more illicit.

The director talks to me about her project and, as I'm listening, I'm thinking that the film business is waging war on me, it doesn't love me, doesn't know what to do with my age, my full figure, or my personality—but I'm waging war on the film business too. I've changed my perspective on the industry to which I owe everything, and which has given me so much—and I'm more surprised than anyone. I've had breakups that were a little like this. Exceptional meetings of minds, magnificent relationships, and one day you realize there's no magic left. It was real. It's not anymore. I've had wonderful friendships that spanned decades, and it's the same—one day you meet up, and as you head home you admit to yourself: I'm bored, I feel alone when I'm with you, you've lost all your sparkle, the friendship is over. That's what's happening to me with the film industry, and until that meeting I hadn't realized how much I had fallen out of love with it. I'm an actress—I've never had to fake enthusiasm for a project. But as I listened to the director talk, I thought: I'm here because I need to work. Almost immediately, she brought up the subject of my weight. That's what triggered my sudden lucidity. From the get-go, she told me I'd have to lose about twenty-five pounds to land the part. I thanked her for being blunt, and without missing a beat I told her it wouldn't be a problem. As though I'd simply been waiting for her and her lousy role in order to get around to it. I say lousy role because the character is a mother, and I always swore I'd never play that sort of thing. She talked about the actors she had in mind to play my sons, and it pissed me off. I'd love to shoot a film with them, she and I share the same taste in young men, but to play their mother? What a waste. I hadn't read the script before I saw her. But I'd been warned. There are scenes of me in the kitchen, cooking. I don't make movies so people can film me doing the dishes. I'm not about to watch YouTube videos about how women bake cakes, I couldn't give a shit.

On the subject of weight, she asked in a sly voice whether there was a particular diet I favored—like she'd know anything, the woman's got at least forty extra pounds hanging off her. I told her I'd do the bulimia diet and said that, unfortunately, I was too old to start shooting up heroin again. She laughed, at once shocked and delighted by my answer. I said the only difference between me and other people is that I talk about these things—but I'm not the only actress who carries a toothbrush in her handbag. She looked at me knowingly. "For your breath." But it's not for your breath, it's for the acids that attack your teeth; I realized she had no idea how actors keep their weight down. I was furious with myself for not shouting, "Who are you to talk, you fat bitch?" when she asked me to lose weight. If your film involves putting me behind an ironing board surrounded by seriously fuckable boys that I don't get to screw, who gives a shit about my figure? That's what shame is: responding pleasantly to someone who deserves a slap in the face. But I didn't do it out of kindness, thinking, poor thing, so young and already ugly, can't be easy going through life with stubby legs, fat knees, coarse hair, oily skin, a nose so turned up you can see her nostrils, and those weak eyes. I did it because I need the work and I know I can't afford to be brutally honest anymore. I resented finding myself in this position, even though she wasn't to blame. Ten years ago, I wouldn't even have agreed to meet with her, so the question wouldn't have arisen.

And in that moment, it occurred to me that this scene was the whole film industry in microcosm—that what she's doing when she talks to me about dieting is admitting she's subservient to a system that doesn't even work in her favor.

I didn't say: I don't know what the hell I'm doing here, I know directors like you and you're all a pain in the ass. You want to cast me in a role that's unlike anything I've already done. Go find someone who fits the role, go find someone who has what you want. Don't come asking me to make myself into something other than what I am. It could be amusing, she could say, I'm doing a remake of *Ben Hur*, I want you to play Ben Hur, it's the kind of role no one's ever seen you play. But that's not what's happening here. What she wants is for me to allow her to film the horrors of middle age. Not the truth of middle age: she doesn't want to film my body as it is, or break into my house when I'm smoking crack. She wants half-truth—as much as she can handle of what she calls truth. She wants to bust my balls, to wield some bogus power over me. Ultimately, what she wants is to know she won't have to pay for a hairdresser and makeup artist for me, and to be able to use slapdash lighting. That's what she means when she talks about shooting the skin and not being afraid of the wrinkles. She's telling me I'll be ugly in a tedious film, and she wants me to say I think it's a radical statement.

So, I didn't give a flying fuck about disappointing her. But I thought of you. My composure comes from the fact that, for better or worse, my reputation for being difficult precedes me, and I have nothing to prove. Everyone in the industry knows that I do drugs. No one asks me to go into the details of my consumption. I have an aura about me—and they love it. It's my rock star persona, I'm putting myself at risk for them. And just watching me do it, they feel like they're being rebellious by proxy.

OSCAR

It's absurd to ask you to play some nondescript woman. Like getting a tiger to play a hamster. And contrary to what you said, it has nothing to do with the fact that you use. To the audience, you're the majestic she-wolf—with or without the drugs. I'm not surprised that no guy has ever dumped you. I haven't been feeling great the past few days. My sister's been messing with my head.

"If you really think you're clean, go talk to your family." It's a cliché I keep hearing at NA meetings. Expecting comfort and protection from my family is like an Escher drawing of a staircase—nonexistent perspectives that look convincing. They lead you in, and you're lost—they addle your brain. At the beginning of the week, I called Corinne because she'd left me another message. For the first ten minutes, everything was fine and I was thrilled that our relationship seemed to be improving. We talked a bit about our mother, who's ecstatic at the moment, and I said, "Maybe she's met a guy." She spends her whole life on Facebook, and everyone knows that's just Tinder for old people. My sister declared that a seventy-something heterosexual woman has very little chance of hooking up with a guy. She was playing it cool—in that I-don't-fantasize-about-celebrities kind of way, but it was obvious she was thrilled to be back in touch with you. I felt a bit offended—this was the reason she was so nice. I told her that I hadn't touched a drop of booze for over a month, and she didn't instantly assume I was about to fall off the wagon. The call started out really well, but it's always the same story—one false step and the conversation goes to hell. I felt comfortable enough to tell her that, on the one hand, I've been feeling brutally alone in this empty, unfamiliar house, suffering from vague panic attacks after it gets dark and wondering what I'm doing here, but on the other hand, sobriety and spartan surroundings are doing me a world of good. They've made it possible for me to face up to things. I laughed as I told her that the worst thing about what's been happening is reading statements supposedly defending me written by lowlifes so utterly vile that I wish they hadn't bothered. Corinne sounded strangely distant. I thought maybe she'd been cut off. Then she said, "The shit that's being slung at Zoé Katana is disgusting," and I said, "What's disgusting is saying that to me." And then I had an intuition, a literal lightning flash. The penny dropped. I said, "Do you know her?" and I could tell from her voice that she'd tensed up. "I've been a feminist for thirty years. It didn't just come on me like the sudden urge to piss. So, yes, I wrote to her. When I saw vicious trolls attacking her, I thought she needed all the support she could get. *You're not alone.* It's the most important thing women can say to each other."

Since going to Narcotics Anonymous, I've been thinking a lot about my anger. How I fly off the handle, lose my shit when things don't go my way or when I feel I'm being attacked. Going completely psycho rather than accepting any level of nuance. And I want to stop injecting so much drama into my life, stop cranking things up to eleven. I want to rebuild my relationships with others.

But when Corinne said that, I ditched the whole rebuilding program. I felt so betrayed and so stupid for thinking I could trust her! In the empty house, I screamed at the top of my lungs, making the most of the fact that I wasn't likely to disturb anyone, as my nearest neighbor is five hundred yards away. I called her a hateful bitch. We immediately stopped listening and started shouting at each other. I vaguely heard her call me a shitbag who acts all shocked when someone calls him out for behaving like a shit-faced entitled prick, adding that my ex-girlfriend had told her I'd raped her, and at that point I snapped, because what the fuck is it with Corinne and all my exes? I hung up and spent the whole night making a list of all the arguments I could throw at her.

I turned off my phone. Then I turned off the internet for the whole house. I want peace and quiet. It's good for me. I don't want to start my day with a torrent of vile posts. It's amazing. A digital detox. Being an addict means having a lack of imagination. You quit one thing and you start wanting to quit other stuff. An addiction to detox... Now I'll be able to focus on my new book. I think I'll tell my own story, in real time. I've wanted to write autofiction for a while now. I've had enough of writing crime novels. It's hard, making up a story that's not real. I want to talk about what's happening to me.

There are several novels by Céline in the hallway. Nobody's bothered to steal them. For all I know, this house has never been rented, and what I'm feeling so intensely is its abandonment. I don't like Céline. His prose is crude, blustering, and mannered, self-consciously intended to shock.

As a teenager, I read the beginning of *Journey to the End of the Night* without bothering to find out that it was by one of the most important writers of the twentieth century, and the first few pages left me dumbfounded—but after that it just circled the drain and I never finished it.

A few years later, when I was inducted into the literary establishment, I discovered that Céline is supposed to be incomparable. A virtuoso stylist. A brilliant innovator.

Writers aren't like soccer players—whatever you think of the French national team, there are objective reasons for selecting each player. You don't see some total wimp wearing the blue jersey. Literature is very different. To be a great writer, all you need is three snobby fucks swooning over your work and screaming *Genius*. And I loathe Céline buffs. When they talk about his unique style, what they are really celebrating is submission to power—when that power comes from the far right. The penchant for submission is a fascist thing. Céline mimicked the language of the working classes in the hope of winning the Goncourt; in other words, he offered the literary salons a vision of the prole as they imagined him: gutless, brainless, thoughtless, anti-Semitic, and a lousy fuck. Later, I read his anti-Semitic scrawls and realized that the Parisian literary world was grateful to him for those, too—a facade of subversiveness pandering to power. That's the thing that turns them on. In the difficult decades of political correctness, it's allowed them to sing the lament for the censored. After all, there was a brief period when being a racist fucking bastard was frowned on. I love Calaferte and I despise Céline. I don't believe that artists have to be respectable. But some are redeemed despite their terrible behavior. Calaferte fell out of print, and that was that. He was forgotten. He and Céline weren't treated in the same way. Calaferte wrote from and for the working classes. Céline was an ass-kisser to those in power whose revered status was stymied by a historical backlash he badly misjudged. I despise Céline. I should write a book about him. I'm short of enemies at the moment.

REBECCA

Comrade,

    Are you still living in your country house? Are you back in Paris? I've got the feeling that pretty soon you'll be able to doomscroll in peace without coming across vicious comments from your haters . . . I'm writing this from an almost empty train.

I went to Barcelona for a couple of days for a retrospective of my films, and the whole thing was canceled. The city closed up shop overnight. My agent told me that the airports were chaos, he got me a train ticket home. It's a six-hour journey. Everywhere, I saw people wearing plastic gloves, others wearing face masks. I'm heading back with suitcases stuffed with bottles, cigarettes and hand sanitizer gel, because apparently you can't find any in Paris—it's only been a week and it seems like the only thing people are thinking about. They say everything in Paris will close too, but that seems a little wild to me. I can't imagine that film crews are going to stop shooting or that my agent is going to roll down the shutters. Life will carry on more or less as it did before. In Barcelona, I saw Las Ramblas completely deserted for the first time in ten years. I'd forgotten what a beautiful avenue it is. That was when I realized that maybe things wouldn't pan out the way I thought. On the phone, a journalist friend said, they're planning to close off the arrondissements in Paris, and he gave a nervous little laugh. I said, don't sweat it, we'll storm the barricades. Still, I can't help but think how complicated it would be to keep us off the streets. But I don't hate this eerie atmosphere. For people like me, who never quite fit in, liminal situations can be strangely reassuring. There's something exciting about changes of setting and perspective.

And in all this chaos I'm thinking about you, my dickhead friend. And I'm thinking you must be feeling relieved. This dreaded coronavirus looks likely to eclipse your MeToo scandal . . .

OSCAR

Late last night, the neighbor who comes over to clean once a week knocked on my door. She told me I had to leave. At first, I didn't understand what she was talking about. She's Polish, probably about my age. I told her that I had two weeks left on my rental. I could tell from her expression that I was missing something. So I turned my phone back on and saw the extent of the disaster. Voicemail full, dozens of increasingly frantic WhatsApp messages—and your email. So I reassured the cleaning woman in the weird French I tend to use when talking to someone who doesn't speak my language, and which I'm sure is completely incomprehensible—I put words in random order next to unconjugated verbs. But she worked out that I was going to pack my bags.

The last time I was online, people were talking about

this virus . . . I'd just told myself I'd be safe here in the middle of nowhere, that I wasn't at risk. But Jesus, the whole country in lockdown—things have moved fast! The people who own the house are arriving later today so they can enjoy the garden. I wonder how long this is going to last? I hurriedly packed, and I was grateful that a taxi driver was willing to come and pick me up. We chatted as though we'd known each other for years, what's happening is so mind-boggling that everyone has something in common. The station was deserted, but there were still trains running. There were about thirty of us on the Nîmes–Paris route. We smiled wanly at each other, as if we were all exhausted. People chatted with each other. The woman who'd just dropped her kids off at their father's because she works in a hospital and can't look after them, the guy who moved back to his parents' place then realized he couldn't stand them and decided to go home, the woman going to move in with her lover who left no explanation for her boyfriend when she left. And me—who'd been living in a rented house with the internet turned off. People laughed at my story. I enjoyed telling it, and the more I told it, the funnier I was, overacting the scene with the Polish cleaning woman, my disbelief when I turned my phone back on.

It didn't make my daughter Clémentine laugh when I called her from the train. She said, "We've been worried sick," and I realized she didn't believe my story and wanted me to know that she didn't care. I blustered on, trying to find out what was going through her head, and she calmly said that IRL I was usually so bombed I had no idea what was happening. That cut me to the quick. I said, "I haven't had a drink in over a month and stop talking about me like I'm an alcoholic, you're making a mountain out of a molehill." She said, "Sure, Papa, sure," in a weary voice. When I hung up, I was furious. It's her mother filling her head with this shit. I don't see why my daughter would think I'm so high that I can't hear what's on the radio. But for the fact that her mother doesn't trust me, my daughter would have no reason to think I'd lie to her. I considered stopping off for a drink on the way home just to spite her.

But then I saw myself at an NA meeting confessing that I'd relapsed because my daughter was lippy. And I realized—it hadn't hit me until now—that it means something, being able to tell people, "I didn't use." And have them clap. I'd thought the whole collective ritual was a bit puerile. But it means something. And I thought about the guy not long ago who said, "I duck out of joint custody with my kids as much as I can," and when he said it, I was judgmental, I thought, what kind of pathetic excuse for a guy does that? And at the same time, it hit me that he was saying something that I couldn't even admit to myself. I haven't had Clémentine stay with me for over a month. I always come up with a good excuse to skip my shifts. And when my wife has a go at me, I blame her. If she hadn't walked out on me, we wouldn't be in this mess. But I'm afraid to have my daughter stay with me—we never know what to do when we're together.

Paris, as you know, was completely deserted. I can't think of a better image than the one everyone uses online: an apocalyptic film set. Strangely poetic. Dreamlike. More awe-inspiring than frightening. In the lobby of my apartment building, I could smell the hand sanitizer. There's a silence in the building unlike anything I've known. Except for the sound of other people's kids playing in the stairwell.

REBECCA

What I find most fascinating is the speed at which we change, the malleability of our realities. It used to be unthinkable, now it's normal. One woman I know is a rich heiress. She's jetted off to her private island. Asked me to go with her. We FaceTimed and she was sitting next to a basket of tropical fruit, surrounded by palm trees. I told her that her idea of paradise was my idea of hell. She laughed, but I could tell she was freaking out about the virus. Her father was a big name in pharmaceuticals.

Since then, I've been reading the outraged comments of people my age complaining that a couple of writers have gone to stay in their holiday homes while most French people are living in cramped apartments. As if being two hours' drive away will make a difference if there's a problem. And I think, it's weird how we never hate above our station in life. We only hate our neighbors, the people we could be. Not those who are truly safe.

I've turned off the radio and TV. There's no point. This apocalypse isn't even spectacular. And it's my turn now to go offline. When I go on social media now, I feel like I'm turning into a wimp. Or a techy little old lady who can't bear anyone disturbing her stuff. I don't like what this is doing to me. The ridiculous oversensitivity, the way I'm constantly tracking down things my friends have said that I find inappropriate, or just plain dumb. I listen to Wagner cranked up to full volume. The neighbors wouldn't dare complain. After all, this is me we're talking about.

My agent dropped by to fill my cupboards before he left Paris. Hours spent sitting in traffic jams, a genuine exodus. I haven't had a credit card in months. So he came and ransacked the grocery store downstairs. I have enough Coca-Cola and Chinese soup to last me through a siege. My agent says journalists have been given a pass that allows them to travel for the next three months. I can't believe we'll be in lockdown for that long. On the way out, he left me a wad of cash. It was like a scene out of *Goodfellas*. I go down every day to buy stuff, more out of curiosity than anything else. I hate walking, but I go for long walks. Especially at night. I've never seen anything like it. A film set the size of a city. No teenagers prowling the streets. I'd have thought they'd sneak out and get up to all kinds of shit. Drug dealers have borrowed dogs so they can go for walks and make home deliveries. They have an extraordinary ability to adapt! We should let them run public services; everything would work much better. You need to put your order in by late afternoon, they stop delivering at seven p.m. But you can even buy face masks from them. I find the idea of only buying drugs during office hours depressing.

My first thought was to ask my dealer to move in with me. Not that I have the budget, but we have an excellent relationship: we've known each other for so long, he'd have let me run up some credit. But I didn't do it. It makes me feel a little feverish. But you've been busting my chops with your whole "I'm clean" shit, so I'm taking that as a challenge. I'm pretty competitive as a rule. It's a pity I never liked sports, I've got the mindset of an Olympic champion.

OSCAR

On WhatsApp, I'm getting messages from people I barely know—all paid-up members of NA—with links to Zoom meetings. I logged in to one the night I got home. It's a shitshow, no one knows how Zoom works. I watched as dozens of tiny windows flickered into life on the screen.

There was the guy in his empty bar, the elderly lady in the stark white office, the girl in a hostel room, the guy lying in bed and framed any which way, the shady character in the garden of his country house, the Senegalese guy sitting at his kitchen table, the pretty blonde lounging in a deckchair, a famous actor in his living room with groaning bookshelves behind him. I felt moved. We took turns talking about what lockdown means in our lives. There was fear, anger, and for some a sense of relief. It made me think about what you were saying. When you're used to living at the edge of the frame, you feel pretty comfortable when the frame disintegrates. I think I've been losing the plot, and this human canvas has been holding me in. For me, lockdown has made things easier. I don't have to not drink at dinner parties, or pretend not to notice everyone slipping off to the bathroom, or look for something nonalcoholic to order in a bar, or turn down an invitation to go backstage after a gig. I'm spared temptation. And I'm also hugely grateful because it's like your drug dealers, these are people you can rely on. In less than a week, they've devised a whole new way to hold NA meetings.

So every day I boot up my laptop and connect to them. I phoned another writer who's in the program because I wanted a sponsor—because during this slump, I want to start writing down my steps. He put me in touch with someone else, who's agreed to be my sponsor during lockdown and has sent me photos of his step notebook. I've never seen anything like it. Here I am, still traumatized by the #MeToo cabal railing against me, and I'm thinking I've never had so much support. It's the polar opposite of Instagram. A place where men and women come together to talk about their weaknesses, their powerlessness, their sadness, and promise to help each other without trying to control each other—and they do it. There is such a thing as male solidarity, but it always comes at a price. You have to prove that you're a real man, that you can hold your own, that you're a winner. You're tough, you're a good fuck, you earn wads of cash, you've got a flashy car, a sexy girlfriend. There's male solidarity—but there's no sense of fraternity. With NA, I go to meetings every day, and every day I show my weakness and no one cracks a smile. I say I'm terrified of being alone. I'm in deep shit and I'm dealing with all the people out there who hate my guts and every day I'm tripping over my own thoughts. And not a single person comes back with a sarcastic quip.

My sponsor is a bit of a lunatic, he looks like he's been transported from the Stone Age to the twenty-first century, but he's twenty years clean and knows everything there is to know about brotherhood. He told me about unofficial NA meetings being organized despite the Covid curfew, but I refused to go. I doused the whole apartment with bleach. I clean the door handle if I go out to buy milk. I find that I belong to the group of people who are completely freaking out about the virus.

But I'm writing the first step. It's a long inventory of my relationship with what they call "substances." I was afraid it would make me want to use. I start every day with a meeting—and it works, at some subliminal level, obviously, and I have no explanation, but I forget to think about drugs, whereas until now I have thought about drugs every fucking day of my life.

REBECCA

I identify too much as a Viking to be freaked out by the virus. I tell myself that with all the shit I've taken in my life, my body has to be a first-class self-healing unit. And it's not like we're seeing corpses piled up in the streets. But I understand other people's fears, and I respect them. Not everyone has fifteen years of heroin and twenty years of crack in their system. The mailman doesn't have a mask. He's a good friend, a film buff. He hates French cinema. Except for the films I'm in, which he thinks are all amazing. He doesn't have a mask, and I can tell he's cracking up because he doesn't want to come into the kitchen anymore, and he's got this sad smile on his face. He told me post offices are still open for business and the counter staff don't have masks either. The police aren't wearing masks. You see them wandering the streets. Four in a cop car. With no protection. All these minimum-wage bodies delivered up to the virus—at a point when no one can say how it spreads. These reviled bodies. I feel humbled. I haven't felt close to ordinary people since I was fifteen, but now I feel humbled. It's difficult to explain. It's the image we have of the country foundering. I didn't realize I loved my country—it's like you talking about how much you love your girlfriend now that she's gone. Now that the France I grew up in has vanished, I realize I loved it.

OSCAR

When they said, "We're in lockdown," and I headed back to Paris, I was expecting anything but this. I'm living my best life. From my window, I can see the neighbors opposite. A couple have set some chairs out on the balcony and spend all afternoon sunbathing. In the evening, after the eight o'clock clapping for care workers, some guy plays the saxophone and everyone stands at their window, listening to him and clapping. Last night he played "Despacito" and I danced by myself.

I'm calmer than I've ever been. I don't know whether it's the silence, being able to smell the trees along the avenue for the first time since I've lived here, or my body finally starting to recover from the shock of being clean.

I spend hours on TikTok. Lockdown has given a veneer of genius to creators on the platform. I've had the app for ages now, but never really got into it before.

One weekend when my daughter was staying with

me, she and her cousin were making this insane racket in her room, even though I'd just politely asked her not to make any noise because I was on a call to the States. I hate it when people speak English on the phone—not being able to see the face of the person I'm talking to leaves me farcically half-deaf. After I hung up, I barged into her room screaming; I didn't even bother to knock, which was my way of saying, if you don't respect me, why should I respect you, and since he was her cousin I figured I wasn't going to find them doing something weird. Besides, from the noises they were making, it wasn't likely to be anything other than a lot of childish high jinks, and there they were, wearing K-Way jackets zipped up to their chins, hoods tied tightly, he was jumping up and down on the bed, arms by his sides, and she was pogoing right in front of her phone's camera. I burst in, screaming, and watched as they realized in real time that this was going to make a hilarious clip for their TikTok channel—they exchanged looks of fake terror that were brilliantly synchronized, then Clémentine stopped recording and apologized, and they collapsed in a fit of giggles, and the more I shouted the more they giggled.

I was jealous. I felt like flushing her phone down the toilet to stop her laughing. This wasn't the first time it had happened. I called her a silly bitch and stormed out of the room because I felt like I might cry. Or smash things. I was jealous of not being part of their generation, jealous of their giggling, jealous of their dancing, jealous that they were talking to me about some app I'd never heard of, jealous of their antics, of their closeness. I was jealous that I wasn't part of it. I was jealous of their youth. And for once, I was clearheaded. I wasn't lying to myself about how I felt. I was sick of being the old man sick of being the father sick of not being able to put on a jacket pull up the hood and pogo in front of a camera thinking I'm Gucci. And I couldn't even tell myself that when I was her age I'd giggled like that, because at her age I was terrified, I was convinced I was a creep and nothing good would ever happen to me, and I always felt I had to be pushy to get to hang out with friends. I carefully hide my jealousy of my own daughter. I can barely admit it to myself. I prefer to think I feel sorry for her or I'm worried about how stupid she is, about how badly she's doing at school. I say it's appalling that young people today are prematurely hunchbacked from being constantly bent over their screens. But this month I'm watching TikTok videos and simply saying to myself: I'm often jealous of her youth. And the way she's living it.

ZOÉ KATANA

I'm friends with an actress. A massive movie star. We chat a lot online. She asks how I'm feeling. I've never faked like I don't care about getting to meet famous people. I'm a complete fangirl, and I don't apologize for it. I get stoked about people I wouldn't talk to in a million years, they're like my imaginary friends, I have conversations with them in my head. And that helps me get through, and I know it's a kid's thing, and I don't give a fuck. I'm friends with a movie star, and every morning she sends me sweet little DMs. And I'm lit. Period.

I don't leave the house much, and I don't see many people, and still I've managed to catch this fucking virus. It scared the shit out of me. I was running this serious temperature and I had these stabbing pains everywhere. Something in me was totally screwed, way worse than just a bad case of flu. I would phone the emergency services and they'd tell me to take my temperature and wait it out because I still wasn't sick enough to be in the hospital. I couldn't ask anyone to come take care of me, and I was terrified I'd get worse and not be able to call for help. I had this permanent migraine that made me want to vomit. It was so weird. On day five, my radical lesbian friend gave my number to Rebecca Latté. Seriously, I'm not hallucinating. My fever broke days ago. I really said Rebecca Latté. The third member of the Holy Trinity: Béatrice Dalle, Lydia Lunch, Rebecca Latté. The women you turn to when you're wondering how to survive as a heterosexual. (Hannah Arendt is fourth on my list, but there's no photo of Hannah Arendt over my bed. Only the other three.) So, when I got this message: "I live nearby, would you like me to leave some groceries outside your door?" I felt like I'd been visited by grace. I read it like a dozen times. I said yes, and I sat next to the window, my fever hadn't gone down at that stage, but it was worrying me less. I saw her. She checked her phone for the code to the front door and I rushed over to the peephole so I could see her. She was looking at the names on the buzzers, and I shouted down, "I'm up here. I can't let you in, but mine's the door on the left." She said, "Hi Zoé," and I just laughed. I hadn't laughed in a long time. And I explained, "It's just weird to think you know my name," and she didn't seem scared of the virus slipping under the door because she leaned against the wall, I could see her in profile. She lit a cigarette, and I was shocked. "Are you smoking in the hallway?" and she turned toward me with a smile: "It protects you from the virus. I've read articles about it."

While she was smoking, we chatted through the door. I recognized her voice, but it sounded deeper, more impressive.

"It's been a week since I talked to anyone."

"That's the idea. Apparently, it's transmitted by the disgusting little flecks of spit you spray when you're talking to someone."

She sat on the floor, leaned against the wall, tilted her head back. Just like in a movie. She has a laugh that's really reassuring, a laugh that transcends the situation, that turns it on its head.

"It's nice talking to you. Makes me feel better."

"Corinne, the girl who gave me your number, you know who she is?"

"Yeah, I'm completely up to speed. At first, I didn't want anything to do with her. But she wore me down—which is just as well, because you're here. She said she's known you since you were teenagers."

"Since we were kids, actually. Did she tell you that I know Oscar?"

"No."

"We message each other. I'd rather you knew."

"Do you get on well with him?"

"He's a dickhead, I know. But he's my friend. I have a lot of dickhead friends. I think that's because I'm a bit of a dickhead myself."

"I don't mind. As long as we don't talk about him."

Jayack has fucked up my life enough as it is, I'm not about to pass up meeting Rebecca Latté just because she finds him interesting.

I heard her go back downstairs and I opened the door. There was fruit and bread and milk and chips and Haribo strawberry gummies. She'd bought all those things for me. I went back to bed and drifted into a deep sleep.

REBECCA

I won't insult you by wasting your time apologizing. I just never expected her to write something like that. That's the problem with kids. You can't bring them a croissant without them bragging about it on their socials . . . Just once, I wanted to prove I could be sensitive. Just goes to show, if it's not in your nature, don't force it.

Corinne has been storming the citadel again, just like you predicted. She's more amenable, more fun. I mean, we're locked up in our homes 24/7 and she's been flirting with me in an old-school way, she's not exactly a wallflower. I let her get on with it, it's no big deal. We chat on the phone a bit. She told me about Zoé, and I pointed out that she wasn't exactly being loyal to you. Corinne snapped back that as a historic feminist (a bit of a legend in her own lunchtime, but that's not nothing) she felt it her duty to offer her support, if only symbolically, to a young blogger being harassed by all the forces of evil on the web, and God knows they're not in short supply. Long story short, I asked Corinne not to bring up the subject again, and she said no problem. I've often been attracted to people like her . . . the ones who say no problem and then do the exact opposite of what you asked. That's how, at the beginning of lockdown . . . well, you know the rest. I thought, I can't just leave this kid who's sick and not visit her. I'm like sunshine, my bounty is all-encompassing. Just because I brought her three lemons and some ginger doesn't mean you don't get to bask in my radiance. When I went over to her place, I felt a bit like Princess Diana. A cross between a princess and a nurse.

When I got back, I read a few of her articles. There's this huge gap between the girl talking to me through the door and the blazing Valkyrie haranguing feminists online, and I like that dichotomy. I realize there's no point expecting you to feel for her, but she's really been getting a lot of shit. As someone who can't stand it when a moron like you calls me ugly in real life, I don't know how I'd cope if I were in her shoes. Nobody's cut out to take that kind of abuse. And the vicious trolling she gets every time she opens her mouth just makes people feel more sympathy for her. So the following day I sent her a little text asking how she was.

I know you well enough by now to realize you're liable to turn this into a huge psychodrama. That would be a shame, given the pleasure you get from writing to me and reading my emails.

OSCAR

I wish I could spew you out of my life like vomit. We've been emailing each other for weeks now, you've become the person closest to me. And there you are, scheming with my sister behind my back, telling me in that flippant way of yours that you let her flirt with you, then you go visit the girl who's completely ruined my life and send me an update to say: she's having a really shitty time, but I'm looking after her. Of course I'm going to react like someone who's been betrayed. And you're right, I will miss this, it hurts me more than I can begin to describe, and you'll say that I'm always moaning and complaining but at least I'm being honest.

Thanks for everything. Bye.

REBECCA

When I got your message, I thought: fine, go fuck yourself. But the problem is I've gotten used to your emails. And given how much time I've got on my hands at the moment, I'd rather keep writing to you than be bored. Since you're so keen on honesty, let me give you some: I was genuinely touched when you said I'm the person closest to you right now, and it made me realize that it's mutual. Let's face it, we're getting to be pretty inseparable.

I listen to you at the morning Zoom meetings. I worked out that's how you start your day. I had to try a few before I found the ones you go to. You rarely turn on your camera, but your first name gives you away. And now I recognize your voice when you speak or do a reading. Please don't think I'm spying on you. I have every right to attend NA meetings. Especially since I still haven't phoned my dealer friend. You should congratulate me. But I log in under a pseudonym and I never turn on my camera. I don't want some asshole making a screen recording so they can poke fun at me on YouTube.

I understand why you went off the deep end about me going to see Zoé. Of all the women in Paris, I chose to connect with the one who makes you want to puke. I could say: "But she didn't do anything, she's the victim in all this," I could say: "Your sister manipulated me, she's created this mess because she's upset that you and I are friends." Or I could say: fuck off, no one gets to dump me, no one gets to be angry with me, and you're no exception. But instead, I'm going to say: I know I fucked up. I wasn't a good friend in this case.

You went off the deep end, and that night I phoned my friend who's got gear, he came over and picked me up on his motorcycle and I stayed with him for two days. His studio has become a five-star crack house, only VIPs get to crash there. I didn't enjoy it. I haven't enjoyed it for a long time now. But it's hard to quit.

But enough is enough, you've been sulking for ten days now. I've unilaterally decreed that we're friends again.

I'm interested in this whole NA thing, and you're the only person I can talk to about it. First off, being connected to the rest of France really does change the feeling of being in lockdown. Whether it's the hoi polloi or the stars, we're all in the same mess. You'll say that's hardly surprising given that everyone's on drugs . . . On the other hand, without wanting to go on and on about it, I didn't recognize many people. I spotted two, to be exact. I find the whole religious aspect off-putting. I don't really like being lectured about God over breakfast. But I log in every day, like a priggish old maid who has shares in a brothel.

Already I've noticed a genuine belief in the existence of people who aren't sick. In a society like ours, it's difficult to imagine there are any sane people. The vast majority are completely brainwashed. All of them. And I've noticed that junkies seem to systematically equate the part of them that wants to get wasted with the part of them that's wild. When I'm listening to you all, I picture the two shady characters from *Pinocchio*, Honest John and Gideon—it's like junkies going to NA are running away from sinister villains trying to manipulate and destroy them even though they're cute, innocent little puppets.

I don't really buy that. Granted, at some point getting wasted is something you do with no regard for common sense. It's bad for you but you keep doing it: so far, so obvious. But when you start using, it's as much about protecting yourself as putting yourself at risk. It's a tactic that works. If it didn't, we wouldn't fall for it, we're not stupid.

Overall, my favorite thing about the meetings is how well they work if you think of them as frameworks to explain the world as it really is. If you think of the world as a crackhead, it works. Imagine saying to someone: "Maybe you should think about putting down the crack pipe and trying something else," and them saying: "You're completely insane; getting wasted in parking lots is in my nature." Now, replace "crack" with "shareholder dividends"; it works. Everyone knows our economy is headed for disaster. And it's fair to say that the people in charge react the same way as diehard junkies: "I'd rather die than go into rehab."

I know I'm being a smart-ass. I'm hemming and hawing because I find it weird, buying into this whole thing. I've never bought into anything. Especially not a program. Let's face it, the word "recovery" makes me want to jump out the window. I'm writing to you because something happened in one of the meetings. I was watching from the sidelines, fascinated but at a distance, and this girl spoke. I immediately identified with her because she's really pretty. And amazingly photogenic, because otherwise with no makeup, staring straight into the camera, she wouldn't have been so radiant. She said the word "crack." I know, usually you don't name the substance. But she did. One of the nice things about the meetings is they bring together people who've spent their lives doing precisely what they're told not to. So, right from the start, she said the word "crack." She said, I smoked crack with my little daughter sitting beside me, and I thought I was doing fine, that I wasn't an addict, because I didn't go through withdrawal between pipes. I remembered you telling me how you cried like a kid at every meeting. I didn't cry. But I felt something inside me break. I understood what everyone meant when they talked about "identifying." I stared at the paintings on the wall behind her, I couldn't see what they depicted.

I don't feel any withdrawal between binges either. If I quit for a few days, like I'm doing now, it doesn't really bother me. And like her, I tell myself that I'm not an addict, because I don't always use the same drugs. I mix and match according to the season, the people, the city, the occasion. I take whatever's available and from that, I assume that I'm in control. But I'm lying when I say, hand on heart, that I never use on a film set. When I'm in my trailer, if I think I've got the time and someone kindly offers, I don't give a shit that I'm going to screw up some takes, that when it comes to editing, the director's going to have a hell of a job, but he'll manage and he'll never dare call me on it. This girl who dared to say the word "crack" was as pretty as I used to be. I was blown away by her sincerity. We beautiful women don't owe anybody anything. Especially not the truth. That she chose to say it so simply left me dumbfounded. Everything she said about how she lied to herself when she first came to NA felt as though it was directed at me.

I turn on my laptop every day to stalk you. But the

truth is, I also log in to meetings that you're not at. I listen to people say "The obsessive need to use has been lifted from me," and on the one hand, I find it annoying, it sounds childish and silly. And on the other hand, I envy them.

And it's also driving me around the bend. I'm wondering where this bloody bullshit is going to end. First, I turn into a feminist. Then I start feeling a connection with the little people who have to work during lockdown. And now here I am listening to people talking about how they manage to stay clean. At this rate, in six months, I'll be buying a pair of trainers and going jogging. It's terrifying, my fans will be so disappointed if I go on like this. But I'm not here to play to the gallery. I want to survive. And I don't know if I'm capable. Of doing what all of you are doing. That's what terrifies me most, I think. Risking failure.

OSCAR

Okay, I admit it, I'm glad you're writing to me. I considered relapsing because of you—because of your disloyalty, your unreliability, I was thinking, she pretended that she was my friend, my rock, but she didn't care about me at all. I was about to do what I've always done—spend a few days shit-faced whining about how nothing's ever easy for me, nobody gives me the support that every human being deserves, yada yada.

And then it was one little satori after another. Not that I like Kerouac. Dumb American jackass who likes slumming it and is obsessed with his own genius. But when it happened, I borrowed the word from him. Little satoris. I've been saved by these daily fucking meetings and by writing the first step. They call it the pink cloud of the first months of being clean. Standard.

And then you wrote me. I wanted to reply to your first email, but I was still too angry. The joy I feel in imagining you attending meetings is hard to put into words. There's something weird about NA—the obsession with other people staying clean. You don't even know these people, but you want it to work for them so much it's like your life depends on it. I didn't really understand how it happened for me. I just know that using was all I thought about, it defined me and the people I was attracted to, it was my way of being in the world. And that's gone. I never dreamed I could feel so strong. So calm. And I never knew I could trust myself this much. I so want that to happen for you . . .

"The only requirement for membership is a desire to stop using." It's a brilliant formulation. For once, I don't have to wonder whether I'm lying, whether I'm an impostor, whether I'm worthy. I belong in this group. Since all you need to be welcomed is the desire to stop using. There are no other preconditions—you need a credit card you need to be clean you need to be able to spell you need to have been born here you need to prove that you're a real man—this is a group where "it's enough." I've never seen so many people who genuinely want to change their approach in order to make things better. Most of them have a long way to go. But that's not the point. It's the effort that matters, the effort of tending toward the positive.

I don't think I've experienced that anywhere before. And I'm so thrilled at the thought that you're behind one of the little black squares on our screens every morning.

My daughter is not doing so well. I feel helpless. Right now, she's staying with me. Léonore needed a bit of breathing space. Clémentine is miserable, and this is the first time I've realized that it's not about me. She's not trying to make me feel bad or blame me for stuff. She's her own person—not some satellite of my life. It should have occurred to me sooner, but it's like I didn't have the time until now. I avoided thinking about her. Too much guilt.

Things between us are going better than I expected. We play Othello, she's crushing me—I'm not letting her win, I'm giving it everything I've got, but I get confused, I don't understand what's going on—she's hammering me. I can see the joy on her face, so we play Othello. Deep down, it hurts to feel like such an idiot and also to see her jubilation, though I can't say it makes me feel any closer to her. I want to say: "Have you seen how mean and pathetic you look when you win?" But I bite my tongue and just suck it up. We play Othello to the kind of music she's into and that's brought us a bit closer. Billie Eilish was a revelation to me. Then I let myself be seduced by Lana Del Rey. I didn't say what I thought of the lyrics—My pussy tastes like Pepsi-Cola—I pretended I didn't understand English, but deep down I thought, hey, someone's put some thought into the lyrics. I like this idea. My pussy tastes like Pepsi-Cola. I tried to get her to listen to PNL, and I could see in her eyes that she was horrified to think of her father listening to a group of young guys, but I put the CD on anyway. I suggested we change the game and got out the triominoes because that way at least it's a level playing field, and she in turn let herself be seduced by PNL. I realized she didn't listen to music performed by guys. It's not a pose, or a decision on her part. But apparently the depressiveness of PNL is feminine enough for it to pass muster. I even put on Bad Bunny. Same thing, she started out appalled but got over it.

At eight o'clock, she opens the windows and claps with everyone else. Before she moved in, I was opposed to it—I think it's disgusting to do this when no one gave a shit about the nurses' pay demands before the pandemic and they won't show any solidarity when it's over. But as soon as she hears the clapping, Clémentine gets up, and I can see that she's enjoying it, so I stand next to her. I was surprised by how I felt—as though I'd been chosen. It's dark by eight o'clock, you can't see the people around you, and I realize that this has nothing to do with care workers. In the darkness, we're applauding ourselves to ward off our fear. I was glad I hadn't told Clémentine I thought the whole thing was bullshit.

We spend the evenings watching TV shows, because that way we don't have to try and think of things to talk about. We eat dinner in front of the TV. It's not ideal. I know that when Léonore comes to pick her up and Clémentine tells her we've been watching four episodes of *Pretty Little Liars* a night, she will have a hissy fit. Not least because, in terms of homeschooling, I'm mostly teaching her to do the bare minimum.

Sometimes I try to talk to her, but it's hard. My sponsor says you have to be patient—that it takes time for your kid to forget you were a junkie and they had to be wary of you.

I'm not a picture-perfect father. But Clémentine isn't exactly the daughter you dreamed of having, either. She's harsh. There's this girl at the Zoom meetings—maybe you've seen her—she always turns on her camera, looks like her parents were North African, has her hair pulled back so tight it must be painful. She's always asking to speak, and it's always something negative. She reminds me of my daughter. She listens to everyone else speak, and then she comes along and says, "This whole thing is bullshit, I think you're a bunch of stupid liars, I wish I could die, you're driving me up the wall."

I like this girl. So I tell myself that, logically, I should like my daughter for this way she has of being constantly negative. On the defensive.

Except that with Clémentine, I desperately wish my attention was enough to make her happy. When I see her sulking, I want to scream at her, I want to say, "What do you think I am? A parent-companion?" Things between us are getting better, but I want it to go faster. I want her to love me and tell me she's happy that we're playing board games, that I'm clean, that we watch TV shows after clapping for care workers. But generally she just goes along with things. I can tell that the only thing she really cares about is what's happening on her phone and she doesn't want to tell me what's happening on her phone.

It just hit me. I was furious with you for going to see Zoé. For telling me my sister was flirting with you and you just let her. And suddenly, it hit me. You're not doing it to piss me off. You're not doing it to humiliate me or to hurt me. Some things aren't about me—even if I find them hurtful, they're not about me.

REBECCA

Listen, if you want my advice, be careful . . . too much bliss kills the bliss, and all this kindness could turn you into a bit of a moron. Then again, I'll never understand this thing people have about wanting kids. It's like, before they go around procreating, no one ever thinks to wonder whether they'll make a good parent or whether it'll be a nightmare. And fathers only ever have to do the bare minimum . . . and still you can't hack it.

Yesterday, a friend lent me his electric bike while he rode his fixie. His plan is to ride around every night at eight o'clock so people can applaud him "like he's won the Tour de France." Now, usually, if someone asks me to ride a bike, I punch them in the face. But I can't stand being cooped up anymore, I think I'd even agree to go jogging. I thought about you, I thought maybe I'd cycle past your window. People on the streets recognized me, we got standing ovations. I've always loved Paris, but right now I feel like I'm seeing it in a new light. There's something sad about it, it's like the end of an era.

When we got to the place de la République, the police were clearing the migrants from the square. We headed in the other direction. Cops love me, they always want to take selfies. I thought the evening was going to be ruined, but as we came to Père-Lachaise cemetery this kid on a scooter started doing wheelies next to me. He must have been about twelve or thirteen, but he was a big lad, and when he saw that his fooling around on one wheel was making me smile, he stayed with us for quite a distance and we rode the length of the cemetery. I adore this part of the city, and it occurred to me that it would make a great shot in a film. I was experiencing a cinematic moment. A moment of perfect grace.

And today, I'm in a tailspin. I know there are important things going on out there in the world, I know I should be outraged because they're destroying everything—the hospitals, the schools, the whole culture. Because Trump is spewing shit 24/7, because Russia is locking up gays, because China is taking advantage of the pandemic to crush the Hong Kong protests, because here in France migrants are being hunted through the streets, and cops are apparently teargassing their blankets to make them unusable. But the real reason I feel like shit today, the thing that made me feel sick and completely crushed my morale, is that this morning I found a pair of pants I wore three months ago. And they don't fit me anymore.

I'm warning you: one word to anyone and I'll kill you. In the literal sense. I'm so furious that I'm upset by this, I'd rather spend the rest of my life in prison than admit it publicly. Me, myself, and I have had a tacit agreement for years: when I get out of the shower, I don't look in the mirror. When I pass a shop window, I don't look at my reflection. When someone takes a photo of me, I take a quick glance. All my life, whenever I've looked at myself, I've liked what I see. That's what I miss about drugs too, the time when we had a good thing going. They claim it's one of the side effects. That we girls like heroin because it gives us a perfect figure. And the more you take, the more beautiful you are. Until you look like nothing on earth. But for the first few years, that's what you're looking for. Cocaine does the same thing if you take it every day. And speed, back when we were kids. We liked those drugs because they made us thin. I don't understand what happened. I spent a few years taking a lot of codeine, maybe that screwed with my metabolism. Or maybe it's just age. Or the obsession with waffles and whipped cream I've developed. I don't care what it is. I don't want to be fat, and I am.

I don't wake up thinking, "I'm fat." I know women whose first thought every morning is "You fat cow, all you do is eat." That's not my style. Because I don't really believe it. I don't identify with the woman I am now. I think I'm waiting for my true self to make a spontaneous comeback. A little older, obviously. No plastic surgery, because I've never thought it worked very well for other people. But slim. I've always had a slim figure and big breasts, so it makes no sense that things have changed all of a sudden. Even ugly women don't want to be fat. I've always thought that was insane. I've met lots of plain women who say, very seriously, "No thanks, I'm on a diet." I used to stare at them and think, if I looked like you, I'd have fries with every meal. I mean, may as well . . . For women, watching your weight is like a form of chastity. A crucial sign of submission. But I never gave a damn, I was getting so wasted back then I never put on weight. I've changed, and I don't want to talk about it. But this morning I weighed myself. In my upstairs neighbor's bathroom. Locking the door so she didn't know what I was doing. I've always been in favor of profanity. But for an actress, putting on weight is sacrilege.

And I feel humiliated that it upsets me so much. I like to feel that I'm above ordinary rules. And being obsessed with your weight is so vulgar. The unhappiness I feel is so clichéd. I try to reason with myself: I tell myself I'm getting older anyway. If I wasn't fat, I'd still be old. Might as well eat fries and stop worrying about it. I want to be invincible. Like a guy. You think Robert De Niro gets teary when he steps on the scale? I don't think so. Does Tony Soprano wonder whether he's too fat before becoming the sexiest guy of his generation? I don't think so.

A gentle reminder, darling: repeat what I've just told you to anyone, and you're a dead man. Just because we've patched things up doesn't mean that anything goes.

OSCAR

You're as beautiful as Sophia Loren. I know that's not going to make you feel better. But fuck it, you've got a long way to go before you're a plain Jane.

I know what it feels like to be ashamed of the body you're stuck with—you'll say it's not the same, but I think it is. The big difference isn't that you're a woman and I'm a man. The difference is that I've never looked in a mirror and thought, Okay, looking good. I'm weedy. I'm not thin. I'm not a lean, svelte, elegant guy. I'm scrawny. The scrawniness that marks you out as poor. Something you never grow out of. My shoulders are narrow, my arms are skeletal, my skin is pasty, I've never seen a six-pack above my waistband, what you see is bones, not muscles. I've always been miserable being me.

Snoop Dogg saved my life. He's taller than me—not to mention Black, American, and a millionaire, obviously—and he's written albums that have completely changed the game, but it was the first time I'd ever seen a guy with a body like mine, really skinny, who's not ridiculous. Snoop's funny, but he's not a comedian. He's got swag. I was stunned when I first saw what he looked like. A guy like me, a stick insect, but not unattractive.

You'll say, Okay, but guys get to define themselves by something other than their looks. You'll say, Okay, but you've always been fugly, so you don't know what it's like to start losing your looks when you've been a stunner. And it's true, I don't have the faintest idea what it feels like to walk into a room and dazzle people with my looks. To have everyone want to talk to you because you're gorgeous.

The relationship I had with Zoé is one I've had with lots of other girls. In fact, I was surprised that no one else came forward. The list of girls I've loved and never won is endless. Luckily, I didn't always wear my heart on my sleeve. A lot of the time, their lack of interest was obvious. Deep down, what I found most devastating about these accusations wasn't people saying, "This is appalling toxic masculinity! He kept pestering this young woman even after she said no." It was people saying: no woman could possibly want him. There's nothing sexy about him. Because there's nothing masculine about him. Women sense it instinctively. They don't want him. He's a creep.

This whole story with Zoé is the one that's blown up

in my face. But it's one I've been through a dozen times. Where I'm convinced that this is the only girl for me, and I love her every gesture, everything she represents, and I'm convinced we could share everything about our lives and our innermost thoughts. And she wants nothing to do with me. She could fall for any moron. Even guys who aren't that good-looking. But not me. It's as though they can sense that I'm defective.

I tell anyone who will listen that the only reason Zoé Katana attacked me is because she was looking for publicity. But I know that she rejected me, just as so many women before and after her have rejected me. Success has made me a little less repulsive to women. But the ones I'm drawn to are never the ones who are interested in me.

REBECCA

I never said physical appearance was less important for guys than for girls. Never. You have my sympathy. But I don't want to talk about this anymore. Seriously, thanks for your reply, it was really sweet. But I don't want to talk about the mystery of clothes that shrink in wardrobes. I really don't have the strength to revisit the subject. All I can do is pretend that I don't care and that I have more important things on my mind.

And I'm feeling better. I've been visiting my upstairs neighbor a lot recently. Walking up two flights of stairs is a welcome change of scene. Her boyfriend has left to spend lockdown elsewhere. They were arguing too much. I should know, my windows are wide open and I could hear every word they were saying. I felt like I was living in an American TV show full of psychobabble. The endless, tedious arguments.

If you run into her on the stairs, she's a beautiful specimen, sophisticated, impeccable, classically beautiful, not a hair out of place. Which is a surprise because her apartment—which is four times the size of mine—is an unspeakable mess. The woman who cleans for them has refused to keep working—her husband is elderly, and she's afraid of the virus. As a couple they haven't exactly adapted to her absence. And let's face it, no one could accuse me of being a neat freak.

For the first hour, we get along well. She's not too sad. She says the relationship has been over for a long time. That they haven't fucked in years. That it was bound to happen, that she wants to be alone. What she really wants is to be left in peace so she can hit the bottle.

She's well bred but not stuck up, when she moves, she has the grace of a prima ballerina. You almost feel there's a spotlight following her and her every move is guided by a melody that only she can hear. I've seen photos of her when she was twenty, and she looked like Audrey Hepburn. She's in her forties now, and while we talk, I study her. She's a woman who has suffered too much and at the same time she's an unruly teenager, two facets that coexist with no apparent conflict, but I'm constantly trying to work out where she is between those two extremes. We have lots to talk about, conversation is easy. She opens the first bottle. I don't like to drink. I put my hand over my glass—it's no skin off my nose—and she makes me another cup of coffee. I can't say at what point things shift, but suddenly there's a different woman in front of me. A drunk. It's not a gradual change, she's like an actress switching roles from one minute to the next. Her gestures aren't clumsy, she doesn't sway when she stands, her eyes don't wander. It's the same body, the same face, but the personality inside her changes dramatically. As soon as the shift happens, I take my rolling tobacco and head back downstairs. I love the girl at the beginning of the afternoon, but I'm exhausted by the nighttime drunk with her litany of horrors on repeat.

She says people frown on women who drink. That they're afraid we'll be too honest. Or too sexual. And I know that she's right. But there's also something about the spinelessness, the ugliness, the frustration suddenly laid bare that makes you want to run for the hills.

I wonder whether I go to her place to witness this transformation. To pat myself on the back for not having used since the start of lockdown.

OSCAR

I don't know anyone in Paris who says, I miss the noise of the traffic, I miss the smell of the traffic, I miss having to wait five minutes for the traffic to pass so I can cross. Quite the opposite, I feel like at least once a day I've heard someone say: the peace and quiet is amazing, it feels so good, and for the first time since I've lived here I can smell spring in the city.

As for the rest, we each muddle through as best we can. There are those who go crazy, those who drink more than usual, those who are discovering their own home, those who want to split up, those who've learned a lot home-schooling their children, those who've written huge tomes, those who've lost sleep and those who've finally found it, those who've injured themselves exercising too much, and those who've streamed every Korean TV series available on every platform.

But I don't know anyone who is missing the life where human bodies have to cut a path through the cars.

I go online and grab the first statistic I can find; it's from the World Health Organization. Every year, traffic accidents kill 1.3 million people. And another 20 to 50 million people are injured.

One million three hundred thousand. It would take just fourteen years for traffic accidents to rack up as many deaths as WWI. Covid has a long way to go. Without lockdown, would we have reached one million three hundred thousand deaths worldwide?

We can't say that the 1.3 million deaths a year—young people as much as athletes, workers, children, women, truck drivers, bus drivers, actors, and the elderly—go unnoticed just because they're poor bodies.

When I was twenty, cars were a big thing. Road trips, a fascination with big American cars, but also with certain old French cars—people were obsessed with cars. We'd do a ten-hour drive without a second thought. We loved to drive. We love cars more than human lives. It's a question of industry. The global oil economy. Road management. Powerful investors who don't want things to change. But still we believe there's something rational about our behavior. Maybe it can be explained by the zeal of the percentage of people who have a vested interest in the status quo. But I think we treat the car like a god. We are amazed by our own technologies. It's not rational. It's no more rational than sacrificing children at the top of a pyramid every year to please the gods or appease their fury. It's infinitely more lethal, it's less deliberate, but it's no more rational.

We believe in brutal gods that we never name. We speak of neoliberalism, we study its machinations—the cruel tragedy of taking work from the many for the benefit of the few. The pillaging of the planet to make ugly, useless things.

But deep down, we believe that without technology our bodies are useless. We believe in the futility of our species in the face of those machines that we have deified. We find it intolerable that a virus should kill because it's not a machine that we have made.

And we all know that we won't suddenly come to our senses after lockdown. Because we believe in these god machines. The God of the telephone the God of the network the God of nuclear power the God of the airplane—all these gods that make us feel useless. Gods that are worth dying for. We are not beings that are improved by machines. We are consumed by them. Amazed by the power of our creations. The machines are no more to blame than the God of the Bible, who demanded that we slit a son's throat to prove we were true believers. The only way we know to prove our respect for some higher power is to die for it. We can't bear to die for some paltry virus. But the car—now, that's a good way to go!

REBECCA

Well, I don't know anyone of my grandparents' generation who ever said, "It was so much better in the old days when you spent a whole day walking just to get to the next town." You remind me of the assholes back in the eighties who were obsessed with Guy Debord and constantly railing against *The Society of the Spectacle*. You could tell they were all bougie assholes. Where I grew up, no one came out with crap like: things were better before television, when everyone was cold, starving, and bored shitless. Just because I've been on a bike for five minutes doesn't mean I'm going to join you in your fantasy of the car-free city. We're fine, we're calm. But we can't wait for things to roar into life again. Especially when it comes to food. I don't cook. I respect people who are passionate about it, but it's not my thing. The man from the grocery store downstairs brings me some of the food his wife makes. He took pity on me. I'm thinking of doing that thing where stars set up an Instagram account and film themselves in the grungiest room in their house to let people know they're going through lockdown just like everyone else. Except that the only thing I have to say is: I'm hungry. Can someone please cook something for me?

On my street, people are starting to go out again. A group of four local boys standing on the sidewalk, one wearing a mask, one with a mask around his neck, the other two without. They're laughing.

I got wasted the day before yesterday. I cracked. An old girlfriend, I thought, "Just this once." It felt good. But the party's over, I can feel it—and I went straight back to Zoom meetings. I spoke for the first time. No camera. My heart was pounding. At the Friday meeting for gays. They're all so buff. It's like a box of chocolates—I just line them up and admire them. I can see that the Chemsex/Grindr combo has wreaked havoc: there are so many of them, and they're so young to be saying they have a drug problem. I've discovered I've got the soul of a queer guy. They can go from a story about a hellish high with oceans of spunk and fist-fucking to fantasies of the Empress Sisi—all crinoline and Strauss waltzes—without a segue, without a hitch, without feeling obliged to choose between the two. I feel seen. It felt great to be part of it.

I've never thought so much about what drugs are. When I get blitzed, I'm rewarding myself the way my mother used to reward me, in an incoherent, anxious way. Like someone who doesn't know how to enjoy herself, someone who doesn't know how to protect herself, someone who doesn't know the difference between pleasure and the sin of pride. Someone who doesn't know what to do with grief and anger and is convinced that they need to be stamped out the way you'd stamp out a fire. My mother was the daughter of a depressive mother. She rewarded us for nothing, blindly—simply to fill the void. She loved to eat—to give me sweet things. She was one of those girls conceived just after the war. That's where I come from, that everyday ghastliness. The succession of terrors of deprivations of separations. Her parents lived through three wars, and in the lull between wars what was required of them was dignity, backbreaking work, and blind trust in the state. It's amazing that everything hinges on the paradox that women are seen as fragile, gentle, and delicate when in fact they split themselves in two to give birth, they survive wars alone in bombed-out cities. That's how I always think of my grandmother. Putting her father and her uncles on a train during the first war. Putting her husband and brothers on a train for the second. Putting her son on a train for the war in Algeria and each time knowing from experience that the man who just boarded the train will never come back. And even if he did, everything will have changed in the meantime. My mother was born into this absurdity—of course she rewarded us in any way she could. Of course she was trying to fill a terrible void, and of course at thirteen I wanted booze smack speed solvents acid weed. I wanted anything that could get me out of there.

I listen to feminists who wonder how the patriarchy has lasted so long. Some say it's fear of rape, a theory from the seventies that's controversial now, but one that right-wing Christian feminists continue to favor. Others talk about the fear of separation, of rupture: we so want to identify with the roles we're assigned that we end up favoring them over truth, even if we're incapable of embodying them. They look for complicated explanations. I don't understand why they treat wars as something so natural that it's not worth taking them seriously. On the one hand they tell you that if you were sexually abused at thirteen, your whole life will be marked by shame. On the other hand, we go through war after war, and they don't see what connection war could possibly have with the pathological nature of patriarchy. I understand that it's grander to say, "Wars do so much damage, we should close armaments factories," than it is to say, "I'm going to have words with my husband because I want him to do the dishes." But war is there, in the middle of everything. I have no problem with blaming men, with saying that it's the only way they've found to beget children out of bloodshed. It costs nothing to construct a theory, so here's one for you: men are so frustrated at not being able to have children that they've come up with something that sprays shit and blood like childbirth. In order to give birth to nothing. Defeated nations and victorious nations. That doesn't get us very far. But over time, I've realized that the feminists I listen to plan to spend a lot more time thinking without bothering to think about war. Like me, they're the daughters of women who packed suitcases for their brothers, husbands, and sons and took them to the train station. Obviously, when they came back—those who managed to come back—the women didn't have the nerve to ask them for equal pay. When you see how stupefied people are by Covid, you need to imagine a gutted, bombed-out city. The trauma of war is too deep. It fuses people together the way bones fuse together after a badly healed fracture: everything is stuck, you can't breathe. We're surrounded by Germans, by Protestants, by Jews, by Algerians, by queers, by Afghans, by Vietnamese, by gypsies, by enemies—no man no woman no anything left standing is other than "We are not the other." That's what war is all about: saying we are not the other.

I've gotten shit-faced with princes, with homeless people, with Black people, with hookers, with government ministers, with ambassadors, with philosophers, with painters, with Tunisian refugees, with actresses. I am the other. And I think that, for all of us, it's the wars that we've inherited that we're trying to get over. The wars the oldest among us have lived through are lodged in our bones. Their fear has been handed down more effectively than language or tradition.

I really believe that. I've been using all my life, and it has nothing to do with what was going on at home when I was a kid or what happened to me when I was older. It's the war I'm nursing inside me. It's the parent in me trying to protect me. The bewildered grown-up who's tossing life jackets to me at every opportunity, even though we're on dry land and I have no use for a lifejacket. But I'm conjuring a fear that isn't mine, one that goes back a long way. We use for political reasons. It's a dialogue with our ancestors. You take drugs to forget the wars they lived through, the wars from which they may or may not have returned, the hunger of the women they left in the cities, the agony of this trap from which there is no escape. Or you take drugs to remind you of the war, of the chaos and the intensity, the daily miracle of still being alive. But it's always war we think of. That's why a lot of people will start taking drugs during lockdown—they'll say it's because I'm scared of being alone, or I've lost my job, they'll invent whatever they want. The agony it brings up in us is the memory of years of war.

And then there's me, I always do the opposite of everyone else because otherwise I don't feel comfortable, but even I have to admit that in the absurd silence of this slumbering city, I've come to the end of my rope. I listen to people on Zoom talking about the efforts they're making to stay clean and, for the first time in my life, it doesn't sound completely stupid.

OSCAR

Every morning I attend a meeting, then I take an hour to work on the first step. I realize I've been protecting my relationship with drugs to the detriment of everything else. Since I joined NA, I've been telling myself that I'm only here because I need to be protected from the whole Zoé Katana catastrophe. That I'm not a junkie like everyone else.

I'm lying to myself. I wasn't lying to my girlfriend just so I could do what I wanted, so I could get her off my back and not have her stick her nose in my business. I was the one sticking my nose—into a baggie of coke. In the chambre de bonne. In my apartment, you can access these rooms via a back door in the kitchen, and when the concierge happened to mention that one was available, I rented it without a second thought. The part of me that wanted to get off my face knew exactly what it was doing. I told Joëlle I needed to store books and manuscripts, I put a few sticks of furniture in the room, and then I said I couldn't write in peace with her kid around all the time, and since I could hardly ask a six-year-old to stay locked in her room all day, the simplest thing for me to do was to go up to the chambre de bonne when I wanted to work. Usually, when writers rent an office to write they use it as a bachelor pad—so they can see other women in secret. For me, it was so I could get trashed without my girlfriend knowing. My other woman was cocaine. I never thought about it like that.

Addiction is always a matter of faith, of wanting to corroborate the impossible miracle: wanting to do the same thing over and over, hoping this time it will work. Anything so long as you're riding the roller coaster. It's a feeling that there's something lacking and being prepared to strain, to push, to force it to happen anyway.

We try to force things to match up to our expectations, to what we want and we think we're entitled to. We dictate terms. Addiction is always about demands that are misplaced. Misguided. It's about imposing your will. People think addiction is about self-denigration. But the addict's hostility isn't primarily directed at the self. It's the success of others that we're denigrating. Their attempts to dethrone us. Their fatuous pleasure in being what they are. In having amassed what they've amassed. It's a declaration of war. You think I'm shit? Look at yourself—at least I'm not faking it.

ZOÉ KATANA

Feminist friends, I've read what you've written about the film industry. Could you stop trying to play the Marie Kondos of showbiz by condemning three rapist film directors who should be avoided at all costs? We believe it would be better to burn the whole thing down. And when a rapist has been outed, let's not put him on trial—let's demand group therapy instead. So that all the people who saw what was happening and said nothing, all the people who remember but didn't speak up, can speak, apologize, make amends. And—most importantly—get another job as quickly as possible. People talk about the "dream factory," and we focus on the word "dream" when actually it's "factory" that counts. A factory producing a dense sort of darkness. Cinema is incapable of empathy. Which is paradoxical, when it prides itself on capturing emotion through close-ups.

Now that I've got a friend who's a major actress, I've been watching her movies. And I think she's magnificent. The fact that she never won any awards for acting seems to me a consecration of her work, proof of her genius.

Having managed to get some codes to be able to watch movies, I decided to keep watching. And I realized why I never go to the movies. That phony, Technicolor, artificially generated clear conscience constantly at the service of the richest 1 percent. Movies are designed to reassure the billionaires who finance it. Film is the art of producing the reality they want to create.

How does one define a master? He decides what exists. Who appears in the frame and under what conditions, and who is excluded, working with the machines, the props, the little people. Cinema panders to its masters. It is a series of humiliations. Everyone tests his power at his own level. To get even. Your industry doesn't fool anyone, gentlemen. Your movies reek of misery, deference, and vicious propaganda.

When I worked in publishing, I routinely saw film rights being sold, and I realized what a film was. A project that requires an endless series of approvals. And guess what? The people who get to issue them are invariably white men with shitloads of money. And all these fat cat white men are unrepentant sons of bitches. They're repulsive, illiterate assholes, morons, half-witted heirs, neurotic imbeciles. All of whom are required to green-light every stage of the project. Let's imagine there is an interesting idea somewhere in all this mess; they find it and ensure it's turned into utter shit.

And we, the audience—we devour what they serve up to us. The spectacle of our own exclusion. Ages, bodies, classes, races—they make the choice, and with our eyes, with our ears, we take it in as a model. We devour our own shame at not being present. The silver screen is a place where we are not represented. We're outside the frame.

A neurotic society has neurotic rather than healthy reflexes. Consequently, it did not take long for cinema to become what it is today: cowboys, superheroes, soldiers, warriors, filthy-rich philanderers. And manic pixie dream girls who are never verbs, only indirect objects—. They don't move the action forward, they don't talk to each other about anything except the male heroes, shit, they barely have any dialogue, and they're always under thirty because they exist only to draw attention to the hero, the powerful, murderous white guy—and don't tell me that kind of hero would stop at just humiliating those girls. You know why men in the film industry don't speak out? Because if they talked about their actual working conditions, people would whip out photographs of them strutting around film festivals with big smiles on their faces and ask them, "Why are you smiling in this photo? Why are you smiling after being humiliated?" If they told the truth about their working conditions, they'd be seen for what they are: dumb fucks who are treated like shit. Well paid. But treated like shit.

Cinema responded to the feminism of the seventies with a relentlessly violent ideology. You want to embrace your sexuality, bitch? I'll serve it up every hour of every day. Whenever you're not filmed doing the dishes, you'll be shown capitalizing on your erotic potential. That's all you're good for. You want to wear short skirts? I'll brutally expose you, let's see how mouthy you are when you see what I've done to you. As close as possible to the little deer, sweetie, the one the hunter dispatches in *Bambi*: you'll be weak you'll be alone you'll be scared and you'll have nothing but your little legs to run away on.

Cinema is always trying to define the feminine. It works by a process of exclusion. The following are barred from appearing on screen: fat women, old women, and women who are too intelligent. Then there are those it tolerates once a decade, in a single movie: a nonwhite woman, a strong woman who fights well, or a woman with a sense of humor.

From the eighties onward, the film industry took it upon itself to promulgate the most repressive and effective response to any and every fight for liberation. It said: girls exist to be desired and coerced, Black people exist to clean and dance, fat people exist to be funny, revolutionaries exist to be assassinated, poor people exist to starve and be pitied before being saved by a generous, rich man, aliens exist to be slaughtered, etc.

The form of the message is seduction, the language of advertising. It doesn't appeal to your intelligence. It's a message that goes straight to your subconscious: three cheers for the rich, three cheers for the powerful, three cheers for war.

This is what I have to say about the film industry: I and my sexuality as an oppressed person don't give a flying fuck whether the banquet was more tempting when we kept our mouths shut. I'm not a parasite; I'm the main course. I'm the person the film industry considers legitimate prey: young, slim, powerless. Someone you don't want to have sex *with*, someone you want to have sex *in spite of*. Always in spite of. If I'm having a ball too, you've got a problem. If I consent, I'm a slut, and that's embarrassing. If I'm enjoying myself, you feel less in control, which is awkward and ruins the fun. At least let's make sure I feel like shit the morning after, so you can strut around while I hide. The pleasure we are celebrating is always your pleasure. The pleasure of degrading, killing, reducing to ashes. Your bullshit war impulse.

You need to put sex in the bodies of women, making sure that it's not their thing. Making sure that they can't avoid it, but that it's not for them. "They," in this narrative, remain on the threshold of humanity, just outside the door, turned away by the bouncers. "They" are not even objects. Because we don't blame objects for the use we make of them.

It's a pleasure that's channeled through our bodies but one in which we should never be an equal participant. Men dance on us. Not with us. We are never partners. Always prey or victims.

In a system of domination enforced through violence, there is no pleasure unless someone cries. All desire must be associated with destruction, otherwise it is not masculine. If you come when I fuck you and you don't feel like shit the next day, then I haven't fucked you like a man. Or maybe I possess you, I've married you and knocked you up and imprisoned you in your role. Pleasure must destroy. That's true of heterosexuality—it's true of everything. If orgasms don't result in destruction, there is no masculinity.

Cinema is the booming authoritarian voice of the rich man, the powerful white man convinced that his arrogance is a substitute for fact. What he has to say in every possible way is hurray for guns, and death to women who are not barricaded in their homes. Oh, the women we've watched fleeing and sobbing, oh, the men we've watched armed and frenzied with rage. The former as prey, the latter as psychopathic predators. What a spectacle.

OSCAR

As soon as lockdown was lifted, I left Paris. I'm in the Vosges now. I'm doing bar crawls with my cousin. There are eleven pubs in a village of nine hundred inhabitants. Three of them are run by cousins of mine. I haven't seen them for a long time. My uncle was buried during lockdown. It had nothing to do with Covid, but no one got to say goodbye to him. I came here to see his grave.

I'm amazed at the warmness of the welcome and how happy I am to be back with my family. I order coffee. I don't think too much about the booze being drunk around me. The women drink a lot. I think about what you wrote—that women your age are all alcoholics. They're the ones who drink the most, silently, invisibly—they knock back bottles of champagne like it's Perrier. And I'm quick to spot the ones who know—the ones who don't insist when I say, "No thanks, no alcohol." My cousins have all been through at least one round of rehab. They get it. And they don't comment. Over dinner, my aunt will insist, "Where there's no wine, there's no love." It's as if I were subtly insulting her by not filling my glass. But I've been hanging out in bars and chilling in Neufchâteau for three days now. At five o'clock, I'll listen to a guy who's already well-oiled talking about helicopters, highly complex stuff, as though he's some kind of senior flight engineer; he's drinking pastis, his friend is drinking white wine. At the back of the room, a few card players in their sixties knock back beers and glasses of red. And at six o'clock, a couple: the woman has crutches, and long, frizzy hair that's somewhere between white and yellow, and the man looks like a deranged hunter-trapper, like he's just stepped out of the Canadian forests. It's a local bar. But for the pinball machine it would look just like it did when I was a kid and my aunt's brother ran the place.

I take a lot of videos on my phone with the sound on, I can hear myself laughing like a half-wit. I laugh just like my father did: to hide my embarrassment and my lack of composure. I hate my laugh, just like I hate my voice. A rather cool brunette in her twenties, in black leggings and a loose red blouse, comes over to my table. When she leans over to talk to me, I can see the straps of her black bra. The local intellectual hottie. I'm cagey. I don't want any trouble. She says: Apparently you're friends with Rebecca Latté? Then she talks about your films in the weary tone of a France Culture film critic. In that moment, I miss the booze. It made conversations like this bearable. She mentions Zoé Katana's most recent post, which she disagrees with, and in general she doesn't like "that kind of" feminism. All this she says in a very supercilious tone. I take out my cell phone as though it's just vibrated and get up, apologizing: "I really should take this." Once outside, I feel like slapping her. What gives her the right to talk to me? And to talk to me about Zoé Katana? I've read her post.

In all the months we've been writing to each other, I've never talked about the film industry. I'm a novelist; I've learned to be wary of your industry. As soon as writers have a little success, the film industry starts circling us like a pretty girl imploring us to find her attractive. Every writer I've seen respond to its advances has been devastated. I told you about the unfilmed script financed by a nutjob of a producer who never paid anyone. These things can't be mentioned in public because our profession is too specific and too privileged. It's hard to convey to people how miserable it is to work on a story, to bring it to life, to be convinced that it will find an audience—only to see it filed away in a drawer. I can't think of anything more humiliating and devastating for a writer than having your work read by people who don't read books or newspapers, don't go to museums, don't listen to music, don't have any experience beyond drinking binges at film festivals—and force you to listen to their pedantic opinions about your writing. And everything plays out exactly as you described it: the awkwardness of responding positively, because you need their approval and they know it, so they abuse the situation and they corner you. What filmmakers are looking for when they approach authors is not whether they can construct a plot or write convincing dialogue, it's whether they're docile—whether they're prepared to humiliate themselves and prostitute their talent to the moronic gods of cinema. They are confirming the power of money over imagination, the corruption of characters in exchange for a little fake prestige. You're summoned in order to pay lip service to the pecking order, and therefore to corruption—and to ensure your silence, your rejection of all sincerity. I can't think of anything more sinister. When the whole MeToo movement exploded, and I didn't yet know that I'd get a turn in the spotlight, the first thing I thought was, it starts with the actresses, then everyone else will speak up to say: this industry is proof that creative people are prepared to humiliate themselves as long as they're allowed to bask in the limelight.

REBECCA

Will you all just chill about the film industry? I've already bawled Zoé out. This generation seems to think they get to publicly spit in your face and you'll consider it part of your job. I told Zoé to go fuck herself. The film industry is like my family—I'm happy to criticize it, but I hate when it's criticized from the outside. Okay, I vaguely understand what you're getting at. I've watched the cinema change. I've seen it turn into an industry. And, in doing so, lose all the magic it had.

I only watch old movies. I've loved everything about this industry from another century, the talent of every person on set. And the alchemy of the ensemble—nowhere has the notion that the whole could be greater than the sum of its collective parts been more apparent than in a movie. But over the past ten years, for us as for everyone else, it's been all about the cash. It's ridiculous, given that we don't have any. We still perform the same rituals—which no longer have any meaning. We're just pretending to make movies the way we used to. And I know we're lying to ourselves—what we're making is pretentious television.

It's no bad thing to warn people what to expect. In the eighties, we were warned that heroin was a problem. Smack is a harsh mistress. You don't negotiate with junk—it takes precedence over everything else. The ad campaigns were designed by morons, and we pretended not to take any notice—but the fact is we stopped sharing needles. We'd been warned. Otherwise, I wouldn't be here to tell you all this. It didn't stop those like me, who had a calling, from doing it again and again. Not because I wanted to die. I wanted to weave between the raindrops, not do myself in.

A lot of people of my generation were wary, they didn't experiment—because it didn't fit with the idea of the life they wanted to live. They didn't want to be actual junkies. Read the biographies of Art Pepper or Charlie Mingus: before all the propaganda, guys used to take junk for days on end then go home surprised to find they had a really bad cold . . . they knew nothing about the idiosyncrasies of heroin, they blindly stumbled, they had no idea. It's good to be warned when there's a risk. It deters the tourists, the ones who don't want to pay the price.

I'd be in favor of similar propaganda about the film industry: it's not for everyone. You have to be tough. It's the same as smack: even if I'd been warned, I'd have done it anyway. And just as I've stood in too many cemeteries saying goodbye to people who OD'd before they turned thirty, I've also watched dozens of young women destroyed by the film industry. The difference is that if you're cast in a role at the age of sixteen, there's no one to warn you to think twice before you risk your neck.

In the Zoom meetings during lockdown, I'd sometimes recognize the faces of old friends who used to use with me, drug dealers who'd gone into hiding, gold-digging starlets I'd met at parties. I never let them know I was there. I was wary. I was ashamed to be there and didn't want anyone to know. But then one day I saw the ruggedly handsome Redouane show up. We go back a long way, he and I. Partners in crime. Such great memories. Redouane's no lightweight, he's a bruiser, an artist when it comes to hard drugs. He used to do hot-wheels drug runs without ever getting caught. Clever, fast, brutal, sexy, and surprisingly cultured for a delinquent. A true prince of darkness. We lost touch during one of his stretches behind bars, but we never fell out. I had his number, it hadn't changed, so I phoned him right away. He said, I've been clean for two years, princess, welcome to the organization. We chatted for two hours. And I knew. If it can work for him, it's the place for me too. I went to an in-person meeting with him the day before yesterday. I thought about that shyness thing you felt before you went. I was more terrified than if I had to do a solo gig at L'Olympia even though I can't sing a note. I've got the face of an actress—everyone recognized me. I sneaked out before it finished . . . You did tell me, and it's true: the amazing thing about this alliance of misfits and maladjusted freaks is that nobody gives you a hard time. So I've decided that I'm going to go to meetings wearing dark glasses, arrive a little late, and leave a little early. Anonymous my ass, I'm a fucking legend. And it's fine.

    I do my own thing. I was of two minds about going to the meeting, but it was right at the end of my street, next to the church. I took that as a sign. I realized that I always thought using made you a more interesting person. Quitting doesn't change that. It's like being a priest, the title is for life. One guy—not young and not old, not handsome and not ugly, completely invisible—talked for ages about his crack habit, and I looked at him and thought, it's weird, because you look like a complete nobody. It's like mentally I'm still fourteen years old, convinced that getting bombed is proof of inner life, of intensity. And it's not untrue. This guy, obviously a coder who earns a good living—you could make a movie about his life. Take away the crack, and I doubt there'd be anything to tell. To me, drugs are a country at war: you suffer, the country is destroyed, but at least something happens.

Apart from that, the clean version of me is in great shape. I haven't gone so long without using since I was thirteen. I'm surprised. It's a lot more enjoyable than I expected. Getting blitzed is a young person's sport. I should have realized that long ago. I'm less pessimistic, less anxious. It's amazing, all this purity. What I thought of as a crutch had started to sap my strength.

I'm going to leave Paris for the summer. I'll go to Barcelona. I hate the sun, but I love that city. I'm taking the train, and I'm freaking out at the thought of wearing a face mask for six hours straight.

OSCAR

I'm afraid of straying from the program. I don't want to go to meetings anymore, or write down my steps. I was excited by the whole thing, but now all I can see is how artificial it is. I'm running out of goodwill. Also, I'm on the sixth step. You start by making a list of all your faults.

I feel like a hypochondriac leafing through the *Diagnostic and Statistical Manual of Mental Disorders*. I'm fed up with sincerity. All I want is to be a complete asshole. To be negative about everything. To hate people. To feel contempt for them. To pretend they're to blame for all my problems. I'm reminded of something I heard at a meeting: "A relapse is something you construct." Some catastrophes have their own architecture.

It's ironic that this is happening just when you're starting the program. I want to be happy for you. But the joy has worn off. I just feel lonely, and overwhelmed. Maybe sad that I wasn't the one to take you to your first meeting. Convinced that the last thing you want is to be seen with me. And you'd be right. I feel like throwing in the towel. A girl at NA came up to me to say she used to read my books. Before. That she really liked my writing. Before. Meaning, before she knew who I really am. A stalker and a bastard. I smiled and said, I don't care, I didn't come here to talk about literature. But I felt crushed. I want to be loved. I don't write to be spat on. Bizarrely, I thought about Zoé. She's really getting trolled with a vengeance. We're both punching bags, for different crowds. But she likes the people who support her. She's writing for the people who understand and accept her. After the girl came up to talk to me, I felt ashamed to be supported by the two guys I was with. I don't want male solidarity. All I want is not to be who I am.

REBECCA

You're a pain in the ass, my friend: here I am getting my shit together and you're falling apart. We're out of sync. Write to me about what's going on with you. It'll be a lot more useful than falling off the wagon.

I'm an actress. My ego is my stock in trade . . . Being loved by the director, validated by the producer, dazzling the critic, catching the light in a shot, nailing every line of dialogue, mobilizing a crew to take a single photo, dealing with scandals . . . No one pays me to be humble. Or to doubt my value. Whether on stage or on a film set, the actor is the one who sets the rhythm for the story. The rhythm of your own ego, in a way. I don't lie about it; I don't do modesty. And it doesn't bother me to see others do the same thing. You spend too much time worrying about your reputation and not enough about your self-esteem. Your reputation, your novels, the affront to your good name . . . You're like a village schoolmistress in the fifties. What will the neighbors think, and what will people say at church on Sunday, and will I be invited to the parish fete? Listen, kid, it's the third millennium, things have changed. You want to write books? Think about the next one. Forget this shit about being the Dr. Dre of the literary establishment, you're too old, for one thing. Try modeling yourself on Casanova. There you go. He wrote his magnum opus so late that he died without knowing people would be talking about it centuries later. That's the advantage of being a writer. Growing old isn't necessarily a flaw. Let's say that tomorrow you write a banger—that you're like Pharrell when he wrote "Happy." Brilliant.

Money, opportunities, fame, a huge ego boost. When it happens, it's fantastic, you wake up and think, what a lovely day, what an amazing adventure, I'm so lucky. I should know. And then, like everything else, it slips through your fingers. Nothing is set in stone. We were told that fame was indispensable. And like sheep, we all got together and said, "I want some of that, I want fame to justify who I am." I get to brag that I've had more than my share of fame. I'm entitled to give my opinion . . . it's like metaphedrone. A designer drug without the spiritual side. A fast, powerful rush that activates every cell, pushing you upward. It's consumer-oriented MDMA—as relentless as it is soulless. Then comes the crash. There's nothing left. Nothing but frayed nerves, disorientation, extreme irritability, misery. And a single thought: let's do it again.

OSCAR

You're right: fame works on me and in me like a drug. It's the same clarity—the first time I used, the first time I knew a novel was going to be a bestseller—giving birth to a different me, freeing a part of myself I can't express when I'm sober. It was an extraordinary revelation. Maybe fame made me a little more anxious than booze—alcohol came with the notion that "all I need to do is drink," and I grew up in a country where alcohol was everywhere, whereas fame was something I would have to seek, find, and nurture. Fame was a more difficult flame to tend, but it lit a fire in my belly. I would make it.

Or at least that's what I tried to convince myself—and I wasn't some young middle-class kid who thinks that he's entitled, that he doesn't have to make the effort or pay the price. It was a war I waged with every weapon in my arsenal. And for decades, the drug factory and the fame factory produced good results. Then they started to run out of steam. Nothing was ever enough. Writing to please people, writing for the acclaim, inventing a version of myself that was more extreme more uninhibited more masculine—less pathetic. I feel the same thing when I read Moby's memoir, *Then It Fell Apart*. I realize the only thing to do is quit. And I remember the friend who's just had heart surgery and whose cardiologist tells him he has to quit everything—the booze, the drugs—who tells me, cardiologists always say that, they don't understand, I work nights, they don't understand, it's my only safety valve, my one pleasure, obviously I can't just quit everything, I can't live without it, it's what makes me feel alive. It's a feeling of unfairness—it's a child throwing a tantrum, screaming this is the only thing I've got I never had anything except this how can you take it away from me? And I listen to my friend and I think, you're not coping, you know it, if you were coping, then your first reaction when you come out of the operating room wouldn't be to phone your dealer and break out the booze. If you were in control, you'd know that you're capable of having fun in other ways, of being alive in other ways. You're not coping, I say to him; if you ever need to talk about it—you never know—you can always call me. And somehow in saying that, I know that I'm breaking our pact. I'm the same way with fame: someone inside me says I can't completely give up. It's the only thing I have that proves I have the right to exist.

REBECCA

Then again, you could say it's moronic thinking. The argument of the coward, a logical fallacy . . . a mechanistic collection of ideas twisted around and fitted together to correspond to your notion of what is right and fair.

Social recognition isn't fair. It creates a yawning chasm of inequality. It's no longer about being well-known in your village or your community. I have no idea what kind of social recognition a silversmith was afforded in the early nineteenth century, maybe back then such people were recognized and admired—something like "You make an effort, you have talent, and if you work as ethically as possible, you'll be rewarded with the respect and affection of those around you." I don't know anything about it. What I do know about is the twentieth century—global media coverage. An individual being thrust into the spotlight by the media, which designates them as more important than those watching: people staring at a giant screen are powerless to change a single thing about what is being played out on it, they are utterly passive. The film progresses as it was intended to progress, as a TV show does on a screen. You can do whatever you like in your living room—it has no effect whatsoever. Online, people feel that the situation is different, they feel they can have an impact. And they quickly realize that the most effective way to have an impact is to insult others.

We actors were larger than life, infinitely reproducible, living, breathing statues, carefully lit and made up to look sublime; writers put scintillating words in our mouths, our every gesture was predetermined, we were timeless. That was the age of cinema. These days, I think we've circled back to thinking of actors and actresses as vain, a little slutty, a little whorish, whose talent is something to be disparaged.

It was music that ultimately created the sort of stars who came into existence in the late twentieth century. Mechanical reproduction made it possible to reproduce the spiritual connection that is music.

Fame goes hand in hand with hard drugs . . . Seeking comfort in fame is seeking comfort in something that is destroying you. You're selling yourself. I've never prostituted myself, in the sense that I've never done anything that I didn't sincerely want to do. But I've never had any reason to. I've never had to bend my desires, force them to conform to anyone or anything. Fame robs you of yourself. It's a privilege. All privilege comes at a price, usually an arm and a leg.

OSCAR

Brutal depression. I feel as though something that never existed has been cut out of me. I've lost a calmness that I fantasize about. I take your advice and decide to write about booze. It unsettles me. Besides, I can't do it as autofiction, the way I planned. Because I can't talk about NA in the first person. I need a drink. When I say this aloud, the desire goes away. Five minutes. Then it comes back. A little voice says, just one glass, it's been a long time, you've changed, you're not like the others, they're absolutists when it comes to sobriety, they can't handle their drink like you can. The voice is like a chess player ten moves ahead of my rational mind. It's patient, a shrewd strategist, it knows me inside out. It is the most highly developed part of me.

I see some friends from Nancy and ask about this girl I know who's trying to quit drinking, she's often talked to me about it, she's a maudlin drunk. They say, "Her shrink asked her whether she thought she'd punished herself enough, and advised her to start drinking again, but in moderation." Part of me is outraged that anyone can call themselves a therapist and believe that it's just a question of willpower, that to stop being an alcoholic all you have to do is decide to drink in moderation. And the part of me that wants to drink seizes on this phrase "but in moderation." My mind is racing as I hurtle down this rabbit hole. What if I could manage to do it? Did I quit drinking just to punish myself? Did I make a deal with the devil because I had a tsunami of hatred sweeping over me and thought I deserved a good beating? You're a filthy, disgusting man—you'll get no more pleasure. From anything.

In moderation. Drink like everyone else. Just an occasional glass. Saying to yourself when you feel a little tipsy: I've got work tomorrow, easing up the way sober people do, casually saying: I've had enough. I'm done.

Like sober people, or like idiots. Amateurs. I have no fucking desire to become a wine buff. I have no desire to drink in moderation.

Life is sending me signals. It's all about booze. I meet up with a screenwriter friend, years ago he and I wrote a screenplay that never got filmed. We were working for a young producer who was handsome and sophisticated but a complete head case, who bitterly argued over every clause in a contract although he never paid us a penny.

The screenwriter and I remained friends, so when I run into him by chance, we go to a café and sit at the counter. We chat. Order coffee after coffee. Like drinkers. It comes back to me. The black-and-white photo hanging in his apartment, he's young, he's with friends, he's sixty pounds heavier, barely recognizable with his air of brute excitement. He quit remarkably young. The way we knock back coffees: we're both recovering alcoholics. Inconsolable widowers, blindly repeating the same empty gestures of the old revelries.

Sometimes it hits me. I feel like giving in, just to be rid of the anxiety. To get it fucking over with. To succumb. Even the word is beautiful. Keel over. Lose consciousness. Fall to the ground, crawl past the bar, wallow in the gutter, vomit. Lose. What you love about drinking, what you love about smoking, is the same thing you love about a love affair, what you love about a well-paid job that makes you miserable: it's loving what is stronger than you.

Yet another day. I'm going into town for a lunch with a group of authors to decide the winner of a small literary prize no one's heard of.

Everyone shows up with a fixed opinion; everyone pretends. They pretend to love literature and to know what they're talking about. We end up giving the prize to pretty much anyone—no one listens to anyone during the deliberations, everyone has their own idea. Some vote for a friend, some vote for their publisher, some vote for a book they liked, some vote against an author they don't like.

Over lunch after the deliberations, the conversation turns to Styron, who I've never read. There's a discussion about translation, about whether or not *Sophie's Choice* is a good book—everyone agrees the first two novels are brilliant. And then alcohol: "He quit drinking overnight, suffered a twenty-year depression, then died. But he never went back to the sauce."

On the way home, I stop off at the bookshop. I buy *Darkness Visible*, his short memoir about his depression. I thought it would be about alcohol. What he has to say on that subject can be summed up in a few lines. "The storm which swept me into a hospital in December began as a cloud no bigger than a wine goblet the previous June. And the cloud—the manifest crisis—involved alcohol, a substance I had been abusing for forty years. Like a great many American writers, whose sometimes lethal addiction to alcohol has become so legendary as to provide in itself a stream of studies and books, I used alcohol as the magical conduit to fantasy and euphoria, and to the enhancement of the imagination. There is no need to either rue or apologize for my use of this soothing, often sublime agent, which had contributed greatly to my writing; although I never set down a line while under its influence, I did use it—often in conjunction with music—as a means to let my mind conceive visions that the unaltered, sober brain has no access to. Alcohol was an invaluable senior partner of my intellect, besides being a friend whose ministrations I sought daily—sought also, I now see, as a means to calm the anxiety and incipient dread that I had hidden away for so long somewhere in the dungeons of my spirit. The trouble was, at the beginning of this particular summer, that I was betrayed. It struck me quite suddenly, almost overnight: I could no longer drink. It was as if my body had risen up in protest, along with my mind, and had conspired to reject this daily mood bath which it had so long welcomed and, who knows? perhaps even come to need."

And from this, I infer that maybe I tried to stop drinking too soon. If I'd waited for my body to say stop, I wouldn't have allowed this thing to take on such importance. I want to drink in the same way I want to go through a portal into a whole world. But Styron is writing from a bygone era, when men were not held accountable for their behavior. I'm giving up going back to drinking. For the time being.

REBECCA

The apartment in Barcelona I've been loaned is so long and narrow that no sunlight penetrates the interior. I'm glad to be away from Paris. Every day, wandering through El Raval, I pass the same rather handsome young Black guy—long hair, battered sunglasses, barefoot, and in shorts—unaccountably stylish. His bike has no tires, the chain is hanging off the derailleur, and there's no saddle—he sits on the bare frame. Over the past two months, I've seen him riding the same bike in the same condition, and every time it takes a moment before I realize there's something wrong with the picture. He's so aloof, so self-assured, that it takes a moment before you notice that both the bike and its rider are missing essential parts.

On the beach, a dark-haired boy was walking with a huge black Gucci bag—as though he'd just stepped out of the shop. From a distance, he looked like an ordinary middle-class boy—and then I saw him take out a cardboard box so he could sleep in the shade, and I took a closer look. He was a kid—fifteen tops—and clearly homeless, wearing old orange Bermuda shorts too big for him. It took me a while to realize that he was hanging out on the gay beach looking for a potential john—or someone to roll, who knows? That's what people hate about prostitution: it's visible.

Everyone wears face masks. For weeks now it's been sweltering—beads of sweat form on our upper lips. The masks are stifling. And probably pointless. Everyone is wearing one, and everyone is out of doors; people wear masks sitting at restaurant tables, and they chat to each other through the masks until their food is served. They're doing their best. They don't wonder whether it's useful or whether it's comfortable. They're doing everything they can to avoid another lockdown.

Like you, I get the impression that life is talking to me, sending me signals. It's showing me a world that looks like how I feel: distraught, damaged, with no clear direction. Coasting.

Let's cut to the chase. You want to relapse; I don't think

you should. The first thing I did when I got here was look for an NA meeting. I don't understand a word they're saying, and since we're wearing masks, I don't even know who's speaking. But it feels good to go. I find it reassuring to be able to cross borders, change languages—and have the same meetings. Nobody here recognizes me, which I don't particularly like. Luckily, a French woman about my age came up to me as we were leaving, and we went for coffee. I'm used to people noticing me, pampering me, being eager little piranhas circling the great actress, each taking a little piece of my time, my attention. But I'm not used to people talking to me like she does. So frankly, about essential things.

It would be a pity if, because of you, I ended up joining the meetings, even though I never wanted to, and they worked for me while you relapsed like some fuckwad. Give up, you dipshit, how many ways do I have to say it? You're not twenty anymore. That's ancient history. Quit arguing. You've had your season in the sun. You're not going to find what you're looking for in booze or weed. It'll be like going back to bed with an old flame you adored and finding it's not the same. Not even warmed-up leftovers. Nothing but hassle.

I too can be nostalgic about my first drinking binges. It was sunny, it was spring. I was drinking plum brandy from a plastic bottle. We were rehearsing a play at the Vandœuvre youth club. I was playing Ondine. We used to make fun of the youth club staff with their beat-up Renault 4s, but we always ended up hanging out there. I adored the theater, but that never stopped me from ending up sprawled on the floor during rehearsals—no one dared to drink with me. Girls didn't dare to do anything. Back in my day, girls were afraid of everything. I was going to be the fourteen-year-old swigging whiskey from the bottle. My role model was the blue-haired girl in the Japanese anime *Albator* who has yellow eyes that look empty and who plays the harp. Her, and Christiane F., obviously. I was living my best life. Sometimes I talk about my teenage years with people who don't have the same kinds of memories, and it's hard to explain that it was a wild time. I'd buy some glue and go down to the back of a parking lot on my own with a little cassette deck, and I'd listen to Queen's "Flash Gordon" and Joy Division and sniff. I'd steal records from the Hall du Livre. I'd forgotten until you reminded me. I'd walk in with an oversize Doro-tennis bag, put together a little stack, slip them inside and walk out. I had cojones, I liked stealing from department stores—in fact, you can add that to the list of things I was sorry I couldn't do after I became famous. I could do it in New York or Tokyo, but when you can afford to pay for things and you steal them just for the adrenaline rush, you feel like an idiot, and it's not the same pleasure it was when you were young and you just waltzed in and took what you wanted. Like you were just taking something back.

I can understand why you feel nostalgic about your teenage years. But that's all over, we'll never be fourteen again. There's no such thing as a favorable relapse. You don't need to go to the movies to know that. I've been around junkies all my life, and I've never heard one of them cheerfully say, "I'm back on the gear." So quit with the melodrama and come back down to earth . . . take up a sport, go on vacation.

OSCAR

I have a potted plant in my living room. It used to have flowers, huge scarlet blossoms like bunches of grapes. This morning I found all the leaves had been nibbled and eaten away, and hanging from them were these fleecy cocoons with tiny green caterpillars inside. I've already picked off about thirty, but they seem to be multiplying by the hour. Every time I clean the plant, I find new eggs. Every leaf has curled up, as though the caterpillar were curling it into a ball. You can spot them because of the sticky white envelope they form; until the caterpillars emerge from their cocoons and start wriggling around—they're exactly the same color as the leaves—it's hard to extract the parasites to protect the plant and make sure it survives the caterpillar attack. When you're in love, that's exactly what it's like: a cocoon, this thick carapace that forms in minutes, sticky, soft, silky but opaque. From inside, you see nothing: you feel you're stuck inside your love affair, you vegetate. And the plant that is our lives can be devoured, devastated, but still we feed on the disaster, we never emerge.

I walked Clémentine to the bus stop. As we walk, we see a black dog, he has stubby legs, pricked-up ears, he looks feisty, I call him Bolt. And I see Bolt's owner sitting at the counter of a little bar, it's sunny outside and inside the place looks like a cozy cave, he's sitting in front of a martini glass—thick red liquid. I see him as we pass, and I know that this is what I miss most about booze: that bars felt like home. That every café had the potential to be a warm haven. Staying with the regulars after closing time, after the shutters come down, and leaving by the back door—looking for an all-night shop that sells croissants. Curiously, it's not the drunkenness I remember most vividly, or the ham-fisted nostalgia—I don't particularly miss talking too loudly and repeating the same thing a dozen times. I see how people are transformed at happy hour, how they become more rounded, how they warm up; after dinner they become touchy-feely, they start to share secrets. The thing I'm nostalgic about is the physical impact: the first sip of whiskey, that burn in the throat, the warm feeling spreading through your limbs. But it's the bars I miss most of all. Having a local watering hole. Knowing the bartenders. Being welcomed. The consolation of a home away from home.

Alcohol meant stability. I've never known any other kind—before, during, or since. Friend, lover, parent, earth, fresh air, and sweetness.

I often think about suicide, sometimes halfheartedly. Ever since I quit drinking, the same thought keeps coming back to me: before I die, the one thing that would make me happy is a glass of wine, a glass of white wine, a dry white wine, followed by a glass of sweet white wine, then a glass of champagne, a glass of red wine, a Saint-Joseph, maybe. And a whiskey. No ice. Any whiskey.

And then I think: what if I had a drink, and then another drink, what if I made up for all the time I've lost—all the missed drinks that haven't warmed me, supported me, distracted me from who I am. Then I'd be drunk and I wouldn't feel like dying. I'd forget the whole thing. All I'd think about was drinking.

I miss the unexpected. I even miss beer. I never liked beer, but now I feel nostalgic for it. Ice cold. On a café terrace. I miss the color. I miss the feel of the glass in my hand. And then it makes you piss. It's only when you get up to empty your bladder that you realize how tanked you are. How many times have I found myself sitting on a toilet, unable to stand up without falling over?

Maybe it's because I'm not drinking anymore that I've stopped writing. I wonder if maybe my problem was that I didn't drink enough. Malcolm Lowry, Scott Fitzgerald, Marguerite Duras, Chandler, Truman Capote, Stephen King, Hammett, Dorothy Parker, Steinbeck, Jean Rhys, Patricia Highsmith, Hemingway, Elizabeth Bishop, Raymond Carver, Georges Simenon . . . the white man's poison. You've got your Black jazz legends and heroin, your Black musicians and any drug you like, you've got Black athletes and Black actors and getting wasted, but Black novelists—whether American, Haitian, French, or Kenyan—never bust your balls about how difficult they find it to write. There's no tradition of alcoholism among great Black authors. So I pull myself together. I think: if James Baldwin didn't need to drink, then you don't need to, to be a good writer.

REBECCA

You're talking horseshit. You're building toward a relapse the way you'd build a lean-to in the woods—cobbling together random pieces of wood. Not that I've ever built one, but I'm pretty sure that's how you do it. Like you.

You cry for help while making sure there's nothing anyone can do for you.

I understand. I so loved getting back with ex-lovers with whom there was no future, I bore the suffering as though I were fated to be a widow, I bore the grief of all my ex-lovers, and as soon as I could, I got involved in another sad affair that was bound to end badly, one that would destroy me, so I understand what you're doing. But we're not cut from the same cloth. I survive everything. I come back from everything. I'm not weak.

And there's nothing I can do to save you from what you desire. In going clean, you become like a fanatical cop, or a gay man back in the day who had to be aware of the subtlest sign if he wanted to hit on someone . . . You develop an intuition, a sixth sense, a hypervigilance. I can tell when someone has been using before I even speak to them, I can tell by their complexion, by the way they smell, by the way they walk. And I see you turning back toward ecstasy—the ecstasy of the lover, but the lover with no consequence, the lover with no human partner, a lover as fool. There's a particular pleasure in fucking everything up, and there's a particular pleasure in reviving your old demons. There's a pleasure in disintegrating. You prepare yourself. You relish it in advance.

I can't lock you away, I can't live your life for you. I think about your daughter, a girl I've never met, who's probably been waiting for this moment for a little over a year because she knows you better than I do and she knows you can't be trusted. I blame you. I blame myself. I know saying "Be careful" never works. I could slam you against a wall and beat some sense into you, I could lock you in a sauna for a month and administer a vitamin C and magnesium cleanse. I could have rolled up with five nymphomaniacs under twenty and had them throw themselves at you so you barely had time to breathe and in doing so given you time to think about something else, I could have hypnotized you, forcibly sedated you, or dragged you to the mountains of Uzbekistan or to see the temples in Cambodia, to Lourdes or to a clinic in Switzerland . . .

And it would do no good.

What can you do for the friend who's determined to relapse? Demand that he get his act together? What can you do for a girlfriend who has hooked up with the wrong guy, when you know she's going to take a beating and you know she won't come out unscathed, but she's under a spell, magnetically drawn to him, and has no use for your warning?

What can you do for the friend who's tired of constantly making the same mistakes, but tells you, I enjoy it? What can you do? You wait. You reply a little too quickly to text messages. You say "I love you" a little too often. You suggest: Have you thought about stopping? Have you thought about changing your approach? Your friend hasn't asked you to stick your nose into his business. The friend hasn't asked you for anything. What can you do for a friend who's doing well but who you can see is heading for catastrophe?

People fuck up their lives. All you can do is go along with it. Or stop choosing friends from among the dysfunctional. It's not the lost souls, the people no one cares about, who fuck themselves up. No, it's people who are loved. It's a way for them to say to those around them: you're useless. Look, you can't even help me. I always side with the nonaligned. What can you do for friends for whom you fear the worst? Nothing. All you can do is send messages saying let's play ping-pong, let's meet at a café. All we can do is think: I hope it will pass. And be there afterward. Praying that there will still be something left of the friend you had. And then let it go. Much love.

OSCAR

I was moved by your email, my friend. I won't relapse. I'm going to change my sponsor because I never feel like calling the one I've got at the moment. And there's a guy I admire who I'm always running into at meetings on the rue de Charonne—I hadn't realized he was in the program, I know exactly who he is.

 This amazing thing happened. Léonore called me in a panic. She and Clémentine were staying with friends she often visits in a suburb of Lyon. Clémentine wandered off with some other kids. They were caught smoking spliffs. Apparently, the cops have been harassing teenagers since lockdown. It's like they've gotten used to it. I realized that Léonore is taking me staying clean seriously. And that it's Clémentine who's been talking to her about it. I didn't think my daughter knew what I was doing on Zoom; whenever she's staying, I lock myself in my room, put headphones on, and never share with the group. I had this weird conversation I'd never had before with my daughter's mother. Whenever I try to convince myself that I was this cool, streetwise user, reality comes around to tell me that I'm the only one who saw myself that way. Léonore talked to me about our breakup. I thought she really hated me, but she mostly hates the drugs. I thought that was sweet of her. I'm not sure I'd have behaved much better if I'd been clean. I let her say her piece. I let her congratulate me on my recent life choices, tell me how she can see the difference, that she can rely on me. It's true that since I got clean, I've haven't missed picking Clémentine up even once. I listened while she told me all this, and I thought about your email—I thought: it's actually pretty nice having these women who care about me.

She wanted me to talk to Clémentine. In my role as a guy who's clean and knows all about life. As a father, in fact. I thought it sounded weird—I could hardly picture myself telling my daughter that weed would lead her to a sleazy life of prostitution and a needle in her arm. Léonore hadn't spoken to me like this for years. I said okay, send her over, and we'll have a snack together.

I went to Chez Picard and bought a tarte tatin, because she loves it. The conversation itself didn't go so well. I said: "I'm going to treat you like an adult, because that's what you're becoming. And you know I used to smoke weed. I know what I'm talking about. It's a soft drug if you only smoke it twice a year, on special occasions. But if you smoke it every week, it's a lot more dangerous than you're led to believe. Taken regularly, weed will undermine your concentration, your creativity, your sense of humor, your pleasure in life, your intelligence, your sleep, your curiosity . . ." She sighed. I was boring her. I became defensive. I felt humiliated. And uncomfortable. I was starting to think that maybe I should have gone about it differently—encouraged her to talk so I could find out why she was smoking weed. But you can't instantly create a close relationship with your daughter at the kitchen table just because her mother's relying on you. Before I knew it, I was calling her a snotty little bitch who'd get her ass kicked by life because she acts like she's tough when actually she's a nitwit. Not in precisely those words—but you get the idea.

She got up to go, I followed her to the door, I grabbed her wrist to get her to turn around, and she screamed, "Don't hit me," not like someone who's scared, more like she was about to punch me. I screamed back. I shook her a bit and she ran downstairs. Like an idiot, I followed, slamming the door without taking my key and caught up with her in the street. She didn't want anything to do with me.

All this to say, things got off to a really bad start. And then, out on the street, she said: Don't go lecturing me I know you're an addict you're going to start taking drugs again so you're the last person who can help me. I was devastated. As though all my rage had been derailed. Instead of coming out with something stupid, I said: "Why are you calling me an addict? Have you ever seen me take drugs?" Her face contorted into a sneer of disgust and disbelief. It didn't suit her. Let me say here that she's really scary when she's angry. Not something she gets from me: I look ridiculous when I'm angry, my face turns sallow and my voice goes wonky. My father was the same when he was angry—the only reason we didn't laugh in his face was because he beat us. And she didn't get it from her mother either, Léonore is hopeless when it comes to getting angry, she sobs, she stammers, she cracks up completely. But Clémentine is like an elegant wildcat when she gets going. It made me think that if our relationship ever improves, it might be worth talking about boys, because I think this is something she's learned from boys rather than from us. But to get back to where we were, her expression of disgust was hideous. And I was genuinely surprised. I repeated the question, "Have you ever seen me take drugs, Clémentine?" She said, "You must be joking. I hope you've got some time because everything I've got to say about you has to do with getting trashed."

It's the first time since she was a teenager that she's ever said something so important and so sincere to me. There are moments in life like this—like in a Wachowski movie, the moment when everything around the character freezes and for a few seconds he breaks away from the situation and into a space of his own. It's miraculous. I felt icy breath on the back of my neck, a hand gripping me, and in that moment I realized that I had been planning to relapse and that I wasn't going to be able to do it. Here, the comparison with a love affair is obvious: it's when you've decided to leave your wife for someone else and then she says something that makes you realize you're not going to do it. Suitcases packed, decision made, and then an invisible hand sends you sprawling on the floor. I wasn't going to have that drink. I wasn't going to snort that line. I wasn't going to backslide. And in that one moment, I felt both distraught at having to give up, and relieved like a castaway finding dry land. And I felt honorable, dazzled by my own glory. What a sacrifice! What an amazing father! Here I was, a rock in the storm, a father prepared to do anything to reassure his daughter. It's rare for me to love myself like that. I made the most of it.

I said, come on let's get a coffee. I knew the guy in the café, and I told him I'd left my keys and my wallet inside, which made my daughter laugh. "You're not in deep shit, Papa." She ordered a Fanta—I didn't know it still existed. It was hard for her to start talking, but she did. In the end, she came with me to the locksmith, then we went back to my apartment building and sat on the stairs while we waited for him to show up—it took all afternoon. She never stopped talking. I was speechless. She remembers things I'd forgotten; things I would have sworn she was much too young to notice. She remembers all the times I fucked up, the lines of coke I'd discreetly snort on Christmas Eve, the arguments with ex-girlfriends when I'd had too much to drink, the nights I'd put her to bed so I could play poker with my friends and when she'd wake up we'd still be there stinking of booze and cigarettes and we'd be talking shit and tousling her hair like dickheads. She remembers the hundreds of promises I broke, the pointless shouting matches when I'd been out partying the night before, my slurred voice when she'd come home, the spliffs in front of the TV and how I was there but it felt like she was alone, leaving her on her own in a bar while I went to the bathrooms with girlfriends, the gear I left in plain sight in the chambre de bonne because I didn't know she was rummaging through my desk. She remembers everything. A real cop.

The locksmith was decent enough, he didn't try to get me to replace the door so he could charge three thousand euros, he took out a card and slipped the lock in thirty seconds. We went inside and finished the tarte tatin. I apologized to Clémentine for having behaved the way I did, and she said, "I'm sorry I said you'd go back to taking drugs. I can see you've changed. You really have. And that's cool. You've never been the way you are now."

She slept over. That night, I called Corinne—it was time to make peace. Corinne always knew how to talk to Clémentine. I was on the defensive, but when I said, "She's been smoking weed," Corinne didn't burst out laughing and say, "It comes with being a teenager." She asked the right question: "Regularly?" She didn't overdramatize the situation or make light of it. She invited us to spend a few days with her.

"I've got keys to the neighbors' house, and they've got a swimming pool."

"I'll check that her mother's okay with it, then we'll take the train down. It'll do me good too. I've only just given up on relapsing."

"You're still a bit of a dickhead, but you're a lot less of a dickhead than before."

I could have taken it the wrong way, but I didn't. I took it as a compliment—which I think it was.

REBECCA

Parenting isn't exactly your strong suit . . . Your daughter is a person, not a crutch. You staying clean shouldn't depend on her. You'll say, who cares: the main thing is that you've come to your senses. I enjoyed reading your email. I can't spend long writing. I'm on a film shoot, and someone will be coming to fetch me soon. I love living in hotels. I love having breakfast in my room. I didn't want to make this film. But I really needed the money. I thought the script sucked and the casting was terrible. But it's turned out okay. The director knows her stuff, and as we move from scene to scene, I get the feeling we're doing something right. We'll be lucky to earn out at the box office, but it will rake in awards at the film festivals. The cinematographer likes me. He spends hours lighting me. I saw myself in the rushes. I look all right. I haven't looked this good for a long time. Such a good idea, this getting clean. Right, I have to go. Give my love to your daughter and your sister. I already knew you were going down to visit her. Corinne calls me all the time. She can't live without me anymore. Love.

OSCAR

I watch the way Corinne is with Clémentine. My daughter's no friendlier than usual. When she arrives, she politely says hello, then instantly disappears, takes out her phone and withdraws, the ways she does with me. She's in the room, but she's not here.

Corinne doesn't react the way I do. She's the one who makes the difference. She doesn't get tense. She's not intimidated. She's not the kid's father—she has no precedents for what their relationship should be. The shit we went through with our father doesn't blow up in her face every time she looks at Clémentine. She goes with the flow, but she doesn't mind roping her in from time to time, into conversation or into things going on around the house. "Get up and go buy some fruit, come help me bring in some firewood." She's not passive-aggressive when she asks Clémentine to do something—seeing her makes me realize how I go about things. When Corinne says, help me peel potatoes, she's not implying: ditch the phone stop being like that think about me for a change give me what I need. She wants the potatoes peeled, end of story. I realize that I add stress to every situation. My stress, my pain, my negativity, my guilt. Me, me, me. I realize that I spend my time forcing my daughter to take account of my unhappiness. But never directly.

Above all, Corinne is enthusiastic. She says, "When I see kids your age, I think that the fascist bastards better watch their backs. We gave them an easy ride, but they're going to have it a lot tougher with you guys . . ." And Clémentine smiles. I'm not capable of thinking such a thing. Still less of saying it while sitting at the kitchen table. When I think about Clémentine's life, all I feel is panic—I'm weaving a sad cloud over her head, that's what I'm doing.

I'm sitting in an old orange armchair right next to the window, and when I look up from my book I gaze out at the garden. I found an old copy of Lorca's *Gypsy Ballads* in the bookcase in the hall that Corinne calls her library. I'm rereading every page several times. And I'm watching them together. Clémentine slaps the bottom of a jar with her hand to get it open, and Corinne sighs, "It's a shame they don't have conversion therapy for straights, you'd make a great lesbian." Clémentine is over the moon.

"Because I managed to open beans on the first try? You're crazy . . ."

"I said it because everything you do is flawless, you don't have the pathetic dopiness of straight women."

And Clémentine is beaming, this is a great compliment. She grabs her phone and fires up Lesbian TikTok to show something to Corinne, who snatches the phone out of her hand.

"Who the hell is this bombshell?"

"Hey, she's my age, you can't talk about her like that!"

"I don't know what else I could say about her—she's a nuclear bomb."

I watch them from ten feet away. And I'm aware of my emotions. My stomach is all twisted up in a mixture of anger and sadness. There's jealousy in there too, anger at being excluded, sadness at my inability to join in, because if I do, I'll ruin the artlessness of the conversation, I'm the father as hack actor miming being casual. It's a weird muddle, and somewhere in it all I can make out a clear line—like the blue streak in the skies over Brittany that heralds fifteen minutes of sunshine to be savored. But there's something new breathing in there, something that breaks down a bit like this: I'm happy for Clémentine, happy that she has a grown-up somewhere who gives her a break from all the adult anguish—and I also realize that it doesn't take much to be good with her.

To allow an event to move through you. To feel an emotion. Rather than running away from it. That's what I want to do. How do I go about it? What do I need to do? Do I go for a walk? At what pace? With or without music? Do I sit down? Back ramrod straight? Take a deep breath? Lie on the floor? Stretch out my arms and yawn? Should I let my parasitic thoughts burrow into my belly?

Bullshit. Emotion is the hole in the ozone layer, it's climate change, it's the magma inside the volcano, the attack by the virus. Emotions aren't a factory or a theater, they can't be contained. That's why you can't just welcome them in. They twist you. You have to brace yourself and ride it out. They turn you inside out. An emotion isn't some sentimental, handmade Etsy thing you fashion according to how you see the world. It's not a pretty porcelain bowl. The emotion sweeping through my generation is despair. It's collective. It's rumbling deep below the earth. Shaking us all. Sure, anyone can come up with a trite little maxim, but that doesn't change things. Emotion is the same whether you're master of the universe or flotsam in the middle of the ocean. We are part of it; it is an implacable chord that will be sounded come what may.

And the only thing you can use to quench despair is hope. Simple as that. Hope is the only antidote to despair. But hope is the one thing that has been taken from us. Dystopia has become the only rational expectation. Believing that things can get better is proof of folly. This is totalitarianism triumphant. Our imaginations have been seized by a single belief: there is no alternative. Hope is for meatheads.

Then Clémentine says, come on, Papa, it's dinnertime, and I stop struggling to put the molten fear coursing through my belly into words, I get up and go sit at the table, and I don't force myself to smile, I don't try to think of something clever to say or something cruel to let them know I feel excluded—and this, this is what makes me sit down with them and say, Lorca is amazing, I haven't read him for ages, and Corinne says, I haven't opened that book in years the girl who gave it to me lives in Australia now I wonder what's become of her, and Clémentine who doesn't give a damn tells me Corinne has made a strawberry tart for dessert, and I can tell she's happy to be back in this world where she has her bearings and everything is simple—and for a few minutes I have this strange sensation, I'm where I belong, everything is fine. I'm not racking my brains for something to say that would make me a better father or a better brother or anything in particular. I belong here. I don't have to do anything in particular to make things go well. Just for today I feel like less of a dickhead than I did yesterday.

REBECCA

Are you sure you're all right, friend? Aren't you maybe getting a little carried away?

I'm writing this at night because I like to spend my days doing nothing. Barcelona is deserted. What's good for the heart is lethal for the economy and vice versa—it's quite the problem, this dichotomy.

Usually at this time of year the streets are teeming. Over the past ten years, the center of the city has lost 80 percent of its inhabitants. Apartments have been turned into Airbnbs, and during Covid they were converted into grow houses for pot. Most of the shops have become tourist boutiques. Whole streets are shuttered up. There are no bakeries, no bookshops, no hairdressers left. Just shops selling tacky souvenirs. All of them closed. Waiting for things to go back to normal. Longwy in the late eighties was a boomtown in comparison. This rush to ruin everything sweeps away everything in its path—it's disturbing watching a whole world fall apart.

You're always saying that you're worried about your daughter. If you weren't worried, you'd be a moron. There are some situations in which panicking is just common sense.

We're all going crazy. It's collective. And yet we still manage to fall out with people we've known for a decade because we don't like what they're saying about vaccines. I say that, but I'd be first in line to grab them, vaccinate them against their will, and tell them to shut the fuck up about their shitty DNA. What do you think is lurking in your genetic makeup? A Picasso? Then I think: Who am I turning into? Who is this person who's taken control of my mind? At what point in all this did I start taking an interest in my friends' vaccination status?

The world is losing its head. It's doing my head in. So all I have to say is hang in there. I'm lucky enough not to have any children, but I get the impression that, as a dad, you're starting to work things out. Better late than never.

OSCAR

At the end of the Zoom meeting there's this guy I've never seen before, but from the way the others greet him it's clear he's been in the program for a long time. He's got

Covid, he's holed up in a room with no natural light. On screen, he looks like he's in a cave because the backdrop behind him is so grim, and at least a dozen times he says, "My mother didn't love me, I just have to deal with it." It's like a litany—he says, "I can't deal with rejection," it's like he's choking on a thought he's trying to vomit up, and as I'm listening, I'm thinking: "Well, go on, deal with it, give your mother a fucking break for a minute." He's a big boy, he's about the same age as I am. Okay, so your mother didn't love you—we can't spend our whole lives dwelling on our miserable childhoods. Get over it. Stop busting everyone's balls. I find him infuriating. I don't identify with him. I overlap, I merge with him, I am engulfed in him. I don't want to be this guy, I categorically refuse to listen to him while he's having his pity party circle jerk, I find him repulsive, I want nothing to do with him. Identifying with someone is graceful, it's like looking in a mirror, recognizing yourself, and giving yourself a little wave. There's a distance—a possibility of putting some thought into what's going on. What I feel listening to him is visceral, it's revolting—it's like swimming in my own shit.

Then I feel a terrible wave of panic, the likes of which I haven't experienced for months. I don't know how, but Corinne senses my panic, and once again she doesn't use it to have a go at me. She sets a cup of hot coffee next to my chair, and I notice that she's picked my favorite cup, the little black one with the thick rim. Usually, she finds these little tics exasperating, me having a favorite cup that I drink out of every day. She doesn't care about objects, rituals, and stupid little habits—so most of the time, it feels like she deliberately doesn't give me my favorite cup, so I get up and change it, and she ridicules me and my "little old lady" quirks. But these days, Corinne doesn't pick fights with me. She sticks around, but doesn't sit down right away. She says, "I overheard, I didn't mean to, I just happened to be passing your window—I heard that guy talking about his mother." I don't have time to respond, I think it's brutally intrusive to listen to what people are saying during a meeting, but I don't have time to say, fuck you, I don't have time to say what I think—she is staring at a point somewhere behind me as she says, "You and I both know that we can't blame them. But it's difficult, as you get older, not being at peace with your childhood." I'm feeling defensive, racking my brain for a way to tell her that I have no intention of having some psychological conversation with her. Instead I say, "We can forgive the pain because, over time, it subsides, we can try to redeem ourselves, we get used to it. But forgiving ourselves for a wrong that's been done to us—that's impossible." And she sits down next to me. We haven't talked like this since I got here. I'm glad we're doing it today, because I'm leaving tomorrow. Corinne says:

"There's this sense that if we hadn't been terrible children, our parents wouldn't have been such bad parents. The wrongs done to us are always the ones we feel most guilty for. If we'd done things differently. If we'd been good kids—we wouldn't have gone through all that. A victim of abuse always feels guilty for letting it happen, for having allowed it to happen, and, most of all, for not having found another way, for missing the opportunity to allow the other person to stop being an abuser. The victim is always the one who believes they missed something."

I shrug. "Let's not get carried away. It's a nice turn of phrase. Maybe if you turned it into a song, it might work—but it doesn't mean anything. I've never been hurt. Neither have you."

"Do you remember the beatings I used to give you? Every time I saw you, I'd think, what is the point of this *thing*? I thought you were a waste of space. In most families, the eldest child hates the youngest for usurping his place as child king. In our family, it was the opposite— you were no better than me at getting anyone to be interested in you. You weren't able to dispel the anxiety that pervaded our apartment—like floodwater trickling under the door and rising day by day."

"You were three or four times my size, and you were always punching me."

"Seriously, bro, have you forgotten? You had only two passions in life: needling me and stealing my stuff. You didn't steal something once in a while to sell it at school— you stole whatever you could lay your hands on as soon as my back was turned and threw it away. Not in the kitchen garbage, you were cleverer than that. You'd race out and toss it in the trash can by the bus stop. Just to piss me off. I can still see you, on your little bike, you can't have been more than eight years old—you were going back and forth. Of course I was constantly laying into you. Living together was hell for both of us."

"I don't remember that."

What she said unsettled me. The pinch-prick game—she wasn't making that up. I hadn't thought about it since. I felt like it happened on a single afternoon, and all I remembered was her brutal retaliation. It was the variety of objects that reminded me it might have lasted longer. Me playing pinch-prick with a thumbtack, with a fork, with a nail. I played pinch-prick with too many things for it to have happened on one Wednesday afternoon.

"The pinch-prick game, are you sure it carried on for a long time?"

"Two years, at least. It was unbearable. I was terrified of being at home with you. You weren't a naughty little boy who got up to mischief occasionally—you never let me alone, and you really hurt me. You pinched me until I bled. If I pretended not to feel anything so you'd let go, you'd do that psycho face, stare into my eyes, and pinch until you broke the skin."

"I always thought I was as meek as a lamb."

"You remember the beatings, but you've forgotten what you did to deserve them? I was fifteen years old, Oscar—if you didn't come bothering me in my bedroom every day, it's not like I would have gone into yours."

"I was little. I haven't forgotten how you mistreated me. And I don't think I had it coming."

"You made my life hell. I don't feel guilty, but I'm not in denial. Things were tougher for you. At least I could tell myself, I like girls, so my parents rejecting me is normal; I'm constantly running away, so my parents rejecting me is normal. At least I can tell myself, I never had a family, I never had a regular job, I've been a disappointment on every level, so my parents being cold to me is normal. But you—you've done nothing to justify what happened to you. You didn't 'deserve it.' You were born a boy, you were good at school, you have a prestigious job, you gave them the granddaughter they always wanted so that they could prove to the neighbors that their life after they retired was normal. And you didn't manage to win their affection any more than I did. That's what I'm getting at: You remember the beatings I used to dish out? What happened when our parents were at home? I'd get yelled at, they'd come into my room, they'd scold me and threaten me. But I don't remember them ever hugging and comforting you. And God knows, you cried your eyes out. But I don't have a single memory of a grown-up hugging you and saying, it's all right, I'm here, dry your tears. I'm not blaming anyone. They just didn't have it in them, that's all. I didn't hate you because you were the little pet, or the youngest, or the boy they'd been waiting for. I hated you because you failed as miserably as I did. Because I knew that someone should have crouched down and put their arms around you, but no one did that in our house. And the wrong done to you—whether it was unfair doesn't matter—it's still a wrong that you allowed to happen, a wrong you deserved, and we don't know how to claw our way out of this banal history of evil."

REBECCA

Back in Paris. The bars have been closed again. My ears hurt from wearing a face mask.

Your emails are always so long, and I don't know whether it's because I'm off-kilter at the moment, but I find them more and more moving. That said, I'm scared of everything. I'm scared to listen to the radio, I'm scared of what I hear on television, I'm scared when I stumble on a tweet quoting Mengele, I'm scared when I see Hungarian police put pink barcode bracelets on refugees, I'm scared when I see cops teargassing demonstrators protesting the death in custody of Adama Traoré, I'm scared when I see photos of Uyghurs, I'm scared when I see how much the richest 1 percent have earned this year.

It was a perfect day to fall off the wagon because this has been a hard week. A role I wanted in a TV series was just given to someone else. She's a good actress, so I can hardly say the decision's unfair or fucking stupid. It's hard to be happy for other people when you're not happy with what you've got. It's something I've never felt before. I hate the hurt I feel at not being cast, I hate the hackneyed emotion it triggers in me, and I despise being relegated to a position of weakness. I didn't open up to my agent and tell him I felt hurt. I said, shit, I really needed the money, and changed the subject.

But at noon, after recording a short interview with a Belgian TV station for a movie I shot ages ago but is only being released now, I dived into the métro so I wouldn't miss the start of the NA meeting in Charonne.

I haven't taken the métro since I was twenty, so to me it's a revelation. First of all, how friendly it is, there are always people who recognize me but they're polite about it. Fans can be incredibly rude waiting around to take a selfie with me, but on the métro, they don't have time to be a pain in the ass. They tell you how much they love you as they're getting off, or they make small talk with you on the platform, but it's not a place where they feel they're entitled to monopolize you. I'm so happy with the way my fans behave on the métro, if I'd known earlier, I would have taken it years ago. At the same time, I should be mourning the fact that it's an indisputable sign that my star is waning. In the eighties, if I'd been blitzed enough to think about taking the métro, I would have stopped traffic—no exaggeration. So that means that today, pretty much no one cares if I'm around. I've got a friend, an actress like me, and not long ago she was telling me she was in a restaurant and saw someone in the street taking a photo but didn't say anything, then some kid at the next table jumped up, absolutely furious, and ordered the photographer to "delete that right now." And she realized he thought *he* was being papped—and his girlfriend kept saying that he had over a million followers, and my friend thought the whole thing was funny because, obviously, no one knew who this kid was. But even though she's been on the cover of every major magazine you can think of, and she's been on the nightly news more times than she's taken out the trash, it was the kid people were snapping. It was the kid and his million followers who were being targeted. He was right. He didn't manage to get the photo deleted, but at no point did the woman taking the photo roll her eyes and say, "It's not you I'm interested in." The woman taking his photo didn't even recognize my friend.

So now I take the métro, and it's a lot quicker than a taxi. I just think they should have a first-class métro where you have to walk a lot less and there are elevators everywhere. Because otherwise, you waste too much time running down corridors—that's the one downside to this thing.

And I got to the meeting on time, I sat next to my girlfriend who was wearing enough makeup to go trick-or-treating. I read one of the basic texts and listened to the others speak, and I wanted to raise my hand, though I was also thinking it might be nice to shut up and listen for a change.

But I wanted to talk about that thing earlier this week: an old friend dropped by and said, I've already had a toke, and, without thinking I said, but I've quit everything, and she said: "That's good, I've been smoking too much since my father died, I'm trying to slow down."

And I was astonished to realize that she had no problem with it. I was expecting bitter disappointment. She'd come to see me, she was expecting to get stoned. I said no, and I saw that it was actually a relief for her. It was completely stupid, there I was feeling kind of obliged to honor some kind of unwritten pact that said we should get wasted, and her doing the same, each trying not to disappoint the other. We should have talked about this long ago. What if it turns out we've been phoning a dealer for years just to avoid disappointing each other?

And I also realized that I didn't envy her. I was surprised it was so easy for her to go without. And I could have thought: I wish I was like her, I want it to be easy, I wish I was someone who could use drugs occasionally and not make a big deal of it. But I am who I am. If I spark up a spliff, I'll finish the bottle of whiskey, snort a gram, and end up with people I don't like, but they're getting wasted too, and I'm not going to enjoy it, I'm just going to feel shattered. I don't do moderation. And that's for the best.

The weirdest thing is that I'm being sincere. I've got a friend who comes and waits for me on the corner every time I go to a meeting. I'm happy to see him, and we talk things through as we're walking along. Because for some reason I don't really understand, I don't get bored with him the way I usually get bored with people.

I wanted to say all these things, but I just listened to others sharing. Besides, I like positive people at meetings, but I'm not about to become one of them, a happy-clappy, hippy-dippy person who says she's thrilled to be there at every meeting. Let's not push it. I'm still a legend.

OSCAR

I said to some girl I barely know, come have dinner at my place, then I'll drive you back, then if we see the cops we can try and sweet-talk them, tell them we're a couple going through some problems and I'm taking you home . . . She said, they'll slap us with a fine, they're making so much money right now, before long they'll be wearing Gucci uniforms with little diamonds on their caps. And then she said, besides, I don't think you'll need to drive me home, I want to sleep with you. The girl I'm into now is ten years younger than me, she does outreach work at night, distributing meals to the homeless, and she says the police will arrest them if they're ten minutes past curfew, that they're aggressive and stupid. She says, I'm going to join ACAB, and I ask her what ACAB means, and she says it's for people who think *all cops are bastards*. The girl I'm seeing says "awks" when more or less anything is embarrassing, and she says "cringe," and her words enter my mouth and for the first time in my life I'm old enough to doubt myself when I use them, I wonder if I sound like an old guy slumming it. But her words are already in my mouth. Her name is Clara. I want to spend all my time with her.

If it hadn't been for the curfew, I'd never have dared ask her over with the implication that we might sleep together. Curfew actually helped my sex life because we were both more relaxed than if we hadn't had that WhatsApp chat earlier in the day. She'd already said, I want to sleep with you, and that didn't freak me out because, given the circumstances, it wasn't a declaration by some bunny boiler who wants to move in with you right away. It was simply relevant.

Clara has a dog. Dogs are much better than kids—they don't complain. If I had to do it all again, I'd get a dog. Especially since, unlike a child, who drives a wedge between a couple and ends the romance, a dog brings partners closer together. It's really easy to prove to the other person that you're good with their dog. Whereas children show you in the worst light—they bring out the crazy in you. Dogs, on the other hand, bring out your patient, tender qualities. Clara's dog makes me cute. Thanks to him, we can take long walks around the block, even super late, like nine p.m., we're out there walking like lunatics. The patrolling cop cars see us, and they don't slow down, but if they did stop to ask why there are two of us, the answer is simple—because she's a girl taking her dog for a walk, and I can hardly leave my girlfriend on her own. No cop could argue with that.

A Deliveroo delivery driver passed on his bicycle, riding very slowly down the middle of the street with Drake blaring from his speaker. For ten minutes, we'd been alone on the sidewalk and we were still wearing face masks. We watched the guy zigzag away on his bike, I thought he looked like he was riding on water, and I pressed closer to the girl, I lowered my mask and she slipped hers down and that's when we kissed for the first time, then we realized the dog had just taken a crap and she laughed and said, story of my life, I always make a fool of myself, and I didn't tell her it was the most romantic first kiss I'd ever had. I don't think I've ever kissed a girl I didn't know well without having a hard-on. So I felt like a kid. And it was really good.

I went to a meeting today and said, I feel really lucky to have gotten clean just before Covid screwed everything up. Ten o'clock curfew? I know I'd have felt justified getting krunked every day after noon. See? I've changed. When it comes to temptation, I've turned the page. One of the guys at the meeting said, "You say tomorrow I'm thinking yesterday and the day before and the day after tomorrow, my head's a mess, you've no idea—and then, like the wind, it's gone." Another guy talked about being sexually abused when he was fourteen. Guys regularly bring up things like that. Stories about little boys and about teenagers. Everyone knows it happens to girls. But unless you're in NA, you never hear guys talking about it.

Yesterday we put on a Wong Kar-wai movie but we didn't watch much of it, I hadn't had sex in a long time—since the shit hit the fan, I hadn't even thought about hooking up with a girl. I assumed it would be a disappointment, I'm not a big fan of first times—I love the idea of the first time, I love the moment when you realize things are going to go the way you hoped, the first time I have sex with a girl I don't know, what I like most is the *idea* of fucking, and I get all girly, all I really want is tenderness, except that I don't feel relaxed, it's like I'm blocked. That was another good thing about getting wasted—never being naked in bed with a strange woman and lucid during sex.

REBECCA

I'd already noticed myself that a lot of guys at meetings talk about being raped. About incest. Or pedophilia. I don't understand why we didn't hear from them during the whole MeToo thing. I can't believe it was out of a sense of decency, to allow women a voice. I think they realized that it would cost them too much to speak out. I don't understand the victim's shame. I believe it exists—but I don't understand it. People say shame goes hand in hand with rage. But that's not true. I've never felt ashamed. I've often wanted to kill people. It's different.

I didn't feel ashamed when I was eleven and my father made me stand on a table, hiked up my skirt in front of his friends, and said, you've got lovely legs, that's the most important thing a woman can have. With a tone and a look in his eyes I didn't recognize. I wasn't ashamed, not even for him. I knew it wasn't normal. I knew that it was dangerous. I never went to visit him again, and he never insisted—given the slippery slope he was on, he knew as well as I did that it would end badly. But I wasn't ashamed. I just thought he was a complete dick. You don't get your daughter up on a table so you can show her legs off to your drunken friends. I didn't need a shrink to know that. My father was stunningly handsome. Think Alain Delon. My mother made no mistake in choosing him as a stud—from the point of view of eugenics, it was a brilliant choice. He was as beautiful as a god, but he forgot to grow a brain. In front of his friends, he lifted up my skirt to show off my legs and said, "That's the most important thing for a woman, being beautiful, and you've got amazing legs." I was old enough to understand that this was inappropriate. And dangerous. But I wasn't ashamed of myself. I knew he was the one being an asshole. I just wanted them all to drop dead.

I didn't feel ashamed when I was raped at fourteen. I knew the fat guy lying on top of me, this guy twice my size who'd followed me down the street, was a douchebag. I wasn't ashamed. Since then, I've talked to women who've told me that *of course* I'd felt ashamed, it's just that I refused to admit it to myself. I hate being told how to feel. I wasn't ashamed. Oh, I felt the urge to kill him, and I felt rage that I was too physically weak to do it. But shame? In your dreams! He was the one who should have been ashamed. I already knew that when it happened to me.

I've been thinking about this a lot lately, about all the times I hear people say rape is something you never get over, and I've been racking my brains. I was talking about it with the wardrobe mistress on the last movie I made, a woman about my age, pretty, with huge blue eyes and a childlike face. She asked if I enjoyed sex, and I said, not particularly. The first couple of times with a guy who turns me on, I enjoy it. Or when you've just had a blazing row and you're thinking, never again, and then it happens and you can't help it and he's fucking you up against the wall, even though you've been together five years and you feel like you're part of the furniture. Sometimes I enjoy sex. Mostly, if I'm honest, I don't care either way. I don't hate it. But I've always been bemused by this notion young people have that it's not enough to be good, you have to be technically brilliant in bed. Look, you're good, that's enough. What next? Tidying the house in a princess dress? Scrubbing down the kitchen in a bustier? And the wardrobe woman said, maybe the reason you don't enjoy sex that much is because of the rape. Even though I didn't say I didn't like it, just that it's not something I'd want to do all day. When did it become compulsory? I think I must have missed that part. I thought for a minute, and then I got angry. First off, "rape" doesn't mean a thing—we have forty-five words to describe shades of blue and only one to describe rape. I'm going to wait until the feminist thinkers progress a little, but most of all I'm going to wait until people let me feel what I want to feel before I talk about it to anyone. These days, you say you've been raped and the politically correct mob are up in your grill telling you you'll never get over it, period. I had a shrink who talked to me about dissociation, like it was a physical thing that could be observed. A woman who's been raped dissociates. I listened as she laid out her case. Then I said, "I'm a woman. How do you expect me to be anything but dissociated?" Ever since I was a kid, I've been told my body belongs to other people's gaze, that it's part of my beauty, part of my attractiveness. Attractiveness—now that causes dissociation. How could it not? I don't know a single woman who can eat without wondering whether it will make her fat. How can you dissociate yourself from your appetite and not dissociate yourself from all that you are? Of course I dissociate. I'm an actress. The shrink listened to me, we were at this big dinner party. But I could tell that she knew better than I do what being raped meant. That she was demanding that I confirm her fallacies. That my word was of no importance. I didn't have the expertise of my own experience; she'd hijacked it in advance.

ZOÉ KATANA

I don't expect much from the shrinks. I don't expect much from the other patients either. We've all got a good reason for being here. Most of us lie when asked why we're here. What else have we got to do except talk to each other? It's not hard to notice. The super cute guy at the far end of the hall who says he's depressed because his wife won't let him see his daughter. You feel sorry for him, you listen to his story, then you listen a little closer and you realize he's just a violent guy who threatened to kill her in front of the little girl. Just a violent guy who abuses a mother in front of her daughter. Just the kind of thug that, being a radical feminist, I'm supposed to despise but—too late: I've already connected with him, and then when I realize that he's a liar and a violent guy . . . it's too late for lectures. The intelligent, pale-eyed girl in the room across the hall who keeps saying that she's not sick, it's society that's sick, and that, when it comes down to it, being committed is proof that you're sane. She's got a major screw loose, and every time they bring her here, she goes off on these wild paranoid delusions. Once she's medicated, she calms down, but she still believes that public radio stations are conspiring against her. Because she posts important shit on Insta. At first you listen, but pretty soon you realize it's sus. The chances that anyone in the corridors of Radio France is arranging the programming schedule to force her into bouts of depersonalization are pretty slim. The sweet old guy who spends all day reading and tells me he's being treated for an age-old melancholy—I found out from the nurses that he took out loans in his kids' names so he could get even deeper into debt because his hobby for the past twenty years has been losing at the casino. And when they challenge him, cuz they've had collectors at their doors demanding they pay debts for bankrupt shell companies they've never heard of, he goes psycho, pulls out a shotgun, and threatens to kill everyone. Everyone in here needs help. And the people treating us don't have a clue what to do. They're typical boomer bureaucrats: good people, good listeners, doing the best they can. You get a couple of fascist psychos, but that's not the norm. Nurses, doctors, psychiatrists—the one thing they know they can count on is sedatives. Beyond that, they're blindly banging out a tune on a keyboard of molecules without the first idea of what's going on with us and—more importantly—how to help us out of the abyss we've fallen into. It's not because they don't want to. It's not because they're not prepared to devote the time to us. But I remember how in ancient civilizations people believed that succubi would creep between the sheets at night to abuse their victims, and I think this was a more apt hypothesis. I talk to people who don't understand what I'm feeling, and it's not because I'm a complicated case that I confuse them. They're just confused, period.

I don't hate the whole shrink ritual—I like talking about myself. Problem is that when they talk to you, right away you can tell they're not hearing a word you're saying. Take my case—apparently being trolled and threatened isn't in the medical manual of serious shit. Now, if I'd been molested by an uncle when I was a kid, they'd hear that. They'd tell me I'd never get over it and let me talk about it for hours. But being a feminist blogger dealing with vicious trolls and rape threats just doesn't cut it. They look elsewhere. What was it about my childhood that's made me so fragile? In my case, there's no point trawling through my childhood. You need to trawl through the political. Trying to treat me by asking whether Papa helped with my homework is like asking a freezing, starving prisoner in the Gulag whether his mother knitted scarves for him. Okay, I bugged out and my sanity is a bit shaky—but that's because the aim of the trolls is to eliminate me, and the tools at their disposal make it possible to do that. Twitter is to blame. Facebook is to blame. YouTube is to blame. Instagram is to blame. My father, my mother, and my great-grandparents can do fuck all to protect me. The masculists on social media have declared open season on feminists, they know that the strategy works, and that they can count on the complicity of the social networks, because they're all owned by masculists. What's happening to me is political. But shrinks think they can treat the patient without treating the politics. If the list of messages on my phone wishing me dead, telling me to kill myself, goes on and on endlessly, I'm being subjected to a form of torture that didn't previously exist, and that's what's making my cognitive system explode. That's what it's meant to do. For once, I'd like to talk to a shrink who has any advice other than: shut up permanently, give in, disappear, stop posting. Do what you're told: quit taking up space in the social sphere and go grow herbs on your kitchen windowsill.

I truly believe that looking elsewhere is the foundation that underpins psychoanalysis. Pile-ons? Think about your mother. Wanting to believe that there's such a thing as a healthy, protective family upbringing. At the start of the third millennium.

OSCAR

The eighth step requires the addict to draw up a complete list of all the people he's ever harmed. Was Zoé's name supposed to be on that list? Until last week, I'd have said no way. In the litany of personal grudges, she's still top of my list. I've done her no harm. She's just making shit up.

I was invited to Stuttgart to give a reading with a bunch of other French writers. The Germans pay for that sort of thing, so I went. On the train, I got a text from the organizer asking if I'd go on a podcast—Fanny, a girl with the Alliance française, hosts a podcast. I said no. I'm not going to submit to an online kangaroo court. The guy insisted: it's a minor podcast, like a fanzine, and she really likes your work. I felt threatened. There's no such thing as a fanzine anymore. These days, if I answer three questions from a girl in a kitchen, it'll be all over social media as if I'd done an interview with *Paris Match*. I say just one sentence that could be misinterpreted, and I'm feeding coins into the machine—a national scandal; a slightly off-color joke, and it's as if I'd pissed on Simone Veil's grave. I was also angry at the organizer's demand because authors are required to set aside one hour for a podcast, one hour for an academic, one hour for a documentary, one hour to visit a school . . . but that's not my job. It's hard enough doing what I do without spending my time doing interviews that I don't give a shit about.

So there we were, all the writers, each waiting for our turn to speak. There were coffee, almonds, and hazelnuts on a low table. We were doing our readings, I was checking over the passage I'd chosen when this girl came up to me, I didn't really notice, she had short blond hair and she was wearing a face mask. She handed me an envelope. Since she was wearing a mask, I couldn't tell she was sulking. As I was talking to another writer, I opened the envelope and it was from Fanny, the girl who wanted to do the podcast. A long, handwritten letter telling me that she was my biggest fan, that she was thrilled to meet me, and listing the questions she would have asked if I'd accepted. She signed off by saying that she wasn't angry. But she said she was disappointed.

I slipped the envelope into my bag and thought no more about it. But as I was doing my reading, I saw the girl staring at me so intently it struck me as worrying. Later, when we were all having dinner in the basement, I saw her hovering. She'd give me this contemptuous look, walk off, then come back. I explained the situation to another writer, and we made a quick exit. To be honest, the girl really scared me. My stomach was in knots as we walked back to the hotel. It was bullshit, it wasn't serious, but it made me really uncomfortable.

At the hotel bar, I had the other writer read her letter. We talked about *Misery*, exchanged stories about demented fans. Then I went up to my room and chatted with Clara for five minutes, but I couldn't sleep. I listened to Prince on my headphones and smoked cigarettes in bed.

I kept thinking about the podcast girl. I couldn't get her out of my head. Suddenly it dawned on me: I am Fanny. That's why she scares me so much. I am Fanny. I remembered the way Zoé used to duck out before the end of any meal I was at. The way she'd avoid me. And I knew she was doing it, I was like a compass with her—I could always tell where she was and what she was doing. I knew she was avoiding me. But I ignored it. I'd write her letters. She wouldn't reply. I'd write again. I am Fanny. But a drunk, drug-fucked Fanny who is entitled to be pushy because I'm a guy and I'm not the kitchen help—the sort of reasonably important author who doesn't have to take no for an answer. One you can't get away from.

Once you've formulated the thought, you wonder how you managed to ignore it all this time. I picked up Fanny's letter and read it again. It made me deeply uncomfortable. And I remembered her over dinner, hanging around without talking to me. And it all came flooding back. My certainty. The conviction that I could impose my all-consuming desire on Zoé. That she had to give in. And I wasn't embarrassed by her discomfort. I didn't care. I thought only about my burning need for her. The overwhelming desire she inspired in me.

I tore up the letter. I felt threatened. Happy that I was leaving the following day and would never have to see the girl again.

On the train home, I went on Zoé's blog to read her posts. Something I hadn't done for a long time. I wonder if you're still in touch with her. I'm sorry for what I did. I'm starting to admit it. I've always known it, but never admitted it to myself. I'm learning to stop putting my defense above everything else. Fanny from Stuttgart gave me a glimpse of something I didn't want to hear. It's excruciating, having someone you're not interested in pursue you. And agonizing to be confronted with a demand you can't say no to.

REBECCA

Zoé is in a psych unit. She's been there for a while now. She's a voluntary patient. She completely cracked up. It seems to happen to a lot of young people. We chat to each other on Signal, because she says you can't trust other messaging apps because the cops can access them and the cops are working with the masculists. I think she's completely delusional. But that's standard when you admit yourself to a psych ward. She says she couldn't deal with the online threats and the trolling. I think she'd been holed up at home for weeks, not seeing anyone, reading everything being written about her online.

I went to visit her at the hospital in the nineteenth arrondissement. A close friend spent the summer there not long ago. The woman at the reception desk recognized me, but I still had to show my ID and wait for a nurse to walk me to the elevator.

I know these places. I wasn't impressed by the grim atmosphere in the day room. A cross between a huge family reunion and a scene from a bizarre movie. As I walked along the corridors, I noticed what was happening in the rooms whose doors were open. One guy in blue pajamas was quietly reading in his neatly decorated room. Another guy stopped me, said we knew each other, he was all smiles. I said I didn't remember him, and he started talking to me about people I'd never heard of. Zoé was wearing her own clothes, which I thought was a good sign. Or maybe just a sign they're short of beds and don't expect to keep her here long. She's not on heavy-duty meds. She was alert and pleased to see me. We'd never actually seen each other before. A girl interrupted us, she had very long hair and an amusing energy. She was talking about classified information she'd dug up about the fluoride added to drinking water by the powers that be.

Most of the patients on her floor are fairly calm—people like this girl, who can't survive in the outside world but calm down as soon as they're under care. Zoé and I chatted as though we were meeting in a café, and I couldn't help wondering what the hell she was doing here. Apart from the cut marks on her arms. It's something young people do, apparently. Another girl interrupted. She barged in, speaking English—she was answering questions in some imaginary interview and acting like she was Beyoncé. Her eyes met mine, and I realized she'd never seen me before. I found it hard not to stare at her. Some people have something special about them—something that makes you want to fix your attention on them. Zoé gently walked her back to her room and came back laughing: "In her mind, she's a star like you." And I thought it didn't really matter, that with a face like hers, she could just as easily be in Cannes as in this hospital.

I didn't stay long. We didn't have much to talk about. I made her laugh. I said stupid shit, the way I do. Sometimes she'd look into my eyes with a mixture of impudence and excitement. I didn't ask any questions. She was the one who told me about the death threats, about how she had no one to protect her. And for a few days, she was in a complete tailspin. She felt like the whole world was made of cotton. That's how she described it. She told me doctors call it depersonalization. She was convinced someone was going to break into her apartment and kill her and no one would bat an eyelash, because femicide is pretty normal, and besides, what other people would say wasn't terribly important precisely because she was terrified she'd be hacked up. She told me she'd been sent pieces of shit through the mail, and at first she hadn't paid it any attention, but once she started to get scared, it seemed suddenly very serious, because she's convinced it's the cops who are sending it, and she added that she'd been doxed and her address was all over the internet. Then she started seeing people in her apartment when there was no one and she'd be sitting alone, screaming, and she said, "It's tough for me to believe there was no one there, but I know it's true. It's weird, because I remember seeing guys in my bedroom, I saw them, I know I was out of it, but I saw them. That's what it's like being crazy, hearing voices, seeing things, remembering every detail and knowing it's not true." I asked whether she'd been taking anything when she had the breakdown. She said, I take pills to help me sleep, and I take anti-anxiety meds, and I said, "Maybe the combination of the two was what did you in," and she laughed. "Considering all the shit they give me in here, I fucking hope it's not the meds . . ."

OSCAR

Sometimes you think you're faking it, only to realize you were being sincere. When I said I was beginning to understand what I'd put Zoé through, I felt like I was being a bit hypocritical. I thought I was playing the good guy but that, deep down, I didn't really believe I'd hurt her. Turns out I was telling the truth.

Nothing miraculous—no heavenly voice summoned me to the top of a mountain to receive some stone tablets. But my point of view is a little broader. I'm admitting to the small stuff.

I can't tell you how angry I am that I'm not some Casanova. How long I've spent choking back my heartache at seeing girls I was in love with pick other guys right in front of me. How often I've been the guy you say yes to because you've had one too many, or because you're trying to get back at your boyfriend, or because you just can't say no. I knew I was furious at the way I have been treated, but I didn't realize quite how angry I was at the guys who get what they want. At the fact that it's easy for them. That they know how to play things and I don't. That they make me feel like a loser by flaunting how easy they've got it. I was aware of my shame, of my anger—I wasn't aware of how scared I am of other guys. Of being judged by them. Of being excluded. I'm so scared of them, I decided to focus on other feelings. And to spend all day listening to rap in the hope it would seep into me—that it would eventually rub off on me. I realize that I'm incapable of snapping at someone who makes me feel bad. I take my revenge elsewhere. I vent my anger elsewhere.

I've never been physically violent because I don't have the muscle. But I've been violent all my life—and I terrorized Zoé. I think a lot about her. She's absolutely right—I treated her as someone who couldn't run away. Of all the things she was, I focused only on one tiny part: the part that rejected me.

It came flooding back to me. I wasn't lying when I said I didn't remember it, that whole aspect was blotted out, erased from my memory of what happened between us. Her voicemail full of messages I'd left. I'd call her every day until her voicemail was full. I'd chosen her because she was vulnerable enough to be within reach. I'd go home wasted and keep on snorting coke, message after message. Affectionate, desperate, insulting. Dozens of voice messages from me when she woke up in the morning. And deep down, what I was thinking was: she's not that pretty she's not that brilliant she's not the most beautiful woman in Paris so she should be grateful that I'm interested in her, it was my gaze that made her exceptional. My gaze, nothing else. I had one of those old cell phones, yellow and blue with rounded edges—it looked like a kid's toy. To type a message, you had to press a key three times to get the right letter. I wrote whole novels to her. Threats of murder or suicide depending on the day, then suddenly I'd be sending jokes, like we were friends and everything was fine. Sometimes I'd be completely deranged in the messages and the voicemails I left—and there was a curious joy to these eruptions, a way of gleefully destroying myself, of looking for a chink in her armor so I could slide my dagger through and make her feel what I felt. With desolate joy. The joy I imagine a rapist must feel. The joy of an office stalker—the middle manager who knows exactly what he's doing and knows his victim can't escape. Zoé said no. She must have been suffering as much as I was. I never wondered how it made her feel. I'm terrified of being a bad person, someone who deserves nothing, someone who shouldn't exist. I tell myself: that's not all

I am. But gradually, I've begun to realize: that's part of what I am. I remember making her cry. I remember making her cry multiple times.

REBECCA

You seem to be making progress, Oscar. Just goes to show, all things are possible. Look, I'm no fan of halfhearted statements, but moderation can sometimes be a good thing. There's a middle ground between "I'm a complete innocent martyr to feminism" and "I feel like a rapist." You behaved like a garden-variety asshole. A guy who uses his power but pretends that everyone is equal. I'll leave it to you to take stock on your own, like a grown-up. You've still got the hardest part ahead: figuring out how to fix things.

I did a TV commercial for the Germans, and the money's hit my account. I've got a credit card again. The joy! I did a shoot with this genius photographer, a punk Polish fucker, pretty old, in his fifties, and the minute he showed up I wanted to sleep with him. Wanting to sleep with the man behind the camera is normal. It doesn't mean you're going to, but it's a good sign. I was dressed all in black. No one mentioned the word "weight" while setting up, but they'd been briefed, it was clearly the elephant in the room, the whole concept of the shoot was how to make a body like mine look stunning.

So, I've just seen the photos—they've done an amazing job. Then again, so did I. When it comes to that, I'm extraordinary. This whole getting clean thing is genius—

I look like I've had three facelifts and fifteen rounds of thalassotherapy. A bombshell. All anyone remembers about me apart from my beautiful face is that my boobs are monuments. Like Gothic cathedrals. People will probably still be talking about them a century from now. It's not just cleavage, it's proof of the existence of God.

I've got a credit card again, and I feel like singing in the street. The getting clean thing makes sense financially, too. I don't owe anyone any money. I went to a bookshop to buy some books for your friend Zoé. I could hardly buy her a sweater. Besides, I don't understand the way she dresses. Or her obsession with fluorescent lipstick. And I bought a book for myself—one of yours. An audiobook—I had to call my agent and get him to send me a CD player since I don't have one. I started listening. I was surprised by how good it was. Writing to me, you sound like a broken-hearted princess, but as a novelist, you're a mensch. People would be amazed if they realized what a fragile snowflake you are. You're like Zoé. You have two forms of sincerity: one when you're writing novels and another when you're being who you are. I didn't hate your novel. Honestly, I didn't.

The new degenerate plan the powers that be want to impose on us is a weekend curfew. So, during the week you go to work, and on weekends you lock yourself away. Because that's all you're good for: keeping the economy running smoothly. As for the rest—your life, your peace of mind, your loved ones, the movies—no one cares. It's a wild ride. Each new measure is harder to swallow than the last. But we swallow it. A little more suppression. Of the little people. Regulate the proles. Anything to make sure the banlieues are hurting just that bit more. These days, the only communication between the state and the less privileged is police, prisons, and parking tickets. The feeling of being guinea pigs observed by a bunch of scientists in the pay of Big Pharma who are surprised by our malleability and our lack of regard for our own dignity.

Luckily, I don't give a shit. I look stunning in the photos. I've got my credit card back. The weather's amazing. A Belgian director wants to meet to discuss a movie. Little by little, life is getting back to normal.

OSCAR

I'm listening to Booba and assembling a bunch of Word documents. I'm struggling to write on anything for more than five minutes at a stretch. "Frérot on ne fait rien quand on doute," and I dream of writing a novel that lands like a French rap lyric—no theme, just punchlines and statements—alternately brutal and vulnerable—all in a single sentence, with no attempt at coherence.

I'm watching Lil Nas X on *Saturday Night Live*. I'd heard about the whole sneakers containing a drop of human blood thing that had Nike throwing a hissy fit. When I heard the story, I didn't know what he looked like, I was imagining someone like XXXTentacion, all hard drugs and facial tattoos, writing emo rap for dark-eyed goth boys, super-smooth, codeine-slick, and disturbingly deranged—sorry, with a childlike charm. Turns out I'm way behind the curve—that was five years ago, the landscape has radically changed since then. So we've got

Lil Nas X on *Saturday Night Live*, and I was thinking, who's this joker, and then I think of Eddy de Pretto, who makes me uncomfortable—not when I listen to him, but when I see him, because I like the way he moves and he's got skinny little legs and physically I identify with the guy and it doesn't bother me that he's gay but I almost wish I didn't know because then I could just think I like the look, I like the whole metrosexual thing. But Lil Nas X is a completely different story—I had two seconds chilling and then I had no choice but to admit that I was blown away by how handsome he was, I've never seen such a buff guy, compared to him Prince was a runt.

So with Lil Nas X, I think it's the NA program, the whole thing about honesty and vulnerability and learning to acknowledge what you feel rather than just bottling it up right away. I think a year ago I'd have changed the channel and maybe gone and written an angry screed about this new generation of sleazy singers who use their sexual orientation just to get attention. But now, I think he's sexy AF. He's twenty-two. I watched him shimmy and I've never seen anything like it, I watched him and his dancers shake it like strippers, but if you take away the pathos of the stripper, it's pure sex. If I were sixteen today, I don't know what I'd make of it all. You'll say, if I were sixteen now, I'd be as ugly as I was when I was sixteen, and there's no way a guy like me would put the moves on a guy like that, okay, but let's say—I think I'd ask myself the question, I'd wonder if maybe I wanted to be queer.

There's a story I never talk about. It's there, but I never think about it.

The first time I saw him, it wasn't love, nothing like

that. But I was blown away. He was dressed all in white, shorter than me, but strong, well built. Actually, he had the kind of body I'd have liked to have. I wasn't confused. He was handsome. He was a hustler—he had style. Anyway, he was helping a friend paint a rehearsal space. I hung out with them for an hour and then left—and I remember the look on his face when I shook his hand. Samir. Back in those days, being gay wasn't an option—especially if you were a hustler. Of course, some of them were, but it was like it was with my sister—I only realized it years later. Samir looked me straight in the eye and said, see you soon, and at the time I was a bit thrown, but I didn't think anything about it. Just, this guy's intense. And handsome. Late in the summer we ran into each other at a bar, played pool, Samir was doing some graffiti and I went with him to his spot, rolled a couple of blunts, and passed him the spray cans. Day dawned. We became friends. He was Muslim. He studied every spray can before opening it. When we hung out together, I didn't eat pork, I smoked spliffs, but I didn't drink beer. We didn't do anything in particular. Then one day Samir drank. I don't know why—some shit with his girlfriend, I think. It was weird seeing him drunk. All that freedom, all that laughter. And the dancing. I'd never seen him dance, and he was hot shit. So that night, he showed up at my house at three in the morning, tossing pebbles at my window—I was still living with my parents. Quietly, I let him in. We put on the Notorious BIG on low volume. He pulled off his sweater and I compared myself to him—my scrawny body with his buff body. The slim, supple waist, the broad shoulders, the chiseled muscles. Then he said, for a while now I've been having dreams about you. He said, I know what you want and I think I want it too. And I swear, I had no idea what he was talking about. He kissed me. I didn't push him away because I thought he'd hate me—after he'd made such a gesture, me pushing him away was impossible. He kissed me the way some girls do when you don't want them to but they're convinced it's what you want. I didn't want him to touch me—I was as embarrassed for him as I was for myself. But right away, I got used to the feel of his skin. I dissociated, as girls say these days. I did something other than what my mind thought I wanted, because I instantly found I liked stroking his skin. I was disconcerted by things like this happening between two boys, and by the fact that he knew exactly what to do. Not long after, he left—to find his girlfriend and make up with her, I think. I was bewildered. Not amused. Bewildered. And when we met up that evening at another friend's house, I expected him to be uncomfortable. But he just seemed a little bit closer to me than before. From the outside, no problem. He sought me out a little more often than before but without it being really noticeable or seeming weird to the rest of the group, and we were all listening to Gang Starr and talking shit. During the evening, I realized that I wanted him to make eye contact. A fleeting way of letting me know that, to him, I was unique. I'd never been fancied by a guy before—and I enjoyed his attention. He had everything I didn't. He had this virile, animal way of being, the way he stood, reacted, smiled, and asserted himself; he wore fashionable clothes, used specific slang words, had a way with words. He didn't ask me to stick around that night, he went his own way and I realized I felt a little disappointed. Two days later, he called me, he was doing a wall in Vandœuvre so I went with him. Things were back to normal except that at the end of the afternoon, he was watching me trying and failing to uncap a spray can and he laughed and said, "You're adorable," and it wasn't intended maliciously, he opened the can on the first try and kept laughing as he went back to his mural. We started sleeping together regularly. I got used to it pretty quickly. We never talked about it. Not with each other, not with anyone. There was never the scene you get in films—where he threatens to kill me if I tell anyone because he doesn't want to lose his street cred. Gradually, I realized that the way he saw it, it was something that sometimes happened between friends. As long as you didn't say anything, it hadn't really happened, so it wasn't a problem. It was like slipping beneath the surface of reality. He was gentle—while we were fucking and afterward, he was gentle. He might be the only person who ever talked to me about love. He talked about me as someone exceptional, endowed with amazing qualities. He revealed a bold new world to me, a world where guys did whatever the fuck they wanted, starting with fucking each other on the down-low, and I realized I knew nothing about the world of guys. Nothing but the surface, what I'd been shown. I felt like an initiate. And I was in love with him. That was something I realized when it was over. One day, he went to see the Talib, who freed him from a spell—made him spit out the small piece of poisoned bread jealous neighbors had slipped into some food. Anyway—that was that. There was no conversation. Just a loss of closeness. He didn't avoid me. But he didn't come by my house every day as he'd been doing for a while.

    Times change. Sometimes I think about him and it's

probably the most romantic affair I've ever had. I don't know what became of him. I never saw him again.

REBECCA

I have to tell you, friend, Booba would be disappointed to find out you're listening to his lyrics while fantasizing about Lil Nas. Though I'm pretty sure you're not the only one. You should tell Corinne your story, it would warm the cockles of her heart to know her brother is half gay. Thing is, I completely understand. Hustlers back then had an irresistible charm. Anyone who hasn't been there doesn't know what they're missing—when the universe invented guys like that, it gave a gift to women. And to men, if I'm reading you right. Those sorts of guys make you feel weak—obviously you don't fall in love with someone just because they're a particular gender. You fall in love, period. The only reason I've never had a relationship with a girl is because I was too busy dating guys and I never had a minute to myself. But life hasn't said its last word—I'm prepared for any eventuality.

I'm still going to NA meetings. I've made lots of new friends. I'm surprised I never run into you. But we don't live in the same neighborhood. At first, when they told me I had to come almost every day, I thought, no way, once lockdown was lifted I didn't need to listen to their self-righteous bullshit every day. But if I don't go to meetings, I have doubts. So I go. I think new things. It's amazing. I feel like I'm traveling to some exotic place, but in my mind.

For example, I see my friend Fabrice, and right away I notice that he's been using recently—before this, I wasn't a sniffer dog, I never wondered whether people had been snorting, smoking, shooting up, or spewing—what they did was their business, not mine. These days, it's like a reflex. I just know. I can see it in people's faces, I even hear it in their voices on the phone. It's worrying. And aesthetically I find it disgusting. Like a drab veil, a dirty blanket. We're not talking moral judgment, it's pure aesthetics. It makes people ugly.

I saw two of them today. There's the one who comes every Monday. He's embarrassed—he never lies, he just reels off quickly I used last Saturday but he doesn't come straight out with it, he thinks before he says it, he never says the word "relapse," he never says I'm falling apart, he says new friends are all very well but they never call me so the wife of this guy I used to use with called and invited me over and I knew I wanted to use, I knew it when I went there but it was all fine. And he's happier than usual—he sounds like someone saying I've been seeing my ex again to a group who've listened to him bitching about his relationship with his ex, but he's happy. He's been waiting for this moment. He says the bus was crowded, he talks about something else, he says I've got it under control, all in all he thinks it went well, he only had a couple of drinks and then he went home, he talks about the storm that was looming, then at one o'clock in the morning he woke up and was sick, and he says that's the price he had to pay, and what we're hearing is that he plans to pay it again, that he's telling himself he's changed, that he's in control. Months after he quit, his face is still scarred by booze—he's excited, he's thinking, here I go again, but he still comes to meetings.

The other guy says I had a complete meltdown and now people are turning away from me, it's painful, I'm repeating the same patterns I experienced as a child, it's the only thing I know, and what we hear is that he doesn't care about the harm he's done—that people are turning away because he lost it, he terrified them. What matters to him is that it makes him feel bad. That it's not a successful strategy.

The backsliders.

And there's another veteran. Sunny. Fabulous. Brings tears to the eyes of everyone there and says I used to spew up my fear I used to spew up my shame and I used to spew up my rage and now I spew up my joy and I paddle in it and I'm alive I'm fucking alive.

Then there's this beautiful, immaculately dressed girl, I see her there all the time, and this is the first time I've heard her talk about her father's incestuous relationship with her sister.

And this guy who has the gift of the gab but never talks about himself, he only talks about the program. He's been clean twenty years, and he's got these killer punchlines. He picks fights with everyone and says that's my recovery.

These are my people. I feel moved to see these people who fuck up as much as I do and who, amid the general slide toward who-gives-a-shit, get together and do the opposite of what people do at dinner parties and on social media: they admit defeat, they admit their weaknesses, they allow themselves to be seen at their worst.

I've changed a lot. This whole thing's getting inside my head. I still have the same reflexes—I used to call my dealer whenever I got good news, to reward myself for effort, to chase away the black dog, to console myself when I'd had a hard knock, to keep from getting bored, to have something to do, to make a friend happy. I used to phone my dealer like you flick on the light switch when you walk into a room. Without thinking. That's stayed with me. Something happens, and I feel the void opening. I take a step to call my dealer, but there's nothing there—these days I walk in the void.

I have too much pride not to stay the course. Never in my life have I thought of sobriety as a state of wonder, but I've shifted. I've decided that this is what it means to have class. I've got too much pride not to stay the course. And it passes. There's a stumble—a moment of dizziness—but it passes.

OSCAR

The train is packed. Apparently it's not a problem, it's all about how the air circulates. For the past year, we've been told it's crucial to keep a safe distance, now here we are in an overcrowded car. I'm keenly aware of my fellow human beings breathing. Windows closed, a relatively small car. Our face masks like shields. I bought a mask in a pharmacy for a euro—it's more comfortable than the disposable ones. I want to rip it off, but if I wasn't wearing it, I'd be terrified.

The girl I met cuts the elastic loops off her face masks

before throwing them away. The ridiculous things we do. In the space of a year, we've polluted the planet with billions of face masks—but we rip off the little elastic bands to protect the fish and the birds. I think she's a bit too sophisticated to be with a guy like me. I'm heading back to Germany for a few days for a series of readings and asked her if she wanted to come, and she said yes. She shrugged and said, if I stay here in Paris I'm going to spend the whole time checking my phone to see if you've messaged. The simplicity with which she said it charmed me.

At the station, I bought a train ticket for the dog. You can't do it online if you're crossing a border, even a European one. I take the train as often as I can. I can see the SNCF changing. One more thing that used to work perfectly that we gleefully fucked up.

These days, when you go to the ticket office at the SNCF, like at the post office and so many other places, someone is paid to greet you at the door, to make sure that what you want cannot be done using a machine. I explain my situation to the woman, who leads me to a touchscreen. I want to tell her I'm not so old that I don't know how to use the internet, but I comply.

We don't find a dog-ticket-to-Germany option. So she directs me to a counter. I have breached the citadel, I am entitled to speak to a human being, the whole thing didn't take ten minutes, I feel privileged. Another woman—I can't see her face because of the mask, and from her eyes, I can't tell whether she's happy or harried—listens to my request, which isn't particularly weird if you think about it. We can't be the only couple taking a dog on a train. She can't find the right code. She calls over another woman, who up to now has been waiting in the wings. She suggests the code ChPO QHeS—or something like that, a string of letters that makes sense only in machine language. It's clearly not the right one, the machine doesn't want to hear about it. A third woman comes to the rescue, appearing from the wings. From this point, the three women spend twenty minutes trying to come up with a code the machine can understand. Two of them on the phone, the third tapping away on her keyboard. I weakly suggest they write me a slip of paper saying I can buy the dog's ticket from the conductor on the train. They tell me that's impossible, that I would have to pay the fine. They're a little younger than I am, and utterly oblivious to the absurdity of a situation in which a human ticket agent cannot communicate with a human conductor using words. They try different codes, they say, "It's grayed out." They're friendly, they don't seem surprised: the machine is a harsh mistress, they spend their days trying to charm her—trying and failing is clearly part of the company's strategic risk. They are not surprised that I've turned up at the station an hour early. I think they feel that for those who want to buy a ticket for a dog, it's the bare minimum.

I feel like I'm taking part in a slightly strange ritual—one that's less precise than a séance. What's needed is to find the code that the machine accepts, to translate a human request into machine language. It's quite complicated, because you can't just explain something to a machine. It uses an abstract language that's even more complicated than the language of justice or science, where it's still vaguely possible to explain a simple request in simple language. Not so in this case: it's the precise series of letters in the precise order, or nothing. These three women don't seem uninformed—and they clearly have a complex network within the company, since they are constantly calling new numbers to find out more. An elegant man joins the group of women to offer an opinion; his masculinity does little to impress the machine, which persists in graying out the relevant zones. Four salaried employees in search of a single code, all that matters is that everyone keeps smiling—that everyone seems willing. Then one of them achieves a breakthrough. She hands me the ticket, advising me to hold on to it since it bears the correct code. It might come in handy next time.

When I go back to join her, the girl I'm traveling with tells me she usually buys a ticket to the last possible station in France and that she's never had a problem. She's younger than I am. She doesn't seem to think it's too much that it takes four people to join forces to perform a simple task.

The ritual in which I've just participated—smiling all the while because every day in every way I'm trying to be less of a dickhead, because I know anger is one of my vices, because I know bellowing like a calf that I'm going to miss my train will only add to the chaos of the situation—was humiliating. For the first time in the history of humanity, the dumbest phone is more intelligent than the smartest man alive. The shittiest phone has more memory, can store more knowledge, process more quickly, calculate more accurately, speak more languages—it's more intelligent than the most intelligent of us. Or rather, it has a different kind of intelligence. One that renders ours obsolete.

We no longer have any legitimate right to rule the world—and maybe that's for the best.

All we're left with is the noise we broadcast on the networks, and even then we're acknowledging that the important thing about this noise is the app we use to express ourselves. Our semantic broadcasts are entirely secondary. Up to this point, our humanity was reduced to its economic value: how to cultivate needs, how to move useless goods, how to sacrifice every waking hour to the death spiral of profit. The next stage is the prostration of the human before the machine. It's one that economists are unlikely to explain, because they're not actually thinkers. We make more effort to learn how to communicate with machines than we ever did to speak another language. With animals, it's long resolved—we're not looking to negotiate, we're just looking for more efficient ways to kill them. But at least this is something we understand: how to exploit living creatures, how to privatize living creatures. Among human beings it's also fairly settled: who's got the biggest weapon, who perpetrates the most violence on their adversaries. It's been a long time since we tried to work out what goes on inside the minds of lunatics; these days, they're just guinea pigs for psychoactive sledgehammers. But the machine. The code it requires. We don't talk about wisdom, about understanding the rules, about moral synthesis, culture, mathematical or philosophical logic—none of the things that defined our lives during peacetime matter anymore. The little scraps of civilization we managed to build between two wars . . . now it's all about code. Finding the code that will persuade the machine to allow you to get what you need.

Armed with a ticket no one will ever ask to see, we head down to the platform. A man who looks about ten years older than me is nervously scanning barcodes; when we reach him, I can see he's shaking. He's probably spent his life working for the SNCF, so at one time he was a self-assured railwayman who knew exactly what he was doing. He's less confident with his barcode scanner. Which refuses to read all the tickets. He doesn't have time to worry about getting Covid from the crowd rushing past him. He is shaking because some of the tickets—which look perfectly fine to the human eye—refuse to be scanned. And every time it happens, he panics. He doesn't know how to say to his machine that it's fine, that he has to let the passengers through, that he can't have people held up indefinitely because the scanner is on the fritz.

I show the tickets on my phone and the code works. I try to catch his eye, flash him a smile, but with the mask he doesn't see it. We're both human beings humbled by the same machines. The man on the platform doesn't look at me—he's concentrating on the tickets, waiting for the next glitch—the moment when he'll be made a fool, caught between the task he has to do and the ruthlessness of the machine that will cut him down to the size of his human incompetence.

ZOÉ KATANA

I've been discharged from the hospital. They need the beds. Ever since lockdown, it's been relentless. People like me have been crossing wires in their brains—in my case the one between "I'm not really coping" and "I'm seeing men in my bedroom." A doctor came by and said the meds are working, you can go home and rest. I'd never seen her before, and I didn't dare say I'd rather talk to whoever was looking after me when I was admitted. I packed up my stuff and walked out.

A friend brought me back. She could see I was looking at the things in my apartment as though at any minute my home might betray me. I know now that the walls can crumble, the floor give way, or my bedroom fill with angry voices. Nothing is stable. She offered to stay with me that first night and I agreed. I felt like an alien in my daily life, I didn't want to be left to my own devices. The most important thing was not to turn on my laptop and log in to my social media accounts. It seems strange to me that we call them accounts. Like bank accounts, reconciling an account, calling someone to account.

So anyway, she's moved in with me for a bit, and it's like living with a boxing coach who, if she sees me hit the deck any time of the day or night, kneels down and whispers in my ear: you're fine you can do it you can get up, you're a champ get back on your feet. And it's working. The doctor was right, the treatment's working. It's my own thoughts, but in solid form. Until one day, a boundless calm coursed through me. I'd found a switch without even looking for it. The panic was over. I knew it. I gave my friend the passwords for my socials so she could make sure there were no nasty surprises lurking in my DMs; she did a bit of disinfecting and reassured me. I was good to go. I went back to work. And back to doing shifts for a cyberbullying helpline.

I got a message from a girl who was being bullied. I didn't have time to worry that it might trigger my anxiety again. I was fully operational, armor-plated, laser-focused. Usually, to do this job you need to dissociate—to put your emotions to one side, see them as outside elements. When her message arrived, I was watching the pigeon out on my balcony. It's always the same one that perches on my window ledge, smaller than the others, gray with a black spot on its neck. That day, the wind was gently ruffling his feathers, and he was nervously preening his neck as he looked in my direction. I wondered whether he was enjoying the music I was listening to. Tina Turner. And I think he was—he seemed to perk up when he heard her voice. He was taking wary little steps toward the apartment.

Anyway, this girl messaged me and I called her right away; she was having a complete meltdown, she was sobbing. At that point I had no idea that something was about to happen that would completely change me. She wasn't particularly likable. A TikToker, just turned eighteen, not very visible before the pile-on. Dark hair, blue eyes, a bit goth, pretty vanilla but a nice kid with a total following of five friends and three fans. No feminist rants, not overweight, she shaves her pits, no videos about Black people or Arabs, no attacks on the pope, no pro-choice posts: most of the flags fascist trolls take as provocations don't figure in her report. Except that one morning she came out as bisexual. She doesn't have a girlfriend. Or a boyfriend. She feels she's bisexual and she wanted to say so. She'd have been better off talking about the migration of monarch butterflies... It started off small, a few standard insults: you're only bi because you're unfuckable you deserve to die you fat slob kill yourself you ugly bitch, etc. Classic. So she did the noob thing. "Help me, I've gone down the rabbit hole on straight TikTok," she says. On the phone, she's sobbing as she tells me that from that point she was hunted down and attacked. It started with a hundred messages in one hour. She thought it would stop there, but the next day they were still posting. And the next. Usually pile-ons like this last twenty-four hours—it's a punishment. Unless the girl posts something else they have a problem with, the trolls move on to some other girl they want to punish. In her case, it didn't stop. Maybe she neglected to tell me that she privately defended herself and hit one of the trolls right in the balls—which, as we know, are delicate. In the end, one of them tracked down her mother's number and phoned and told her that her daughter was a slut, shamelessly flaunting herself on the Internet, and the mother didn't try to understand, she turned on her kid.

I know I shouldn't, but I compare the hell I've been

through—the hell that hundreds have to put up with, the constant, nonstop abuse—with the bad week she's had and I feel numb to her pain. Maybe it's the meds. I give her robot-level support. And I'm aware of how relieved I feel that I can do this without having a full-on panic attack. I tell her not to read the comments, that I'll take screenshots to keep as evidence in case she needs it, or in case she decides to read them later after the shitstorm is over. Can she ask a friend to delete insults and block comments for a while? I tell her, turn off your phone and get out of the house, do something you enjoy, I ask, are you afraid to go outside, are you afraid for your safety, she says she'll go and fetch her friend. I tell her again: don't go on social media together, even late at night, do something else, protect yourself; in the meantime, give me your passwords, and remember to change them afterward.

So I log in to her account and the repetitiveness and the absurdity of the shit gets to me, and also the fact I'm wasting my time helping someone who's not political, who's not a feminist, someone I can't empathize with. But at the same time, I'm relieved that I'm able to do my job. I'm feeling better. I don't feel sick to my stomach, I'm not hearing voices, I don't feel like I want to die. I go through the comments and DMs to make sure there are no serious red flags—the name of her school, her mother's address, her little sister's phone number—and I open a file in her name. I meticulously take screenshots; that's protocol. I don't know much about the manosphere, but I know they don't usually spend a week avenging a fellow "Alpha."

And suddenly I realize I'm not suppressing my emotions. I'm not working on autopilot. And I feel pity. Not pity for us, the victims who are systematically hunted and harassed. For the first time in my life—all glory to the drug treatment—I feel sorry for them. The alphas, the trolls, the abusers. They've posted thousands of comments on this girl's TikTok page. Spent endless hours trolling her, trying to bring her down.

They have org charts: lists of volunteers to whom they send details of the target of the day, and who pass the information on to their contacts, and so on. An efficient chain of anonymous hate. When it first started about ten years ago, it seemed shocking because we weren't used to it, and we were surprised by how organized and violent they were. Back then, the courts had never convicted anyone for posting online messages, so there was no limit to their viciousness.

These days, they're more cautious. The accounts exist—these are real people acting openly, so you can easily find out who they are. There's no typical profile. There are the incels and uglies you expect, but there are lots of fathers and older men, all socioeconomic groups are represented, some live in cities, some in the sticks, some are functionally illiterate, others are university professors. They know there's no payback. They do whatever the fuck they like online. No masculist has ever checked himself into a psych ward because he's been trolled by feminists. If someone insults them, they bitch about it for months. In a pile-on, they're like the droogs in *A Clockwork Orange*, but if we dare clap back, they're cucks. They can't stand being contradicted, they fiercely defend "their" territory: they expect everything online to pander to their point of view, they don't like to be challenged.

We, on the other hand, are pretty magnanimous. When it comes to men, we won't abort them, deprive them of an education, burn them at the stake, kill them in the streets, kill them while they're out jogging, kill them in the woods, kill them in our homes, shame them for being born male, we don't starve them, we don't rape them, we don't grope them under the table, call them sluts for enjoying sex, ban them from public spaces, exclude them from the corridors of power, we won't genitally mutilate them, stop them from dressing however they like, force them to have children, make them feel guilty if they have a hobby that takes them away from home, declare them insane if they're not good spouses, commandeer their sexuality, monitor their every word and gesture as though they belonged to us, we won't demand to see their hair, shame those who disobey. When we talk about equality, that's not the equality we mean. If it were, we would understand very well why they're so enraged by our demands. But they're so delicate. And used to defending themselves. The White manosphere has its own strategies of resistance.

And I realize they don't scare me anymore. It's a shocking epiphany. I read their comments. They've been told to troll, so they troll. They rely on numbers. Taken individually, their messages are dumb, lame, repetitive. I scroll through them more carefully. A hundred copy-paste comments about the troll who phoned the girl's mother: "This Chad is the GOAT," a hundred "Bitches be needing re-educating," a hundred "Cud'n pay me to rape u, fuckin femoid slut." And I feel sorry for them. Abject. That's what they are. Abject. Mediocre. And they're proud of it. Their imaginative world is barren. A grotesque travesty of joy, friendship, and solidarity, but mostly it's an expression of sordid abjection. "Bitch needs a beat down—slutz think they can get away with any shit—hope her mama sorts her out—this boujee bitch probly got a betabuxx, bet he dumps her and makes her a skank—fuckin genius, man, fuckin genius." For fuck's sake. The militia of minuscule masculinity. Toxic minusculinity.

I don't feel like throwing up. I'm not scared. This is real suffering. This exhibition of the emptiness, the nothingness of these anonymous little foot soldiers. This is raw human suffering. They're aware. They know they're nothing. They know they're worthless. That they deserve to die like cockroaches. They're terrified of being what they are. They know they're useless, so they crawl around in the dark, banging into walls. A disgusting little pile of shit, and for the first time I can clearly see what it is they're saying: they know it, and it's killing them.

OSCAR

Got my royalty statement this morning. I've hit the fucking jackpot. This novel has brought in three times as much as my previous ones. You told me—any publicity is good publicity. But I wasn't expecting this. All hail Zoé Katana: this wannabe terrorist skank has galvanized my readers. At least I didn't go through all that shit for nothing. Given how cheerful my publishers have been, I kind of figured it wasn't going to be a bad year. But I was too overwhelmed to call them, I was ashamed. In the meantime, sales were skyrocketing. Apparently, buying my book has become a symbol of resistance against feminist attacks. I found out I got a lot of letters of support. And not just from men. Women have my back too. Being supported by morons is depressing. But it's hard not to be thrilled when I look at the royalties coming my way.

I read Zoé Katana's post and feel a fleeting sense of shame. I know what it's like. So I can imagine her spending her days avoiding her phone and gritting her teeth while she gets expressions of sympathy that leave a bitter aftertaste. I'm familiar with the self-pitying message from the friend who's actually patting himself on the back because he's not in your shoes. And I also understand the obsession with saying that everything's going to be okay, that it's over, that you're stronger than that.

For the first time since she screwed up my life, I realize that she's been viciously attacked as well. I was so preoccupied with my own suffering that I didn't try to understand what was going on with her. But reading in her post about the girl being bullied, I thought about my daughter,

I realized this could happen to her, it could happen to any kid online. And there's nothing I could do to protect her.

I read Katana's blog, and I'm so relieved that she's not kvetching about me anymore that I actually start listening to what she's saying. And it occurs to me that I've never mentioned a single woman in the list of authors who've influenced me. And no one has ever called me out on it. I never mention women because I know it would stigmatize me. It's just not done. I could mention Marguerite Duras's *La Douleur*—one of the books that most influenced me as a teenager. Besides, I love her megalomania. I could mention Anne Rice, I read the early trilogy several times. But I don't—it's instinctive. I don't leave out Stephen King, but I leave out *Interview with the Vampire*. Because I know that, when you're a guy, other guys are suspicious of your relationships with women.

It's not rocket science—you don't need to claim it's hormonal or it's complicated. It's right out of the elementary school playground. We've all been through it. You've been playing with girls because they're your friends and the school bully grabs you in the hall, yanks your ears until he lifts you off the ground, then drops you on the floor—"Look at the little faggot playing jump rope with the girls." And everyone laughs. Boys and girls. Everyone laughs along with the bully. And in every school, there's a bully who tells everyone else how things are going to be. And a little gang of thugs waiting for him to target someone. And an audience—all the kids who watch and laugh. That's all it comes down to. Once it's happened to you, you know the score: if a girl asks you to play, you say fuck off. Her friendship makes you look weak. If you go over to play at her house, you do it on the quiet. You don't want to be the bully's next target. You want to be with the others, laughing at the kid who's being bullied. Even now we're grown up, I can spot that guys like me, who were weak and puny kids who didn't understand the rules of the playground, but have managed to win the approval and respect of the bullies—by writing a book, for example. Beneath the mask of the virulent polemicist I can see the face of the kid who was humiliated back when he was playing marbles; now that he knows how, he's giving the bullies exactly what they want, still desperate to be accepted into their gang. That's all we're looking for: the approval of bullies.

On TikTok, young Colombian boys mime shooting guns to protest the crackdown on protests. In the next video, an American guy says: "Today I destroyed someone's dreams. I work in HR and it's my job to check people's résumés before they're hired, and this girl had the perfect résumé for the job, it was impeccable and her online presence was amazing, but I found this one video that had been erased—but these days nothing is ever really erased." He doesn't describe it, but it's clearly a porn video. She wasn't the one who posted the video, but nothing is ever completely erased and her name comes up, so he says, sorry—but if it wasn't me, it would just be someone else—all the big companies check for red flags. And he says the company is right not to hire her, that it's an important role, the video could resurface at any time. It doesn't occur to him to say, and who gives a fuck? It's a sex tape. It's not a video of her torturing refugees, or setting a homeless guy on fire, she's not spouting death threats to the Asian community, she's not giving a Nazi salute—she's probably sucking cock. Or flicking the bean. Or maybe she's having a wild time on ecstasy in a hotel room with four guys she's just met. It's consensual sex. There's something very fucking wrong about this—and I identify as a guy, and I identify as white, meaning I can't figure out how to stop being part of the problem and start being part of the solution.

REBECCA

I'm worried that Zoé is carrying on with what she calls her "online activism." It's insane that girls of her generation have to express themselves in a space that's so hostile to them. Systemically hostile. Facebook Twitter Google Amazon Microsoft Apple—all white men. It's not in their interest for things to change. I feel privileged to be the age I am, to have made a life for myself without feeling obligated to sell myself online, because I see what it does to young actresses, the abuse they get every time they post online, I'd never have stood for it.

Usually, you can count on me to be in favor of anything that qualifies as behaving badly, but it's a damning indictment of your publisher that they're congratulating you on your record sales just after Zoé was released from a psych ward.

I still don't feel like calling the dealer. It's become a point of honor. For one thing, too many people in my circle seem convinced I won't stick it out. It hurts my pride. I'm going to hold out, just to prove that they don't know shit about me and that they'd do better to keep their traps shut. On the other hand, some of my other friends are starting to bitch that I'm no fun since I stopped using. I realize they think I exist to amuse them. And guess what? Fuck 'em.

I don't want to get wasted, but sometimes I'd like something that would knock me out. I'd like a little peace and quiet. I'm not the one who's screwing up. It's the world.

I'm not finding staying clean too difficult, what I'm finding difficult is recovery. This constant effort to do things correctly. I feel like doing stupid shit. Like ripping the head off the guy who's asked me to make a movie with him. Maybe because I'll be well paid for once and that gives him power over me, so I feel like screaming abuse at him. Or maybe he's just a pain in the ass, a petulant kid who demands to be treated like a great and benevolent artiste. His films truly suck. But he's filthy rich, so everyone is nice to him. I feel like giving him a slap—just for the hell of it.

It comes and goes. Right now, I'm wound up, but other times I'm completely fine. I look around Paris with its makeshift café terraces springing up everywhere, where as soon as there's five minutes of sunshine, they're mobbed with people drinking and laughing together, and I realize I love this city. It's full of mopeds, Deliveroo scooters, bicycles of all shapes and sizes, sleek black town cars. Every neighborhood is being defaced by construction work. And when I feel good, I walk. I walk through every street of this city—ever since the first lockdown I've developed a funny relationship with this city. I remind myself that I love it, the way you love something you know you could lose.

OSCAR

I was going to write and tell you not to be so flippant about the idea of taking meds to get some peace and quiet. When I was heading toward a relapse, you were worried about me, now it's my turn to worry about whether you're coping. I was going to write about that, and also tell you that my brief moments of empathy for Zoé have become more and more frequent, and I'm overwhelmed by a sort of nagging guilt . . . But Corinne collapsed. She's been admitted to the hospital. I didn't even know she was in Paris. She hadn't told me. One evening, she had pins and needles in her legs, and during the night she woke the girl she was staying with because she couldn't move her right leg and her arm was going numb. She realized how serious it was when she was rushed straight through at the emergency room.

It was her girlfriend, Marcelle, who called. Corinne had been transferred to François-Quesnay Hospital in Mantes-la-Jolie. She's had a stroke. She's paralyzed down her right side. Marcelle teaches PE in a high school—she told me she wouldn't be able to visit Corinne on Monday. I was a bit of a dick when she called, I said I had a really busy week ahead and promised to go visit her as soon as possible. It was only after I hung up that I realized I had to go on Monday. I was obsessing about all the things I'd have to cancel, but what really scared me was that it would turn out to be very serious. That, and going inside a hospital. And watching my sister suffer.

Getting there is a complete pain because it's miles from anywhere, but it's nothing like you'd imagine a hospital to be these days. The building is spacious and quiet—it reminded me of when I was young and France was a relatively rich country with public services we weren't afraid of. I easily found her room, on the top floor, and Corinne wasn't as bad as I'd feared. She was sitting up, reading *Viendra le temps du feu*, though she still looks pretty rough and her speech was a bit strange—part of her face is paralyzed. First she said, "I wasn't expecting you today," but since we've got a bit of a weird relationship, that didn't set alarm bells ringing. I said, "I didn't realize you were in Paris, actually I came as soon as I could." She'd just had a stroke, so I didn't think she was looking at me funny, and I didn't sense her embarrassment. Marcelle had told me that the most important thing was to help her into the wheelchair so she could go downstairs for a cigarette, so I offered to take her for a walk. I could see that she was dithering about saying something, I just assumed that her tiredness had got the better of her longing for fresh air. In the bed next to hers a lady was playing Candy Crush with the sound cranked up. I politely asked her to turn it down, and she was friendly, but she was so out of it she couldn't find the volume button, so I helped. And when I turned back to my sister, feeling smug about my little intervention, I saw Zoé standing in the doorway. Corinne said again, "I wasn't expecting you today." I'm always complaining that I'm not in touch with my emotions—well, not anymore. Within seconds I was served up a whole buffet: fear, shame, anger, anxiety, cowardice. I was reminded of what it felt like as a little boy when you're barraged by powerful, conflicting feelings you can't control.

I also had time to think that Zoé was still pretty. All

the time I've spent thinking about her, I had no idea how she'd aged, and I had time to think, the ten extra years suit her. For several seconds, she didn't move, allowing herself time to hate me to her heart's content. Years of accumulated bitterness compressed into a single look. Not a word, it was all in the eyes.

Then Corinne raised her good hand to get our attention, wriggled on the bed and said, "Okay, so this is a shitty situation, but I'm too weak to mediate," and, without saying a word, Zoé went into the corridor to get a wheelchair, brought it to the bed, and helped my sister into it.

I stood up. My legs felt like cotton. The three of us found ourselves in the huge elevator, and my sister had decided to pretend the situation was tolerable. She said: "I was crashing at Zoé's place when it happened. That's why I didn't tell you I was in Paris. Actually, I didn't even tell Marcelle who I was staying with because she might have gotten the wrong idea . . ."

Marcelle and Corinne have been together for years. I don't know if my sister has ever been unfaithful. I don't think so. But she feels the need to lie. In the same way I've been letting drugs get between me and my girlfriends for decades, Corinne also has her own little secrets. We're both terrified of intimacy, so we invent ways to avoid it.

Corinne still chain-smokes. She insisted that Zoé stay with her, and told me to go buy some bottled water and doughnuts in the cafeteria. They sat on a bench in the sun. When I joined them, with my little plastic bottles and my bag of greasy doughnuts in hand, I was thinking that this encounter I'd fantasized about a thousand times in infinite variations—I slap her across the face, or I tell her what happened from my point of view, or I make her cry by telling her about the hell I went through because of her post, or I remind her that we got along pretty well together and that she betrayed me, or I beg for her forgiveness and she sobs in my arms and tells me that she's been waiting for this moment for so long—was not going the way I'd anticipated. Life's like that, you rehearse scenes and when they finally happen they're nothing like you expected. That's another reason I love writing novels.

Zoé didn't seem agitated. She ignored me. Her eyes never met mine. The two of them were chatting. I rolled a cigarette, but I didn't sit down. Like them, I pretended I wasn't there. They were talking about TERFs, I didn't discover what that meant until I looked it up online when I got home.

Corinne, her mouth slightly twisted, still had all her wits about her. "It's classic right-wing shit, you stigmatize a minority group for who they are rather than what they do. And casting them as rapists is classic too. It used to be Black men, then Arabs, then Roma, then the poor; now it's trans women. All rapists of the respectable cis white woman, who lives the way God intended." Zoé nodded in agreement. I found it painful to see them in agreement. Me, I was the cool, stoical decent guy who knows the world doesn't revolve around him. That the important person here is my sister, not me. Corinne went on: "And their presence is a constant in the history of feminism. It's Sojourner Truth, again and again, Ain't I a woman?" Then Zoé challenged her: "But the abuse that TERFs are subjected to is just as unacceptable as the abuse I get. It's all the same. You can't use the weapons of the enemy and expect to get different results." Corinne shook her head. "Fuck them." "You're only saying that because you're not on social media. You don't know what it's like, it drives you insane." I hadn't realized that all this feminist crap was so complicated. I waited for a moment of silence the way you wait for a bus that never comes, so that I could get up and take my leave. Okay, I'd just spent an hour on public transportation for nothing, and now I was about to do the same thing in the opposite direction. It didn't matter—the weather was fine and my sister seemed to be making a remarkable recovery in a pleasant environment. I got up, told Corinne I'd come back, and added, "And this time I'll let you know before I come," and then I made a mistake: I turned and smiled at Zoé, and since she wasn't expecting it, she didn't have time to turn away.

I ducked into the cafeteria for a coffee. I didn't think they'd see it as a provocation, given they were sitting on a bench away from the entrance, so I could hardly be accused of strutting around in front of them. I ordered an espresso, the barista set it on the counter, and at that point Zoé Katana burst in without warning. She was in a blind rage that was completely inappropriate given the situation—between you and me, I'm not sure she's on the right meds: the difference between the nice, calm girl who had been talking to my sister five minutes earlier and the Fury staring me in the face was alarming. She wasn't shouting. She was shrieking. She was like a machine gun, it was impossible to interrupt. "Here we go again! You say you're leaving, then I look up and see you hanging around—what are you waiting for? You want to get me alone? It's been ten years, and when I see you, my stomach is in knots because I'm scared of the shit you're going to pull when no one's looking. I want you to fuck off, Oscar Jayack, I never want to see you again, is that clear? And that little smirk of yours, I'm going to make you choke on it."

I kept my cool. I shouldn't have. I said, "Don't worry, I choked on what you call my 'little smirk' a long time ago..."

I should have kept my mouth shut, but since she just stood there staring at me, I thought I should say something, that this was the perfect time to say: "I'm sorry, Zoé. I've had time to think about what happened. I had a rough time of it when you gave your side of the story, and it took me a while to understand. The way I behaved toward you was appalling. And I never thought about how it made you feel. I'm really sorry. I apologize."

That was it, pretty much word for word, and with every word I regretted saying them. When I said, "I'm sorry," it was like I'd whipped my cock out and wiped it on her coat. She took a step back. She was incandescent, she spluttered, "I don't want your shitty apologies, you think you get to walk away with a clear conscience? Who's going to give me back the person I was before you destroyed me? Who's going to give me back the years of depression? Your apologies? Take your apologies up your ass, motherfucker."

Then she stepped up to me, I could smell her perfume, could almost feel the warmth of her body, and there at the counter of the hospital cafeteria, she spat in my face.

Outside in the sunshine, my sister was sitting in her wheelchair, chatting on her phone with her back to us.

Zoé walked away. I took a paper napkin from the counter. The waiter was texting and smiled at me; I don't know what he made of the scene, but he was clearly amused. I paid for the coffee and he said he really liked my books, which pissed me off because it meant he recognized me. I'd rather have been spat on anonymously.

REBECCA

I saw Zoé again. It was the first time I'd been to her place since the first lockdown. On the way, I stopped off at the same grocery shop and bought some fruit, some chips, and some cans of Coke. She opened the door, and Alicia and Jay-Z were singing "Empire State of Mind." I looked around her tiny apartment. I liked that it was a mess, it looked like my place. There was a soothing light in the living room, and I felt right at home.

She was in a complete state. I've grown fond of the kid, and it upset me to see her like that, but I didn't know how to calm her down. The only miracle solution I know is junk.

I didn't really understand what had happened. I knew that someone had posted photos of you and her online. I realized they'd been taken when you were at the hospital. So we see you from a distance, smoking cigarettes, and it looks like you're chatting. And then we see the two of you in the cafeteria, standing really close to each other— and it doesn't look like you're arguing. It looks more like you're about to make out. The whole thing lathered with vicious comments: the fibber and the fuckhead, the two compulsive liars who cooked up the whole story so they'd go viral, etc., etc.

Zoé spent the whole night getting into Twitter spats. Somehow she mostly got into arguments with other flavors of feminists—and at that point, I admit, I stopped trying to keep up. Too many feminist movements kill the feminist movement, if you ask me. All I know is that it looks like a Mexican standoff. And that I found Zoé utterly destroyed. When you read the stuff she posts online, she's a goddess of war and destruction. And when you see her IRL she's this exhausted kid who's about to fall apart.

I tried to distract her, to comfort her. But let's be honest: I'm a diva. Normally people comfort me, not the other way around. I didn't know how to go about it. We did a Zoom call with your sister. Sitting in her hospital bed, her face half-twisted. I hadn't seen her in years and I thought, even after a stroke she's looking a lot better than most people in their fifties.

We talked about you, obviously. Zoé says that when the photos of you started circulating, you sent her a private message to apologize again.

Stop apologizing, buddy. It's not your thing. At her age, let me tell you, she doesn't give a shit about our stories of rehabilitation, forgiveness, and serenity. Big time . . . What she says is contradictory. She'll say she dreams of putting a bullet in your head. And two minutes later, she'll say that the fact that you've admitted it happened, that she didn't lie, that she didn't make it up, has helped her to calm down. If this is what she calls calm . . . Then she'll say you're like Windows 95, impossible to update. Then she's back down the rabbit hole saying that if she had the cojones, she'd go straight to your house and stab you to death.

I'd rather let you know before she posts something about this on her blog. Given that she's got absolutely no filter and is pretty much keeping a private diary in public, I suspect she'll write about the scene . . . Personally, I suggested she ask you for money. I could see she was livid that you had dared to apologize. I said:

"Play it like an American. Like this Valerie Solanas you're always carrying on about. She'd have demanded compensation. Tell him you want half the royalties from his book. After all, you did all the promotion."

Corinne was adamant.

"No way. You demand every penny he's earned in royalties. Minimum."

I said:

"How much do writers earn? Really, that little? And you call that a bestseller? Corinne's right: you should demand one hundred percent of the royalties."

I thought the money angle was a good one. It's an easy way to work things out mathematically. You just have to work out how much it's worth, how much you owe her, given you're so keen to settle your debts with her. But I noticed that Corinne and Zoé were more ambivalent about the idea. Zoé is one of those girls who is afraid that accepting money will make her look like a woman of easy virtue:

"I like the idea because it's going for the jugular. Guys only ever think about money. That's all that matters to them. And I do need it. But his money would destroy me, it would be tainted. As though he'd bought me. He'd feel we were even. And I'd feel dirty."

I didn't push it. Once I realized what you called "the jackpot" was actually worth, I realized that we couldn't take your money, because you don't have much. You literary titans are happy with fuck all . . . Zoé's right, at that price, it's better not to negotiate. I made another suggestion:

"Tell him to make a public apology. That's what public apologies are for. They're humiliating."

"I don't give a damn about his apologies. He'll just apologize and do it all again tomorrow. It's too easy . . ."

That's when your sister, who's not exactly short of stupid ideas, came up with this:

"Ask him for a finger. Ask him to cut off a finger."

We didn't know what to say. Corinne went on:

"He's robbed you of something that made you whole. You take something of his. You say he maimed you? Let him maim himself. He'll think about it every time he looks at his hand."

If your sister had to choose between justice and her mother, she wouldn't think twice—she'd demand her mother's head on a plate. Clearly, blood isn't much thicker than water in your family. But for the first time, Zoé laughed.

"In that case, I'll ask him for a kidney. I mean, it could always be useful to someone."

Sorry to come out with it like that, especially as it's your body we were talking about, but it lightened the mood. It didn't get us any further, but we went through all the forms of self-mutilation that could be demanded of you. And, no, we didn't talk about your prick. It seems none of us wanted to imagine you cutting your dick off. Everything else was fair game.

In the end, what she liked best of all the things we said to her was the so-called Chinese proverb "Sit by the river and wait to see his corpse float by." It gave her some comfort. She said she'd wait.

In all this it might sound like I'm not on your side, like I'm not choosing sides—and that's true. I've got a bruise on my ass from sitting on the fence. I hate seeing her like this, because she's sweet and she makes me laugh. And I can see that she's angry with you, but that what's most hurtful is suddenly finding herself the butt of so much online chatter again. It's inhuman, all those voices speaking simultaneously, and yet you can hear it all in detail. Your brain can't keep up. But it's you she's focused on. On the other hand, the idea of you having to sacrifice a finger to pay for past misdeeds doesn't exactly thrill me. Because, whether I like it or not, I'm fond of you. But also because, in the back of my mind, I'm working out the number of people who'd be entitled to demand a finger from me, and I can tell you right now that I'm not about to fess up to my mistakes.

We turned off the laptop and I sat there for a while, listening to Cardi B, and Rah Digga, and Kae Tempest with her. Zoé said, I only listen to female artists now, and I said that didn't surprise me. We didn't mention you again. In fact, I monopolized the conversation because I wanted to distract her from thinking about you and the feminists she's arguing with online, and the fusty old men insulting her.

But I know that the minute she closed the door behind me, she was back on her keyboard, pouring fuel on the fire of her rage.

 I decided to walk home, and it was nice seeing the crowded café terraces and the people in the street, the city emerging from its anguish. I didn't tell Zoé that what most shocks me about her relationship with you isn't so much the damage you did to her. You behaved like a standard-issue asshole who finds a defenseless person to take out their frustration on. What shocks me most is that she didn't resign on the spot. It could have played out that way. You tell her you fancy her, she tells you she's not into you. The next day, you try again. She gets another job. And if you show up at her door some night, she punches you in the face. I feel so privileged that I never had to have a real job. From everything I hear, it sounds like a disaster. I've had directors come on to me on set. But I'm in the same situation as you: if I don't like it, they have to fuck off. You don't replace the lead actress. You replace the director. That's privilege. So I don't actually know what it feels like to be a twenty-year-old girl when she has to go to a job that makes her want to slit her wrists. I just want to say to her: stop going.

ZOÉ KATANA

If Valerie Solanas came back, I think she'd give up on her project of cutting up men. That's utopia. Pretty hard to achieve (although we could just systematically abort them, introduce a conscience clause and transform abortion into the ethical practice it should already be) and difficult to defend. Because seductive as the idea of a world without men sounds, it would inevitably make us the unwitting agents of patriarchal culture—the culture of death, authority, and the belief in two distinct humanities: those who have the right to kill and those who get to die.

If Solanas came back, sixty years after the *SCUM Manifesto*, I think she'd give up on the fantasy of human dignity. If Solanas were to come back, I think she'd say: fuck off and die. Beat each other, bomb each other, judge each other, infect each other, shit on each other, and let's put an end to this once and for all. Just fucking die, the lot of you.

If Valerie Solanas came back, would she still be so eager to support her feminist friends? It's hard to imagine her at the general assemblies of bougie feminism, joining in the clap clap clap and the grotesque chants of "Feminists unite!" bellowed by middle managers with ambitious career plans. I don't know what she'd make of a liberal feminism that's forgotten to be revolutionary. And directs most of its hostility—surprise, surprise—at others in its own camp.

I sacrificed my peace of mind for this dream. Feminism. And today, I've decided to be honest. These are the winners of the revolution I dearly believed in: Arms-dealing feminists. Heteronormative feminists. Feminists who believe in the importance of bosses, feminists desperate for promotions, rewards, success, and social recognition. Feminists who are pro-police, pro-judgment, classist. Identitarians. The self-professed virtuous. In other words, the feminism of the respectable, the well-groomed, the screws, and the prigs.

Sisters, just one more little push, already we're almost as dumb as men. Except without the power. We mimic the same stupid assemblies. The same fake indignation. The same urge to imprison, the same love of authority. The same passion for a Father who sagely listens and then metes out his justice. Change the name to Mother if you like, and we'll call it quits. It's the same game. And I no more intend to forgive you for what you've done to me than I've forgiven men. Let's be precise: no more, no less. It's the same shit. I recognize it, I've been forced to eat it for long enough.

Some of you started piling on when I wrote the post about minusculinity. Too easygoing for your taste. I hadn't created the perfect little post to match your handbag, so you started bitching and piling on. Just like the guys. You didn't offer criticism, you didn't engage in debate, you didn't come to me with ideas. You attacked me. Your methods are more basic, you're not as organized as they are, your networks are outdated. But it's the same aggression that seeks to cancel, that doesn't want to hear. The voice of She Who Shouts the Loudest, the one that silences everyone else. You didn't try to find out why the post went viral, or why there were so many comments on it—you weren't worried that a lot of it was coming from the far right. You just jumped on the bandwagon as it passed and went for it. That was my fifteen minutes of fame, the start of my party.

Then I was papped next to Oscar Jayack. This time, yeah, you wiped your hands a little before you slapped me—a lot of you remembered to say that you condemned the person who took the photo and posted it. But you still had to give your opinion about the incident. An incident about which you knew nothing.

In passing, let me say I could have reveled in the fact that you were more vicious to him than to me. That you mocked him more than me. But all of you, without regard for gender, headed for the same place: the shitter. It's the manosphere: it loves to wallow in shit and loves to stir it up. These people have no boundaries—they're pragmatic. They want power. It's all they think about. Just a little power. Wipe your hands before you slap them if you like, ladies: you're still covered in their shit.

And these days I'm rediscovering a feeling I'd almost forgotten: that wherever I go I'm being hounded and the danger could come from anywhere. Let's face it, I had it coming: I wrote a post about them. They didn't take kindly to my post about minusculinity. I'm used to the fact they're sensitive creatures. I deleted the comments. I don't read my DMs. So they indulged in a little transference—

they trolled and threatened anyone who liked or shared my post. A meticulous operation. The one thing they're good at. Retaliation. Effective, disciplined, predictable. Boring as fuck.

No, the surprise this time was the feminists. And women who don't call themselves feminists, but who feel implicated. And they're right. We are all feminized. Even when we don't like it. Even when we'd rather it wasn't our business. Femininity is a prison, and we've all got life sentences.

So these women felt they had something to say. About the post and about the photo. They didn't think, she's just come out of a psych ward. She's at the end of her rope. Her chest is damaged. She's been wounded in battle and she's weak. They didn't think, we share common enemies. Though that's about the only thing we have in common. Our enemies. As for the rest, we are humanity, too numerous to constitute a homogeneous group. But we have the same enemies. And they're watching us. And they know. And they are thrilled when we turn on each other and shoot at each other, in a circular firing squad. Today, I'm joining that circle, because for months I've weathered your attacks without saying a word, in the name of activism and out of respect for our commitments. Silence has never saved anyone. So I've come to tell you what I think of you, and then I'll shun you. Just as I shun our old friends, men.

Your messages were interspersed with those left by trolls. Some came from friends, relatives, or girls I'd met at demonstrations; all of you had something to say about my alleged friendship with Oscar Jayack. Few of you bothered to contact me privately. You had to make a three-ring circus of your opinions about my presence in the hospital room of the sister of Oscar Jayack, the man who sexually harassed me. My closeness to him in the photograph. My moronic posts. Suddenly I was just a figure, a target to be shot at. You didn't exactly outdo yourselves in terms of originality. The important thing was for you to make a statement. Which, for the most part, meant trashing me. Some women came to my defense. I'll remember all your names, because that took courage. A lot of others found it funny. At last! The mask has slipped, they'd seen the real me. They'd sort me out. I was a turncoat, I was spineless, a weak link, easily led. And—obviously—a little slut. In the end, we always end up being little sluts. A variety of judgments was passed on who I am, what I was doing there, what I represent, what I write. Sisters, it was a bonfire. With all the flickering shades of a fire—ranging from hatred to contempt. And fun, of course. A great opportunity for a bit of a laugh. The laugh of the guy holding the camera while a girl is being raped. Don't get me wrong—it's the same laugh. It was rhizomatic: you were groping toward each other in the dark, damp earth of your subconscious—the poisoned earth. You knew what I'd been through. You knew I'd been tricked. You knew it was a lie. That I never saw him again. That I'm not his friend. You knew all that, but it didn't matter. What destroyed me in this whole circus was that I felt respect or affection, or both, for so many of you.

And now I find myself in this weird-as-fuck situation where Oscar Jayack is sliding into my DMs, saying: "I've seen what people are writing about you, it's disgusting." Now that we're at the center of the same shitstorm, he starts up again with his lame-ass apologies. I don't want his apologies.

And whatever I say to him, I'm trapped. You can't undo events. You can't rip them from your body. He peddles the same old sanctimonious line about regret and self-awareness. And I tell him, "When I hear your voice I want to throw up." And that's not a figure of speech. The fear of him is rekindled. The fear that it will happen again. Because that's how this whole thing started. Whatever I do, I'm feeding the web that's suffocating me. If I speak out, I trigger a wave of hatred. If I stay silent, I suffocate. And if I write what I'm writing today, I'm binding myself to him in an even more intimate way. What I want is to forget him. And for him to forget me. And I think, dear feminist sisters—and those who aren't feminists but who are feminized and feel they have to have an opinion on this issue—I think about the wave of your hatred about to crash down on me. You wear me out because you've gotten inside my head, and now whenever I write, I'm terrorized by that hatred. It isolates me, cuts me off from my own voice. The game of threats. We've moved from one situation where it's impossible to speak and say anything into another situation where it's impossible to speak and say anything. So we're still dying of the same asphyxiation. The walls may have changed, but the prison cell is just as cramped as ever.

When I decided to tell my story of being sexually harassed, that is to say, when I decided to add my voice to those of thousands of other women, I thought, the important thing is to create a safe space. And I was convinced that we would learn to listen to each other. To listen to these words that had never been spoken and to ask ourselves, what do we do with these voices? With these stories we'd never told ourselves?

In my case: What are the mechanics of sexual harassment? What has it broken in me? What is this thing no one prepared me for, this thing that has no vocabulary, what is this mounting panic I feel every day while I wait for the request, the insult, the unwanted compliment, the veiled threat? When will fear overwhelm me? At what point will my abuser take over everything I am, taint everything I am? At what point will the inability of those around me to hear my cries for help leave me helpless? What could have been done? At what point does the perpetrator's impunity make me feel utterly abandoned? At what point will I make bad decisions? What is this day-to-day destruction that's so unrelenting? So methodical. That claims to be desire for but is really a desire to do away with me. A tentacle that burrows its way into your everyday life, stubbornly groping, searching for your weak spot and finding it—and you say nothing because the very nature of harassment is feeling that whatever you do, it will make things worse. What is desired is that you keep quiet, permanently. You know this instinctively. You keep quiet. It goes on for years.

And so, when I spoke up, I felt as though people were listening to me. I heard all the cries of "Me too" and "That's my story," and I heard the cries of "You're not alone," and I welcomed the cries of "I believe you" like so many balms and cures, as though maybe I'd finally found a place where I could put down roots.

But at the same time, as soon as my words—amplified by my detractors—became important, I also got the impression that they were being taken from me, exploited by people for their own ends. My words and those of others. And I said nothing. We had to stand together. We shared the same enemies. We couldn't make a public spectacle of ourselves. I'm done with that silence. So let me tell it to you by quoting a man: "You don't like me? I don't like you either."

And don't think that means I'm leaving you to define feminism. Feminism is a sprawling house with room in it for all women. All of us who share the same enemy. The same torturers, the same murderers, the same rapists. The same stalkers whose friends all rally round.

It's my house, too. And I don't intend to leave just because you're trying to take away the keys. The keys are in the door. And they'll stay there.

I'll leave you to create whatever mess you like in your wing of feminism. To demand your pound of flesh: the subsidies, the privileges, the prestigious jobs. Every woman for herself, staking her claim, comparing her intersectionality with that of the others. Your political pragmatism knows no bounds when it comes to sating your personal ambitions, which you call demands for justice. Do you want to keep working in the same supermarket selling the same old shit just so you can gain positions of power? Suit yourselves, good luck and go fuck yourselves.

I'm going to find the quiet corner in the house of feminism where women want to learn to listen to each other, where someone else's words can shatter our myths and our preconceived ideas, where I will support the presence of others. No matter what or who they are. Without trying to find ways to use their weaknesses to further my career. To see whether I can heal, and if that's impossible, to feel useless and deal with that, too. I'm going to love my neighbor big time and I'm going to eat the fucker's face off whatever the cost. That's my feminism.

I'm leaving your club and moving to the one place in the great house of feminism that suits me: the trash heap, with the rats and the rest of the ornery girls.

OSCAR

A glittering anthill. Back in Paris at rush hour—night falls in broad daylight. On the ring road, an uninterrupted string of white lights on my left, and in front of me an endless stream of red lights—I'm listening to Prince Rakeem. Each in their own car, gripping the steering wheel. I dream I can hear what's going on inside each car, radio stations, soccer commentaries, telephone conversations, news reports, opera, golden oldies, anguished silence, Collège de France lectures, work conversations, the audiobook of *In Search of Lost Time*, arguments about vaccine passports. A mosaic of our differences in this visual homogeny, this rushing torrent of headlights. All of us, at the same time—heading home. What we thought would forever be our lives, snuffed out, without so much as a whimper. We comply. It's not difficult to tell ourselves we had no choice.

Apart from that, everything's fine. I'm taking another online pile-on because that dipshit in the cafeteria published photos of me and Zoé at the hospital. And another, right afterward, because she told everyone I'd apologized. Men can be so fucking pedantic . . . Male solidarity works perfectly as long as you follow the rules. But step out of line, and they'll let you know. They're really laying into me. So that's good. My sister suggests I cut off my finger. My best friend thinks I should have all my money confiscated. I'm fine. I'm feeling supported.

And it's true. I am fine. Not overjoyed, not in denial, but this time I know that this will pass. The most important thing is that Corinne pulls through. That I stay clean.

That you're all right. So yeah, my friend, I'm making progress. I don't bitch like I used to.

I spent five days on vacation with my daughter. I suffer from worthless father syndrome. When I'm with her, I'm uncomfortable and bored. The understanding we developed on the day I locked myself out of the apartment is long over. We don't hate being together—we've just got nothing to talk about. She spent the whole weekend on her phone. She's a cliché, a typical girl her age. The minute someone clicks "like" on something, she has to pick up her phone and check it out. She's constantly taking selfies. The one time I saw her excited was when she said on the Sentier des Douaniers, "Let's do a photo shoot," and even then, it all went wrong, I tried to share some funny memories of photo shoots I'd done and she clammed up like an oyster when I told her to stop staring into the lens. I felt like an old fart, and at the same time I was angry with her because she's not interested in anything. I can't deal—and I can't tell you how guilty I feel for not wanting to try anymore.

Clara comes to join me, with her dog. I'm fine with them. She shows up late. I'm getting to know her. She has her little quirks. She's perfectly capable of getting off the métro, crossing to the opposite platform in a blind panic, and going back home to check that she unplugged the iron. On her phone, she has a whole folder of videos of her locking the door. To prove to herself that she's done it properly. But it doesn't work: when she looks at them, she wonders whether maybe she went back, reopened the door, and forgot to relock it. There are other videos of her unplugging things and closing windows. She says:

"I can't help it. I know it's ridiculous. I leave an hour before I have to because I have to deal with this thing. And after three stops on the métro, when I have the uncontrollable urge to go home and check because the video isn't enough, I start to have doubts, I wonder if maybe I opened the door again to get something or do something. The other people on the métro don't think about these things, even though some of them have probably forgotten to switch something off, and in most cases, it won't matter. I know that. But I have to do it, I have to do it anyway. I've already lost jobs because of it, because I show up late, but also for the state of panic I get into if I don't go back and check." It's tough to deal with. But I like it. I like it because I think at least she knows what it's like not to have control over her own thoughts. And I like it because I can picture myself helping her through it, and I know it's as much of a pain in the ass for her as it is for me, and who am I to judge her? And I also know that it's not all she is. In the same way that I don't feel I'm just the sum of my faults. She's this slightly wacky girl who's tough to take on a weekend getaway. And she's also this brilliant girl who constantly surprises me when we've just watched a film or documentary together, because her intelligence is the complete opposite of her obsessive compulsions. Her analysis is solidly backed by an understanding of politics that I don't have and am incapable of expressing without her. I can't remember ever being so comfortable with anyone.

Clara loves you in all your films. My knowing you is part of my charm. She read somewhere that you're shooting a new film with a major director soon. I wonder if he's the guy whose head you wanted to rip off. And I wonder whether you wanted to scream insults at him because you were afraid that his film would be one of the ones that didn't get made. There are lots of things I want to talk about with you, but I'm starting to feel a bit restricted in these emails.

Clara loves all your movies, and she also loves Zoé Katana's blog. Gotta move with the times. Back in the day, girls read women's magazines with features about fashion week and diets; now they read feminist blogs.

REBECCA

I called Corinne. She's fine. She flirted with me, she was smooth, direct. She's got a way with words, I like her compliments. I let her get on with it. For weeks now she's been telling me that she's in an "open" relationship. Open to all kinds of bullshit, I thought. I offered to come visit her in the hospital and she said, "Absolutely, I'd love that." So three days later, there I am in this one-horse town, an hour from Paris. It's a loooong way. Her girlfriend, Marcelle, was there. Who is this hottie? I took one look at her and before we'd said a word, I realized I wasn't heterosexual anymore. When you reach that level of sexy, there's no straight no gay no nothing: she's beyond categories. Corinne sat in her wheelchair, smiling like a queen. People often tell me that dykes age better than straight women, because they're less unhappy. And she's aging well. Okay, about Marcelle, I'm not going to lie, we'll be talking about her later. I don't think this is the right time to steal your sister's girlfriend, but I'm tempted.

Zoé doesn't talk to me about you anymore. I think she's doing better. She's setting up an online magazine with some girls her own age, and they're talking about moving to the country somewhere. She doesn't write to me as often, and she doesn't visit your sister anymore. And that's fine. We remind her of bad things.

Last night, I watched *The Crown*. All night long, I kept watching until it was dawn, and I cried. I cried to think I'll never play a princess again.

I was so depressed I wanted to die, but I didn't think of looking up the number of a dealer.

Like an abandoned train car, the drug machine has been shunted over to a siding. And I stayed with this painful emotion, I didn't use.

I'm over fifty, and this is the first time since I was thirteen that I've been like this—I haven't gotten wasted for months now. I'm finally emerging from a fog, and I can't say I'm happy about everything I see. I know myself—so I'm not exactly surprised. But my weaknesses, the intensity of my mood swings, the loneliness, the fear of growing old, and the fear of dying mean that I'm not happy about everything, and I don't see a solution to every problem. I think of the NA prayer: the serenity to accept the things I cannot change. And I understand every word. I am here. Present and accounted for.

Lockdown helped me keep going. This pandemic may have screwed up the whole planet—but it helped us. I've been able to get used to all this. I didn't have to deal with the dinner invitations you can't refuse with the booze flowing and the people talking louder and louder and glasses being filled with red wine or golden bubbles and everyone laughing about nothing and talking passionately and everyone's intense and the party's in full swing then there's the whiff of weed from the corner—and the little late-afternoon beer—the champagne corks hitting the ceiling and the excited shrieks after a premiere, the sound of glasses clinking—and the dealers hanging around, you know them or you can spot them, so often they've got this look about them, they can hook you up, give you their cell number—and the film shoots, the guy who rents the dressing room trailers and always has something on him because he's got time on his hands, there's the helpful makeup artist whose boyfriend's a junkie, the producer who's trying to be your bestie and asks if you need anything—the gigs, your friends are playing and you're backstage and all sorts of shit is being passed around and it's easy just to join in, you just need to get wasted. We were spared all of that. There were no bars open, no bathrooms to queue for, no dressing rooms, no waiting, no panic attacks to deal with, no rehearsals, no one-night stands. We went through it all together, you and I. Life has a sense of humor. When I think back to our first emails, it seemed unlikely that you'd change my life. And that you'd change yours.

Something I've realized only recently: no one can take my life away from me. The only thing that can do that is amnesia. It was a revelation—something happens inside you and there's no going back. I was sitting on a plane staring out the window at the clouds, the radiant orange glow, all that tranquility, and, as though I'd accessed a portal into my consciousness it all came rushing back: the hundreds of times I've felt happy on a plane. I've always loved flying. And it was all there in that one moment—a glorious life, from every point of view, made up of sated desires and passions that shatter me, fill me, create me, encounters like sweet collisions, and curiosities, and it all exists in me. It's real, and it has happened, and it's all there for as long as my memory holds out, etched into me as surely as sadness. It's the opposite of nostalgia, the things that happened are with me forever—and no one can take that from me. I am that past and I cherish it.

I'm home now, Paris is raucous once again but hasn't quite recovered its arrogance. The city will come through this, it's solid. I'm clean. Zoé can call if she needs to. Corinne can call me. Marcelle can call me too, but she hasn't summoned the courage just yet. And you can call me. You can count on me. And, yes, we could meet up someday. You're right, these emails are starting to feel a little cramped.